Breaking Barriers

A Mending Shattered Hearts Novel #3

Nikki A Lamers

Frey Dreams

For more information, address: freydreamspublications@gmail.com

First edition, July 2025

Editor, Dina Huessini

Cover Model, Ren Taylor

Cover Photo Photographer, Dennis Theoharidis

ISBN 978-1-951185-36-7(paperback)

ISBN 978-1-951185-35-0(ebook)

www.nikkialamersauthor.com

Other Books By Nikki A Lamers

All books are standalone novels, except the first two books in the Home Series.

<u>The Unforgettable Series</u>

The Unforgettable Summer (#1)
Unforgettable Nights (#2)
Unforgettable Dreams (#3)
Unforgettable Memories (#4)
The Unforgettable One (#5)
Unforgettable Mistakes (#6)
An Unforgettable December Novella (#7)

Home

Dreams Lost and Found (#1)
Finding Home (#2)

Mending Shattered Hearts

Breaking Cycles (#1)
The War is Over Novella (#2)
Breaking Barriers (#3)

Piper Falls: Station 28

Leave of My Duty (#5)

Love Canyon: Blind Date with a #BOOKBOYFRIEND

Blind Date with a #FORMERPLAYER (November 2025)

Waves Crashing

The Lost Princess (Coming 2025)

Breaking Barriers

Mending Shattered Hearts
#3

Nikki A Lamers

Chapter 1

Declan

Stale beer hits my senses as I make my way through the crowded room. Dropping down onto an old stool at the end of the bar, I heave a sigh and take in my surroundings, grateful for the peace among strangers. I love my family but between Finn not only winning his first game of his senior year as the starting quarterback, but slaughtering the other team, Charlotte landing a lead role in a musical at a local community theater and Ella, getting engaged to her long-time boyfriend, Grant, who's also Finn's football coach, I need some time devoid of family celebration.

Maybe I'm the oldest, but their accomplishments seem to be all I have to celebrate. Just because I'm happy for them doesn't mean I don't start wondering what the fuck I'm doing now. I've spent my whole life focusing on them. I wonder if they realize everything I gave up to be there for them. Don't get me wrong, I would make the same decisions in a heartbeat because my family needed me, but sometimes I wish things could've been different, admittedly for selfish reasons.

Growing up, I gave up nearly everything all throughout school from sports and clubs, to dances and dating, focusing on academics. Settling for a college close by instead of Yale, my fucking dream school was the toughest blow. I was close to accepting it, my family even encouraged me to do so, but when Ella had a relapse, I knew I would be consumed with worry and guilt. There was no way I could go through with it, no matter how much I wanted it.

After college, taking the job at a nearby marketing firm instead of a corporate job in the city; leaves me unfulfilled. It's been a great resume builder and good experience, but it's a job I don't even want anymore. The problem, I have no idea where to go from here.

Avoiding relationships at all costs has been my only viable option without losing my mind. How can I commit to a woman when I can't give anyone besides my family my time? Impossible, so I don't. But I'll be thirty in a couple months, and I don't know if I can keep going like this much longer. Breaking free from old habits could prove to be difficult.

Is that even what I want?

"What can I get ya'?" An older man stands behind the bar, eyeing me while wiping his hands on a bar towel.

"Bourbon, neat, please." He nods and steps away. Reaching into my wallet, I grab my card, placing it on the bar.

My phone vibrates in my jeans pocket with an incoming text. I pull it out and glance at the message from my best friend, Laine.

Laine

> Where did you disappear to? Thought we were going for a beer.

I heave a sigh and run my hand through my light brown hair, a couple lightened streaks still apparent with summer barely gone and the warm temperatures hanging on in North Carolina. I text him back as the bartender sets my drink in front of me, swiftly followed by a receipt. Grabbing the pen, I scrawl my name across the bottom and hand it back. "Thanks." I nod in appreciation and take a sip, enjoying the burn down my throat.

> Sorry, man. Had to get out of Genesis Beach. At a dive about ten miles west of town if you want to join.

Laine

> Sounds like you need a break. Maybe you should get laid and I'll catch up with you later.

I huff a laugh. He knows me better than anyone.

> You sure?

Laine

> I'm on at the Breaking Cycles center early anyway.

A smile tugs at my lips thinking of the new center inspired by Laine and now employing Ella as a social worker. Its mission is to assist kids in tough situations and help them break the cycle, giving them not only a place to go, but recreational tools, support, activities, and medical support with a variety of doctors and therapists. Laine is not only a physical therapist, but he organizes and participates in some of the activities with the kids regularly.

> Sounds good.

Laine

> Later.

I slip my phone back in my pocket and take another sip of my drink. Leaning on the bar, I look around, filled with a mix of mostly twenty somethings and an older man in the corner who appears like he's spent most nights on the same stool. A pool table sits on the opposite side of the bar. My eyes are drawn to a woman about five-six with long wavy violet hair as she saunters confidently around the table. Pointing to the corner pocket she leans over the table, cue stick in hand, the curve of her ass looking perfect in faded, ripped jeans. The guy behind her stares, his mouth falling open in shock when the black ball drops. Setting the cue on the table, she spins around, holding out her hand. Her sly grin looks sexy as hell.

The guy gives a shake of his head, and slowly backs her into the pool table, leaning down. Her eyes go wide and my muscles tense, preparing to pounce. But she's quick. Slipping under his arm, she steps away, crossing her arms defensively over her chest, pushing up her pert breasts. He laughs and points to a dart board hanging on the wall at the far end of the bar. She shrugs and they saunter over together with another couple, making me wonder if they're all together. She doesn't seem that into her date to me.

"They have a bet going."

Turning my head, I glance at the owner of the feminine voice with a slight southern drawl to my right as she sets a blazer on the stool and sits down next to me. Her short, pencil skirt slides up her long slender legs, my gaze sliding up with it. Her low cut tank shows more than you'd expect, but I imagine with the blazer, she works hard and I enjoy a smart woman.

I quirk a brow, meeting her gaze. "A bet?"

She nods towards the woman my eyes have been fastened to since I walked in and the people she's now playing darts with, my gaze gladly following. "I'm not exactly sure what it entails, but it started with whoever wins the game, then it went to best of three and he apparently got the point after going to best of five and losing three in a row. Game two was close, but only because he went first."

Chuckling, I watch her, pulling the darts from the board and take another sip of my bourbon, asking, "Friends of yours?"

She shrugs. "Him, I grew up with. Her, I don't know." Her head tilts to the side as she spins on her stool, openly staring at me. Out of the corner of my eye, I see her lick her lips while her gaze roams my body, possibly here looking for the same thing as me—one hot night. "I don't know you either. I'm Evie."

The corners of my lips twitch up. I give her a slight nod in acknowledgement and again let my eyes blatantly travel up her body. Sure, she's pretty. Tall, thin, dark brown hair and probably a few years younger than me. She's the kind of woman I'd usually spend the night with, likely too busy for a relationship and focused on a career. But is she the one for tonight? Something tells me not to make that decision quite yet, my head already wanting to turn back to the beauty on the other side of the bar. Holding out my hand, I grasp hers.

"Declan," I state before letting go.

Her smile grows at my introduction, her hand falling to my forearm. "Well, Declan, it's nice meeting you."

Cheers erupt near the dart board, drawing my attention. The woman with long violet hair smiles, turning towards the target, and lighting up the room. She bites her lower lip in concentration and aims, while I fight back a groan at the simple action. When she releases the dart, her tongue juts out, freezing until the dart lands near the bullseye, my skin prickling in awareness. Her arms go up in triumph. She spins around, giving a blonde woman a high-five. Her head falls back in laughter, the motion causing my breath to catch and my dick to stand up and pay attention.

The guy clasps his hand around her wrist and pulls her towards him. Her hands slide up between them, attempting to push him away in protest. I watch her body go rigid as his arms wrap tightly around her, pulling her close. She glares at him, trying to twist away. Everyone else seems to be paying attention to everything but them, toasting, cheering, drinking, singing, dancing, oblivious to the sudden chasm in their midst.

"Excuse me." My body rises before I have a chance to think about it and I'm across the room in a few long strides, forcing myself into their business.

"Is there a problem here?"

"We're good," he claims, never taking his eyes off her.

"I've got it," she hisses through her teeth, warily glancing in my direction.

I don't budge, I can't. Not until I know she's safe. This guy is obviously an asshole who doesn't like to lose. Who knows what he might do. My eyes narrow. "You sure about that, darlin?"

She huffs a humorless laugh, the sound shocking my system. Looking in my direction, she glares. "I'm nobody's darlin." Her knee flies up, connecting with his groin without hesitation. Instantly, his arm falls from around her waist and he folds over, grunting in agony. "Get over it. You lost to a girl. Again. Doesn't mean your ego takes whatever he wants."

I hold back a laugh, my eyes widening as she steps around the asshole. She brushes past me, electricity shooting right through me, leaving me off-balance. The bar falls relatively silent taking in the scene before the cacophony of voices ensues, like the scene is typical for a Friday night. She walks up to the bar, easily catching the bartender's attention. "Two shots of tequila, please? The douchebag on the floor is paying when he stops whining like a bitch in heat."

My lips twitch in amusement, not able to take my eyes off her. Watching while he slides her the shots with salt and two lime wedges. She hands one to me, her light hazel eyes meeting my blue ones, a crooked grin tugging at my lips. "To needless heroes."

I huff a laugh, my breath catching as I spot a tattoo on the inside of her wrist a moment before her tongue slips out, covering it. Makes me wonder what else she's hiding. She downs the shot and sucks the lime, eyeing me in challenge.

Taking a deep breath to help my dick calm down, I swiftly follow suit, setting the empty glass on the bar. "It's been a while since I've taken a shot."

She shrugs, unapologetic. "Well, if you plan on keeping up with me tonight, you might need it."

I quirk a brow. Maybe this woman is exactly what I need right now. She's feisty as hell. I like it. "I'm Declan."

"So, Declan, do you not like anyone here, or did you just come to drink amongst strangers?"

Laughter erupts from my chest, helping my shoulders relax. "I'm not from here."

"Well, that makes two of us."

"What's your name, firecracker?"

"Alex." My heart lurches watching her suck her bottom lip between her teeth making me fight back a groan.

Taking her hand in mine, my thumb glides gently over the back of her soft, velvety skin. "Alex," I echo, her name a low rumble, attempting to elicit a reaction.

Her cheeks tinge the perfect shade of pink, giving me exactly what I want.

This could be fun.

Chapter 2

Alex

Damn this man is gorgeous. Standing about five inches taller than me with broad shoulders and a narrow waist, I can imagine how defined his muscles must be under his long sleeved, white cotton shirt. The two buttons hanging open at his neck giving me a peek at his tanned skin underneath are merely a tease, taunting me. His fingers run over his strong jaw while he eyes me, assessing me, causing my heart to pound against my ribcage. I don't like it, but I sure want it; want him.

I reach up to the bar and grab a beer from the bartender. "Thanks." He nods. I tip the beer back and take a drink. "Are you sure you don't want something else?"

Giving me a crooked grin, he claims, "I'd rather find something else to do with you than go drink for drink."

My eyes widen in surprise. This man just made tonight a hell of a lot more interesting. Besides the sexy scruff of his five-o-clock shadow, my first impression is he's more classically handsome and probably always does the right thing, but maybe I'm wrong. I tilt my head to the side and force myself to remain flippant. "Careful pretty boy. I might be more than you can chew."

"That's alright with me. I prefer my tongue more than my teeth." I spew my beer, spraying it all over him and the guy behind him.

He bursts out laughing as he wipes his brow, but the guy behind him doesn't look happy. "What the fuck?" he bellows stepping towards me.

Declan sidesteps, blocking him from getting to me. "Haven't you learned your lesson? I can handle myself."

Declan smirks while the guy on the other side of him fumes, ready to fight. "Then why is your beer and spit all over me?"

"Sorry." I shrug, struggling to hold back a laugh, but I don't succeed and it slips out without my consent.

He reaches for me, fighting to get around Declan, but he continues to hold him off. "You can't hit a woman asshole."

"Then get your girlfriend away from me."

I step towards the guy, determined to stand my ground. Strong arms wrap around me, picking me up like I weigh nothing as Declan tosses me over his shoulder. "Put me down, you ogre!" I yell, smacking his firm ass. The action only makes my body heat.

He chuckles, striding towards the back of the bar into an alcove by the restrooms. Carefully, he sets me back on my feet, my body rubbing against his on the way down. Damn him. "You're trouble, firecracker."

I glare at him. "It's your fault."

His head falls back in laughter, making his body vibrate against mine. I bite my lower lip, a groan escaping. "My fault?" He quirks a brow, not playing fair.

"Yeah." I nod, defiant. "Between your hero complex and your innuendos..."

"What innuendos?" he taunts, his breath picking up its pace.

"You're not denying the hero complex, but I guess looks can be deceiving. I pegged you for a smart man."

He laughs again the sound going right through me. "I'd love to see what else you can do with that smart mouth."

"More than you'll ever know," I declare a moment before I grab his head with both hands and pull his lips down to mine, desperate for a taste.

He moans, allowing my tongue to slip inside and tangle with his. He slides one hand down to the curve of my ass, while the other holds firm at my back. Teeth clashing, tongues licking, mouths moving and gliding, frantic, desperate to get closer. I lift my leg, curling it around his back, his hard length pushing against my belly making me gasp.

"Get a fucking room!" The same asshole from earlier grumbles, breaking us apart. My feet drop to the ground the moment he slams the door to the bathroom open, banging it against the wall and stomping by us.

"Sorry," I mumble, suddenly timid, afraid to meet Declan's gaze. What the hell is wrong with me?

"I'm not." He chuckles. I lift my head and narrow my eyes, ignoring the frantic beat of my heart. The look in his eyes takes my breath away. "That was more fun than I've had in a long time."

"Now that I believe," I snap, smirking. "Wanna get out of here?"

"I don't take advantage of women when they're drinking."

I roll my eyes. "I'm not drunk. If you didn't notice I just beat some guys at pool and darts. Besides, I'm the one who asked you. I'm only here for tonight."

His eyes narrow. "Winning a few games against a couple drunk frat boys doesn't mean much. I don't know how much you've had to drink. How do I know you're in the right state of mind?"

"I'll challenge you to a game."

He huffs a laugh and shakes his head. I grimace. "You know what? I'm never in the right state of mind, but I always know exactly what I'm doing. And you're starting to drive me crazy."

"So, you're telling me you pick fights often and you want me?"

With a shake of my head, I mutter, "Something like that, but not for long."

He licks his lips, staring down at me, his heated gaze turning me into a puddle of hormones. "Damn."

"So, you in or not, Cowboy? I'm staying at a motel down the road."

A look of distaste crosses his face and he quickly brushes it off, shaking his head. "You don't want me to fuck you there. My place is only a few minutes further."

A hum vibrates in my chest with his words before I process what he said. "Wait, I thought you weren't from around here."

"I'm not. I'm a couple towns over."

Shaking my head, I huff a laugh, rethinking my stupidity. "I'm not going home with a stranger."

"But you'll bring me to the motel that you shouldn't be staying at. Trust me on that. I'm starting to feel used."

"We're not there yet."

He gives me a sexy crooked smile making my blood boil for him. "Take a picture of me and send it to a friend so they know where to find you."

"You and your driver's license."

He nods, pulling out his wallet and handing it over without question. "I could just run now."

"You wouldn't make it far, Darlin."

"Wanna' test that theory, Cowboy?" He chuckles as I pull out his license. "Declan Howard. At least I know you weren't lying about your name."

I snap a picture of his license, followed by a picture of him and send it to Sloane before I second guess myself. Then I hand him his wallet and push him back, stepping away. "Coming old man?"

I hear his laughter as he catches up to me and we walk out of the bar, side by side. "Old man? How old are you, Alex?"

"It's Alex now? I'm twenty-seven," I respond honestly. "And your driver's license just told me you're old."

His eyes go wide. "I'm twenty-nine."

Technically he's younger than most of the men I've hooked up with recently, but I don't need to tell him that. "See? Old." He chuckles, the sound giving me goose bumps.

"This is our cab." He gestures to the lone sedan pulling into the parking lot with a magnetic sign sticking to the side of the car.

"No Uber?" I slip into the backseat, and he slides in right beside me, the heat from his body causing my breath to pick up its pace.

"Not likely 'round here. They're around, but may take a couple hours, or days..." he trails off, his hand falling to my thigh, and giving it a gentle squeeze.

My heart stutters and thrashes against my ribcage. He barely moves his hand, my core heating almost instantly. I bite the inside of my cheek to hold back a moan. What is this man doing to me? It's impossible to hold myself together around him.

After what feels like an eternity, but is only about fifteen minutes later, we pull into a long driveway, a large southern Victorian sitting in front of us. "This is your house?" I step out of the car, wide-eyed.

He shrugs, not answering and leads me to the front door, pushing it open. "What the hell do you do for a living?" I take in the open living room, with a massive brick fireplace and an expansive, stainless-steel kitchen just beyond. A soft sigh escapes his lips letting me know I've asked the wrong question. "It's not illegal is it?"

Shaking his head, he huffs a laugh. "Definitely not."

I spin to look at him. Surprising me, he stands staring at me with his hands in his pockets, appearing vulnerable. My need to take control and help him relax skyrockets. Swiftly, I close the distance between us. Reaching out, my hands run up his chest, slipping underneath his shirt at his neck. "I'm clean. I promise."

"Me too."

"So," I mumble, dragging out the word, "what are you going to do with me now that you got me here? It is only for tonight." I don't want there to be any question on what this is. Then again, men like Declan never take a woman like me seriously. It's part of the reason why he's perfect for one night.

Pushing up on my tiptoes, my tongue juts out licking up his throat, a salty, masculine taste tickles my senses. I'm only halfway to his mouth when his head tips towards me and his lips crash down on mine, igniting me. *Finally.* A moan falls from my lips as he kisses me hard, his tongue tangling with mine. With each swipe of his tongue, he walks me backwards until the back of my legs hit the couch. He lowers me down, ripping his lips from mine. Hovering over me, his eyes flare. My gaze remains glued to him as he reaches down with one hand, and yanks his shirt over his head, tossing it to the floor.

"Damn," I mumble, breathless taking in the hard ridges of his chest, his arms, his shoulders, his abs with a light splattering of hair leading beneath his jeans.

The corners of his lips twitch up in amusement. "Your turn."

Without hesitation, I sit up and pull my shirt over my head, tossing it to the floor. His mouth falls to my neck, his teeth grazing my skin, making my head fall back, my entire body aware, heated, and wet. "That feels so good." His hand skims my side, pausing near my chest. I grab his hand and cover my breast, arching into his palm. He obliges, giving me a gentle squeeze before slipping his hand underneath the silky fabric of my bra, pinching my already taut nipples between his thumb and forefinger.

He kisses me and I moan into his mouth, arching my hips towards him, my body in desperate need for the friction. His hard length presses into me. My head falls back to the couch as I gasp for breath. His lips move down my chest while he slips the straps off my shoulders, kissing and licking. The instant his mouth covers my nipple, I cry out. Needing to touch him, I reach for him, rubbing him through his jeans. His body jerks and he pulls back slightly, groaning, running his teeth over his bottom lip.

"Too many clothes. Dec, help me with my jeans."

He pushes away from me, and I instantly feel the loss. My shoes fall to the floor with a loud thump. Grasping the bottom of my jeans he yanks hard, a soft yelp escaping my lips as I slide on the couch along with them for a moment before they come off and he tosses them to the floor. His own soon follow, pulling a condom out of his wallet before dropping them.

Pausing, he looks into my eyes. "Are you sure about this?" he asks breathless.

"Yes, please."

"Damn, you're sexy." His fingers reach down, running through my core. I moan, my body arching into his hand. "And so wet."

"That means I'm ready," I moan sassily.

With a growl, he rips the condom open and rolls it on, filling me in mere seconds as if in punishment. "Ahh..." Halting he waits while I adjust and begins to move, his actions deliberate. His mouth finds the crook of my neck again, biting while he thrusts inside me, harder, deeper, and slowly picking up the pace. My entire body tingles, coming alive. My back arches towards him, greedily meeting each hard thrust.

Pushing further up on his arms, he hooks my leg hanging off the couch, holding it between us and getting an angle I don't expect making me ignite, shooting sparks of fire through me. I pant, breathless, "Oh, my, Dec," I mutter, stuttering each word.

"That's it, firecracker. Let me feel you."

The sound of his voice is like a fire starter to my senses, setting me ablaze and I soon feel my body shattering all around him. He quickens the pace and closes his eyes, thrusting into me, chasing his own orgasm while I come down from mine, watching him, wanting more in the glow of the aftershocks.

A guttural moan leaves his lips as he hits the back of my pussy, his movements becoming wild. He thrusts again and again, pausing deep inside me, finally following behind. Exhaling, he pulls out, immediately removing the condom and disposes of it.

I'm salivating for another orgasm compliments of this beautiful man and at the same time, wondering if this is already over. Halting my internal battle, he reaches down and picks me up with one arm around my waist and the other boosting me up by the ass. "Wrap your legs around me."

I do as he says. "Where are we going?"

"Upstairs. I need more condoms." He nips at my neck again, bringing a smile to my face, in hopes he'll do the same in other places.

* * *

Rolling over, I glance at the man lying next to me, almost wishing things were different. Last night sure felt unlike anything or anyone before. That's not the case, though. It can't be. I'm not that person.

I let my eyes roam his ridged muscles, appreciating his fine form, the sheet covering him from the waist down and his arm resting over his head. A small tattoo I didn't notice last night sits over his heart, making me frown. I wonder what those initials are for, or who. It doesn't spell anything. It must be initials.

The next instant I shake my head, brushing the thought away. It doesn't matter. I won't be here to find out. Placing a soft kiss on his chest, I carefully sneak out of bed to go in search of my clothes. It's time for me to leave before he wakes up. I hate the awkward morning after conversation. And for some reason, the thought of it with *him* leaves me feeling uneasy.

With my hand on the knob I whisper, "Goodbye, Declan." Walking out, I quietly close the door behind me, making my escape.

Chapter 3

Declan

Pushing the door open, Laine follows me into the bar. "So, this is the place you met this girl?"

"Alex." I shrug as if it's no big deal when everything in me is telling me it's a very big fucking deal. "Yeah."

"Why are we back here again?"

I barely give him a cursory glance out of the corner of my eye before I scan the bar, looking for any sign of Alex. "To have a drink."

"This is your third time here since last weekend."

"So? Work has been stressful."

"Right..." He huffs a laugh and arches his eyebrow in challenge. "You're telling me it has nothing to do with the woman, Alex, that you hooked up with last weekend, the one you can't stop talking about?"

Frowning, I heave a sigh and stalk to the bar, sitting at a stool near the end so I can see more of the room. She told me she was only here for the night, but I was hoping she'd come back anyway. Unfortunately, everyone I've asked doesn't seem to know anything about her. If I knew her last name, like she knows mine,

I'd have a starting point on where to look. In the past, I never cared, so I didn't think to ask until it was too late; until she was already gone.

Why is she so different that I can't seem to get her out of my damn head?

"I feel like I'm losing my mind," I mutter.

Before Laine has a chance to respond to my comment, the bartender saunters over to us, looking at me with a knowing smile. "Back again, huh?"

Laine bursts out laughing. "Oh, this is too good."

"Shut the fuck up," I snap, glaring at him. Looking back at the bartender, I say, "Yes, anything change?"

Shaking his head, he confirms, "She hasn't been back."

Ignoring Laine's laughter, I say, "Thanks."

He nods. "What'll it be?"

"A bourbon neat, please."

Swinging his gaze to Laine, he arches his eyebrow in question. Laine wipes his hand down his face, trying to stop his laughter. "Whatever draft you have on tap would be great. Thanks."

"Got it." Turning around, the bartender moves swiftly, getting our drinks.

Laine sits down on the stool next to me and spins to face me. Smirking, he leans his elbow on the bar and asks, "Are you going to admit it?"

"What?" I snap. "That she has my head all fucked up?" Exhaling harshly, I attempt to let go of all my frustration. "Yeah, I admit it, but that doesn't do me a damn bit of good when I don't have a clue who she really is or where the hell to find her."

"This is damn entertaining," he mumbles, chuckling.

The bartender comes back with our drinks, and I pull my card out, handing it to him. "Will you start a tab for me? This asshole can pay for his own damn drinks," I add, tipping my head towards Laine.

He bursts out laughing and grabs my card before the bartender can take it and hands him his. "Then, I think tonight can be on me since you're providing the entertainment."

I glare at him out of the corner of my eye and take a generous sip of my bourbon, slipping my card back in my wallet. "Fuck you."

"I'm sorry, Dec, but I've never seen you like this," he claims, taking a sip of his beer. "I'm the one that usually falls hard and fast, but you have always kept your emotional distance when it comes to women. Knowing you and how much you care about your friends and your family, I honestly always wondered how you did it," he concedes, shrugging. "Remember prom?"

"That was a lifetime ago," I mutter.

Chuckling, he nods in agreement. "True. But that's probably the closest you came to losing your mind over a woman–until now. Then again, your empathy was only because you were friends, and you didn't want her to feel bad because you didn't want to date her."

"I'm not an asshole. And I'm always honest about what I'm looking for whenever I hookup." I take another gulp of my drink.

"True, but this is the first time you've had a woman walk away from you. Am I right?"

I run my hand through my hair and grip the back of my neck, trying to relieve my growing tension. "Yeah, so?"

"So, unfortunately, liking someone can fuck with your head whether you want it to or not."

"Yeah, I know that. It sucks—first time I actually thought about letting my guard down, and she's gone before I even get the chance to tell her how I feel."

"Well, from the sound of it, she only did what you normally do, so she likely wouldn't have given you a chance."

Setting my glass on the bar, I glare at Laine. "Thanks, asshole. Why are we friends again?"

He grins, looping his arm around my neck. "Best friends."

Shoving him off, I scoff. "You sure about that?"

"Yup." He nods, confidently. He's right. Sighing, my body sags against the bar in defeat. "So, tell me, Dec, why this girl? Why does she have you so twisted up?"

Taking another sip of my drink, a vision of Alex and her violet waves flashes in my head. "Well, there's the obvious–she's gorgeous, sexy as hell and the sex was off the charts."

"Expected all that," he mutters, urging me for more.

Grimacing, I give him a look out of the corner of my eye. "She was so much more than that. Alex had this energy and passion about her that you could feel. I watched her bounce from the pool table to the dart board and kick everyone's ass." Pausing, I take another sip of my drink, a smile tugging at my lips. "Her laughter was contagious. She befriended other women and didn't put up with any shit when it came to the men. It was obvious she's independent and strong. The fire visible inside her is reason alone that I want to know more about her."

Offering me a sad smile, he says, "Sounds like she was a good one."

I huff a humorless laugh. "Pretty sure she was so much more." Setting my glass on the bar, I turn, facing him. "Since you know so much about relationships, what the fuck am I supposed to do?"

"Give it time and you'll feel better." He shrugs.

"Great," I grumble, finishing my bourbon.

"I know it sucks, but there's not much you can do when you don't know where she is."

How do I forget about her when she's everywhere I look? Every time I see anything purple, especially someone with dyed hair, I have to stop myself from chasing them down. I never knew a simple color could be such a trigger.

"Ideas on finding her?" I ask, almost afraid of his answer—I'm desperate.

"Seems to me she doesn't want to be found, or you would already know that answer. I can't believe I'm saying this, but if you're never going to see her again–"

"Fuck," I mutter under my breath at the thought.

He winces, giving me a look of pity, but that's the last thing I want. "Maybe you're better off moving on. At least now we know you have a heart beyond family and friends." He smirks. "There just may be someone out there for you."

Heaving a sigh, I shrug. "Maybe."

Although, if I don't find Alex, I'm not holding my breath for that to ever happen. No one else has ever consumed my mind like she has. I order a second bourbon and take another look around the bar, searching for a distraction when it seems that's the best I'll get. Swiping my drink as the bartender sets it in front of me, I try to push Alex out of my head.

"Dec, you know it's okay for you to have a relationship. You don't need to be the one to watch out for all your siblings until they're all married off. Ella is doing great. As for Char and Finn, they're old enough to take care of themselves."

I run my hand through my hair and drop it onto the bar. He knows me better than anyone. "Yeah, I know. Thanks, Laine."

"Hey," a twenty something woman and her friend smile at the two of us. The one with blonde hair focuses on me. She's cute, wearing a short jean skirt and a crop top that looks to me like a bra, but what the fuck do I know? "I think I've seen you before. Weren't you in here last night?"

I nod. "I was."

"Are you from around here?" the blonde questions.

Laine chuckles.

"Not exactly," I respond, frowning.

Laine interrupts, likely trying to pull me out of my funk. "Hi, ladies. I'm Laine and this is Declan."

"Hi," the same blonde one speaks, staring at me. "I'm Annabelle. This is Bea."

"Nice to meet you both. You ladies up for a round of darts?" Laine asks.

They both grin, glancing at each other. "Sure, thanks."

Smirking, I add, "Why don't you order a drink on us?"

If he's going to try to get me off my ass, he can pay for it.

Chuckling, Laine waves the bartender over and gives me a hard pat on the back as they both order a drink. "I'm sure you didn't forget how to be friendly."

When we all have drinks in hand, Laine holds up his glass and waits for us to do the same. He grins, toasting, "To new friends and a good night."

I laugh, finishing my drink and setting the glass on the bar, reluctantly following them to the dart boards.

Maybe getting out of my head will be a good thing. I glance at the blonde, wishing it were violet and frown.

Then again, maybe it won't do a damn thing.

Chapter 4

Alex

A Month Later...

I walk into the kitchen dressed in ripped blue jeans and a long-sleeved purple shirt, a shade darker than my hair, perfect for my first day at the garage. My brother stands at the stove, making eggs and bacon, his red hair wet and sticking up in all directions as if he just ran a towel over it; the same hair I used to have before I dyed mine. Guess I won't be able to do that much longer. I'll have to look into that. His jeans and black t-shirt tell me I'm wearing the right thing.

"Mornin', Aidan."

He glances in my direction, his blue eyes meeting mine. "Morning, Sis. Want some eggs?"

My nose scrunches up in distaste. "Maybe just some toast and a little coffee for now. I'm not hungry."

He nods and turns back to the stove, giving me a few minutes of quiet while I make myself a cup of coffee and swipe a piece of his toast before I sit down at the small round table in the corner. He plates his food and makes his way over, sitting next to me. I feel his eyes burning a hole into the side of my head and look at him, rubbing his neatly trimmed goatee as he stares at me, assessing me.

"What?" I snap irritably.

"You going to tell me what's going on with you?" Aidan asks, arching his eyebrow in challenge.

"Can't your favorite sister move in with you and beg you for a job without you thinking there's something going on?" I smirk.

He huffs a humorless laugh. "I just want to help, Alex."

"I know Aidan and you are helping. You let me move in with you and work for you, no questions asked."

"Alexa…" he warns.

"Don't call me that."

The feminine voice on the smart speaker sounds, "What would you like me to call you?"

Aidan laughs as I groan in annoyance. "Alexa, off," I snap.

"It's been a while since I heard that. Apparently, I like telling you what to do, although she sounds nothing like you." He chuckles. I glare at my brother, his grin growing. "Fine. Tell me what has your panties in a twist and my smart speaker will no longer have your name."

My shoulders sag as I heave a sigh in defeat. "Don't ever say that word again. It's vile coming out of your mouth."

"Panties?" He quirks a brow.

"Do you really want to go there?" I challenge. His cocky smirk drops and I heave a sigh. "I'll tell ya Aidan, I will. Just give me a couple of days. Please."

He frowns, his concern only making me feel worse. As I look away, the scraping of the chair on the tiles lets me know he's scooting closer to me. He wraps his inked arms around me, pulling me close. "Is it Dad? Have ya seen him?"

I grimace. The thought of our father making my stomach turn. He's likely the last person either of us want to see. I shake my head, trying to shove him out of my mind.

Aidan's entire body tenses. "What happened? What did he do?"

Turning my head, I cross my arms over my chest and narrow my eyes at my brother. Although I love it when he goes all big brother on me and I've used it to my benefit in the past, now is not the time. It's better if I don't say anything yet. He can come to his own conclusions until I'm ready to talk.

Groaning in annoyance, he shakes his head. "Alright. Fine. I'll give you time."

I lean into his five-feet, ten-inch frame, resting my head on his shoulder, feeding on his support. "Thank you," I whisper into his chest.

"But no more than a couple days. After that if you don't tell me, I'll hold you down and tickle you until you do."

"Wonderful," I mumble sarcastically, pushing out of his embrace. "Can't wait, big brother." We fall into an easy banter, as we finish our breakfast and get ready to leave for the garage.

"Let's go. We'll take my Jeep," Aidan announces, slinging his arm around my neck.

I shove him off. "You don't want to take your bike?"

"Not today."

"Don't change your day for me."

He gives me a look. "Get in the damn car, Alex."

I stick my tongue out but do as he says, making him laugh. It's not long before we pull up to G & A Cycles, my brother's specialty motorcycle shop with his partner, Grant Young. Aidan does a lot of the design and artwork, while Grant takes care of the mechanics and builds. They make a great team. Business has been going well, but they're still relatively new and both work other jobs. Grant coaches the high school boys football team and Aidan works at a tattoo shop a couple nights a week to supplement their income.

"Are you sure y'all are okay with me working the desk?" I ask, stepping out of the car.

"Yeah, I'm sure. Grant and I talked about hiring someone and hadn't gotten around to it." He shrugs like it's no big deal.

"Did you tell him I'm coming?"

"Yup." He yanks the door open, gesturing for me to go in front of him. I step inside, finding Grant standing behind a tall gray Formica desk with their black, white, and red G & A logo embedded on the front. A few black chairs sit to my right along with three basic gray tables, one on each wall and along the window facing the front–a simple and masculine space.

It works.

Grant pushes his dark brown hair out of his eyes as he lifts his head and smiles behind his light stubble, his golden-brown eyes lighting up at the sight of me. This man could give me ideas if he wasn't all in with his fiancé, Ella. He's a little taller than my brother, strong, with tattoos peeking out from underneath his black sleeves, shoved up to his elbows.

He nods to us in greeting. "Morning, Aidan. Alex, it's good to see you again."

"Hi Grant."

"I hear welcome to the team is in order?"

I give him a half smile. "Yeah, are you sure you're okay with that?"

"You're helping us out. Hell ya, I'm okay with it. And Ella will be thrilled to have you around here too."

I smile. "Aidan told me about your engagement. I left last month before I had a chance to say congratulations to you."

His grin grows as he bites his lower lip, getting lost in thought. "Thanks." He shakes his head as if bringing himself back to reality. "Yeah, we should get you set up here. This area will be yours."

"Okay. Thank you." I glance between the two of them as they move around the space, attempting to clean up the area. "So, you guys want me to answer calls, handle your calendar, files, bills, and stuff like that?"

Both men nod their head in agreement, Grant affirming, "Yup."

"Do I get a shirt?" I ask, glancing at my brother.

Aidan chuckles, "I can do that."

I shrug. "All right. That's not so bad."

"It's not, but our stuff is kind of a mess at the moment," Aidan admits.

"Sorry about that," Grant apologizes, sheepish.

"No big deal. Aidan knows I like things organized. After I get that part done, it will be easy."

"You should even have time to write songs, or jingles or whatever else you want to do," Aidan suggests.

"Sounds good." If I have any artistic bones left in my body with everything going on. "Do you guys mind if I just look around to get an idea what I'm looking at with the files and calendar?"

"No problem. I've got a motorcycle to work on. Glad you're here, Alex."

I smile in response and glimpse at my brother, arching his eyebrow in question. "You're good?" he asks.

"Fan-fucking-tastic, Aidan. Go do your damn job."

Chuckling, he spins on his heel, moving towards the door for his private workspace on the right, with the garage door on his left. Without another word, he disappears into his office, leaving the door ajar, likely in case I need anything.

Softly sighing, I sit and begin digging through the files to see what I'll find, ready for the distraction from the chaos in my head. My turmoil is drowning my creativity and burying it in cement leaving nothing but bones and ash. Hopefully, working here will do something to calm what feels like madness to me, and resurrect my imagination.

Maybe then, I'll finally feel like myself again.

Chapter 5

Declan

Relief floods me the moment I step out of my office, and I quickly try to shove the disastrous morning out of my mind to no avail. It sucks that I'll be the one stuck picking up the slack and leading one of my teams on his marketing campaigns. Granted, I'm their boss either way, but now I'm stuck doing a lot of fucking busy work. The worst part about this job is without a doubt firing someone but losing one of our clients is a close second. Without consistent advertising and marketing clients and contracts we'd all be gone in a heartbeat.

But would I honestly give a fuck? Doubtful. This job started as my salvation so I could stay close to my family. Doesn't mean it has stayed that way.

I climb into my car and start it up, the check engine light popping on, followed by a notification informing me I'm due for service. Great. I don't need this shit. My cell rings, Gabriella calling. Swiftly, I connect it through my stereo before pulling out of the parking lot.

"Hi, Ella."

"Hey, Dec. I just tried your office. Where are you?"

"Keeping tabs on me, Sis?" I chuckle, attempting to lighten my mood. "I just left for a lunch break."

"Good. I'm glad you're leaving the office. You work way too much anyway."

"Nah, I work hard when I have to. That way I can take off whenever I need."

"True, you are lucky they love you so much."

"Yeah." I bite back a sigh knowing it would only make her feel guilty and that's the last thing she deserves. "What's up?"

"Grant and I wanted to have some people over Saturday for dinner. His brother and sister-in-law will be in town and with Finn's game on Friday..."

"There's no way any of us are missing Finn's game."

"Except maybe Char. She might have rehearsal."

"True. Anyone else coming Saturday?"

"Just our family and Grant was going to invite Aidan and now probably his sister since she just moved to town, as well as his assistant coach and his wife."

"Sounds like a full house, but you know I'll be there." My car beeps and I glance down at the dash, grimacing. "By the way, Ella, my check engine light has been on for a few days and now I got a service notification. I have an appointment at the garage next week, but do you think Grant would take a look at it for me this afternoon? I need to make sure I'm not going to make things worse waiting a week."

"You know he will fit you in, even if he can't. Why don't you stop by and see him. He doesn't always answer his phone right away when he's working."

"I thought they were going to hire someone to help them out."

"They did. Aidan's sister started today, but it is her first day."

"Good. Maybe I'll stop now and bring them all some lunch."

"Bribery. Nice."

"As long as it works." She laughs, the light sound bringing a smile to my face. It's good to hear her so happy. "I'm sure I can find something Grant will like, but any suggestions for Aidan or his sister?"

"Aidan eats pretty much anything, but I'm not sure about his sister. I've met her a couple times, but I don't really know her."

"Okay, I'll figure it out. Thanks."

"No problem. I have to get back to work. I have a little girl coming in to see me in a few minutes that's been in and out of the hospital like I used to be when I was her age." My chest tightens suddenly flooded with memories. "I want to be ready."

"We both know you're the best person for that job, Ella. Have I told you how proud I am of you?"

"Yes, Dad."

"Mock all you want, Sis. You're just reinforcing my belief that I'm the boss of all four of us."

She barks a laugh. "Whatever you say, big brother." She clears her throat. "But thank you, Dec. I'll see you later."

"Bye, Ella." I disconnect the call and turn towards the deli to pick up some food before heading over to G & A Cycles.

About thirty minutes later I climb out of my car carrying a box of sandwiches and salads for more than just the four people I planned on, me included, but I know they have a refrigerator here they can use for the leftovers and eat them tomorrow.

Balancing the box in one hand, I pull the door open, and step inside. "Hello?" Nothing greets me but silence. Maybe Aidan's sister didn't start yet. "Grant? Aidan?" I pause before trying again, "Hello? Grant? Aidan? Anyone here?"

The clear sound of a chair scraping the ground, followed by the slap of something hitting a desk, and approaching footsteps echoes. "What the hell, Al–" Aidan looks down as he steps out of his office, his gaze quickly swerving and meeting mine. "Declan. Sorry about that. I thought my sister was out here manning the desk."

"No worries. It's great you hired someone. I'm sure the paperwork was starting to stress you guys out."

"Yeah, I'm grateful my sister is here. You looking for Grant?"

"Yeah, but I brought lunch for everyone. Your sister too. Ella told me she moved here and started today."

"Thanks, man. You can set it on the top of the desk. He'll come in here to eat. You stayin' for lunch?"

"Probably." With a nod, I ask, "So, is Grant around?"

"He is." Aidan steps towards the door for the garage and yanks it open. "Grant, Declan is here to see you."

"Thanks, will you send him in?"

I smile. "Thanks, Aidan."

"No problem. I'll see you later. Maybe next time my sister will be around so you can meet her and thanks again for the food."

The door closes behind me and I step closer to Grant, standing over a sleek motorcycle. He's dressed in his normal attire–dark blue jeans, black work boots and a black t-shirt, his tattoos peeking out from underneath.

"Did I hear something about lunch?" He glances at me, grinning.

I nod. "Yup. I brought lunch for all of us from the deli."

"Sweet. Thanks." He pauses, setting down the wrench in his hand as his eyes narrow on me. "You need something, Dec?"

The corners of my lips curve up. "Why do I have to need something to stop at your garage and bring my future brother-in-law lunch?"

He chuckles. "You don't, but this is a first when Ella isn't here."

I wince. "Well, maybe I should change that."

"No need on my account." He smirks. "But seriously, is there something I can do for you?"

"I was hoping you'd take a look at my car. I have an appointment next week for a service, but my engine light is on and now I'm getting warnings on the dash, and it keeps beeping. I don't need you to service it, but I don't want to fuck anything up before I get there."

"You don't have to bring it to the dealer. You know I'll service it for you."

"Thanks, Grant, but you don't have to do that." He glares, his lips pinched in a firm line. Clearing my throat, I nod. "Thanks. How's my sister feeling?"

He grins. "Really good."

I breathe a sigh of relief. It doesn't matter how many times I hear it, it's like a heavy weight lifts off my shoulders every damn time. "Good."

"Do you have time, or do you have to get back to the office?"

Shrugging, I claim, "I have time. Honestly, I don't care if I go back at all today. My car breaking down isn't a far reach after the morning I've had."

"That bad?" he questions, arching his eyebrow.

"Let's just say I'm already looking forward to the weekend."

"Why don't we grab lunch and you can tell me about it?"

I huff a laugh. "Sure, I could eat."

He chuckles as we walk towards the door to the front office. "I'll wash my hands and meet you out there."

Lifting my gaze, I step back into the front room. A flash of violet draws my attention before Aidan's door clicks shut making my breath catch. Could it be? No fucking way. I shake my head, refusing to believe it. I've never thought much of anything any shade of purple, except that both my sisters love the color, but now my brain short circuits anytime violet touches anything. It was likely just a shirt and even if it was someone's hair, that doesn't mean it was *her*. A lot of people dye their hair that color.

The memories from that night flood my senses just thinking of her making my dick twitch. I would take another night, or several, like that one in a heartbeat. Unfortunately, she walked out without ever giving me the chance.

What is Aidan's sister's name again? Did anyone even say it? I glance around the room as if I'll see a sign telling me who she might be, but no such luck.

Grant walks into the room and starts going through the food. "So, what did you bring us?"

Instead of answering, I shrug, grabbing my own sandwich and sit. "What's Aidan's sister's name?"

"Alex," he responds without looking at me, grabbing his own sandwich and it's a damn good thing.

The blood drains from my face, not because she's here, but because I fucked Aidan's sister. I would do it again, and again, *and* again if she'd let me. A smile tugs at my lips. The tension leaves my body for the first time in over a month.

Two words scream at me inside my head: she's here.

Chapter 6

Alex

I'm finally getting control of all the paperwork for Aidan and Grant, wondering how the hell they've survived without help although it hasn't been very long. There is no way they would've made it much longer. "You're damn lucky I came when I did," I mumble, loud enough for Aidan to hear through his open door.

He laughs. "Just wanted to keep you busy."

"You didn't know I was coming until two days ago."

Out of the corner of my eye, I catch sight of a man with light brown hair and a familiar build through the window making my heart stop. I turn my head, my eyes widening at the sight of Declan striding towards the front door in tan dress pants and a navy-blue button down, the sleeves rolled up to his elbows looking sexy as hell.

"No fucking way," I mumble under my breath.

The moment before he pulls the door open, I drop to the floor and slip under the desk, grateful for the counter blocking his view.

"Hello?" he calls out as he steps inside. "Grant? Aidan?" He pauses before trying again while I remain frozen. "Hello? Grant? Aidan? Anyone here?"

I hear my brother shove his chair out and slam something on his desk, his footsteps following. "What the hell, Al–" His eyes widen as he sees me hiding under the desk, his gaze quickly flicking to the man on the other side. "Declan. Sorry about that. I thought my sister was out here manning the desk."

"No worries. It's great you hired someone. I'm sure the paperwork was starting to stress you guys out."

"Yeah, I'm grateful my sister is here. You looking for Grant?"

"Yeah, but I brought lunch for everyone. Your sister too. Ella told me she moved here and started today."

"Thanks, man. You can set it on the top of the desk. He'll come in here to eat. You stayin' for lunch?"

"Probably." He nods. "Is Grant around?"

"He is." Aidan steps towards the door for the garage and pulls it open, blocking my view and hopefully me. "Grant, Declan is here to see you."

"Thanks, will you send him in?"

I hold my breath, watching as he grips the door and Declan steps through. "Thanks, Aidan."

"No problem. I'll see you later. Maybe next time my sister will be around so you can *meet* her and thanks again for the food." The door closes behind Declan.

My brother's black scuffed boots step in front of me. Exhaling harshly, he growls softly, "Get in my office now."

Scrambling, I do as he says, sinking into a chair in the corner opposite an art board holding various sketches.

He follows me inside and sits in a chair next to me instead of behind his desk. Staring at me, he probes, "You want to tell me what the fuck that was about?"

"Aidan–"

"Don't. I've never seen you hide from anyone but dad. I've always thought Declan was a good guy, hell I only hear good things about the man, but you and I both know that doesn't mean shit. Did Declan do something to you?"

I gasp, my eyes go wide. "No!" Vehemently, I shake my head, scrunching up my nose before I admit, "Well, not anything I didn't want him to."

Grimacing, he runs a hand through his hair in frustration. "Don't tell me that shit. Do you even know who he is?"

"Obviously not."

"You know my partner, Grant? He's engaged to his sister."

"Declan is Ella's brother?"

"Why the hell were you hiding from him, Alex?"

Heaving a sigh, I avert my eyes and explain, "It happened a little over a month ago and I haven't seen or talked to him since."

Aidan's jaw clenches, his muscles ticking as he attempts to control his breathing. "I'll fucking kill him."

Grabbing his wrist, I blurt out. "It's not what you think."

"No? So, you didn't sleep with that asshole?"

"He's not an asshole. You just said so yourself."

"He is if he took advantage of my little sister."

"Aid, he didn't take advantage of me. If anything, it was me who took advantage of him. I left before he even woke up."

He winces, quickly schooling his features, repeatedly clenching, and unclenching his fists, while regaining control. "So, again, why the fuck were you hiding from him?"

Closing my eyes, I take a deep breath, exhaling slowly, attempting to relax. "Because I wasn't ready to see him."

He scoffs. "You do know you moved to Genesis Beach. This place is as small town as it gets. You can't hide from him for long."

Shaking my head, I stare into my brother's eyes, begging him for support. "I don't need to hide from him forever. I just need a day or two to wrap my head around everything before I talk to him."

His eyes narrow, assessing me. "There's something you're not telling me."

"You're right."

Suddenly, his body stiffens. Sitting up straight, he stares at me with eyes full of concern causing my heart to plummet to the pit of my stomach.

He knows.

"You're pregnant," he states, not bothering to ask.

My chest tightens and I close my eyes, taking a deep breath. I nod my head, a single tear slipping out of the corner of my eye and running down my cheek, betraying me. "Yeah," I squeak, my voice cracking on the single word.

"Shit," he mumbles under his breath, his hand grabbing the back of his neck. "Didn't I teach you to protect yourself? Fuck, didn't *he* use a condom?"

"I did protect myself and you know condoms aren't one hundred percent effective, right? Well, apparently I'm a statistic. But do you really think it's a good time to lecture me about having safe sex?"

Crouching next to me, he heaves a sigh, wrapping me up in his protective embrace. "I'm sorry, Alex. Do you know what you want to do?"

"Not exactly." Pinpricks rush over my skin, my nerves consume me. Fear churns in my gut, unsettling my stomach once again. The thought of telling Declan and making a decision, no matter what it is, terrifies me. It makes it real.

"Alex, it's going to be okay no matter what you decide," he asserts, his voice low, insistent, comforting.

Breathing a sigh of relief, my heart clenches, grateful he knows and as always, he's on my side. "Thanks, Aidan. I think I needed to hear you say that."

"Whatever you need, whatever you want, I'm here for you."

Gulping down the lump in my throat, I nod against his chest. "I know. Let me talk to him first."

"That's why you wouldn't tell me."

"Yeah."

"Do you want me with you?"

I huff a laugh. The noise sounding more like a choked sob, making him pull back to look down at me. "Hell no. I can handle myself."

Grinning wide, his eyes shine with a pride I've only ever seen from him since our mom died. Damn, I miss her, but I'm thankful for my brother. I was only ten and he was fourteen the day our world shattered and everything we'd ever known changed forever.

"You sure as hell can, sis."

"Besides, I'd rather you not kill him before I tell him."

He presses his lips together, his lips twitching in amusement. "How about after, then?" I laugh and he quirks his brow. "No?"

Leaning forward, I give him another hug, another tear slipping out of the corner of my eye. "Thank you, Aidan. I love you."

He sighs, resigned, and determined, kissing me on the forehead. I don't know what I'd do without him. "I love you too, Alex. It will be okay. I promise we will get through this no matter what."

"I know."

A knock on the door startles us apart. My eyes go wide wondering if it's him. "Declan brought a ton of food if you guys are hungry," Grant calls through the door.

My body sags in relief.

"Thanks, we'll be right out."

My eyes widen. "You said we?"

Arching his eyebrow, Aidan prods, "Yup. You gonna come out?"

"Of course, I am," I retort, knowing I'm not ready, but I'll push through like I always do.

"Don't you want to get this conversation over with? I think the universe is telling you running and hiding is no longer an option."

"I'm not hiding or running."

"You sure about that?"

Narrowing my eyes, I glare at him and emphasize. "I'm here."

He chuckles, holding up his hands as if he's innocent when I know he's anything but. "You're right, Alexa."

"Thanks for telling me," his speaker sounds.

"You promised you'd change it!"

"Weren't we talking about the one at home?"

I swipe a stress football off his desk, throwing it at his head. He ducks out of the room laughing, pulling the door shut behind him.

Of course, he's here.

This one-night stand is turning into everything it's not supposed to be, but then again, in one night he proved he was not like any man I've ever been with. For that reason alone, I had to leave before he could talk me out of it, if he even wanted to.

You can do this Alex.

Taking a deep breath, I trudge towards the door, my hand resting momentarily on the handle as my doubts surface. What if he doesn't remember me? What if he does and he thinks I set him up?

Straightening my shoulders, I shove my doubts out of my head. It doesn't matter what he thinks. I have to tell him. I'll deal with what comes next after I confess.

"Fuck me," I mutter under my breath, yanking the door open.

Chapter 7

Declan

Aidan steps out of his office, his smile faltering the moment his gaze lands on me. Shit. He clenches his jaw and steps towards the food, grumbling as if he's pissed off at the gesture, "Thanks again for bringing lunch, Declan."

Grant pauses mid-bite, glancing from Aidan to me and back again, his eyes drawn down in confusion. Eventually, he shrugs, taking another bite of his sandwich.

Desperate to know if I'm right, my entire body tenses, at the same time, confident and elated I already know. She's not someone I'd forget. My foot bounces, anxious to lay my eyes on her again, but Aidan's reaction leaves me teetering on a different kind of edge, at the same time confirming my suspicions.

Alex–the woman my head or my dick can't shake since our night together–is here.

"Ah, yeah, no problem. You're welcome," I stammer like a fucking tool.

The chomping and chewing sounds of the three of us eating becomes deafening while my gaze burns into the door to his office, wondering what he knows and what she'll say. She told him something. I'm sure of it. She has every right to tell whoever she wants, but when I hook up, I have my reasons I don't want to be with anyone around here and this is one of them. Ripping my gaze from the door, I clear my throat, desperate to break this awkward silence. "So, Ella mentioned–"

Aidan's office door opens again, my mouth closing as my eyes fly to the entrance, waiting with bated breath. Confirming my suspicions, she steps out dressed in ripped blue jeans, exposing small slices of her silky skin, my fingertips tingling at the memory of what it felt like. The fabric of her long-sleeved purple shirt are tugged down, her fingers gripping the edges, her hair a shade darker and falling over her shoulders. Glancing at me, she holds her head high, looking sexy as hell. I thought I'd never see her again after I woke up alone, but she's here, standing in front of me. Gulping down the lump in my throat, I remind myself where I am.

"You good?" Aidan asks, staring down at her.

She nods as her gaze lands on me, her eyes flashing in recognition, but no shock. Of course, she knew I was here.

"Hi, Alex," I say, my voice a low gravel. She tilts her head to the side, assessing me with a question in her eyes, prompting me to say more. "It's good to see you. I didn't know you were Aidan's sister."

Her shoulders visibly relax. Maybe she wasn't sure if I'd remember her or if I'd admit it. "Hey, Declan." The sound of my name on her lips makes my dick twitch. Thank fuck I'm sitting down. "Didn't know you were so connected to my brother through Grant either. What a surprise."

"Wait. You two know each other?" Grant questions, arching his eyebrow, looking back and forth between us.

"Yeah," I confirm, nodding my head, keeping my focus on Alex. "Running into you is the kind of surprise I can get behind." I give her a crooked grin. She rolls her eyes, arching her eyebrow in challenge.

Damn, I love her sass.

"You'll get behind more than that," Aidan grumbles irritably. Alex huffs a laugh before glaring at her brother, her lips still twitching.

"So, Dec, what have you been doing since I saw you last?"

Contemplating what and how much I want to say in front of these two, I begin, "Yeah, about that–"

Aidan interrupts, "Alex, you should eat something. You barely ate breakfast."

"Got it, Dad," she mutters, sarcasm thick on her tongue.

"Don't–"

"I said I got it," she snaps, grabbing a paper plate and looking at the remaining sandwiches.

"I wasn't sure what anyone wanted so I got a couple extra. Hopefully there's something you like."

She doesn't respond, but suddenly she drops the plate her face flush. Covering her mouth, she mumbles, "Excuse me." Spinning on her heel, she slips into the bathroom and slams the door, the water instantly turning on to cover the unmistakable sound of retching.

"Is she all right?" I ask, my eyebrows drawn down in concern, my protective instincts kicking in.

Aidan glances at the door before turning back to me and holding my stare. "Maybe that's something you should ask her."

Instead of adding fuel to the fire, I nod my head, keeping my eyes on the door, debating if I should get up to check on her, when the door opens, and she steps back into the room looking worse for wear. Standing, I take a step towards her, but she retreats, taking a step back.

Stuffing my hands in my pockets, I ask, "You okay?"

She pastes a fake smile on her face. "I'm fan-fucking-tastic."

"Maybe you should go home and get some rest," Aidan suggests.

"I'm fine, Aid." She glares at her brother.

"I could take you," I offer.

"Thought you wanted me to take a look at your car," Grant reminds me, arching his eyebrow.

Exhaling harshly, I mumble, "Shit, yeah."

"Take my Jeep. Drop her off at my place and bring it back here to pick up your car," Aidan offers, catching me off-guard. "I'm sure Grant will be done by the time you come back after... catching up."

"Don't I have a say in this?" Alex questions accusingly.

"Go, Alex. It looks like you've done enough today already. Besides, we've gone this long without you, I'm sure Grant and I can make it a few more hours." Aidan gives his sister a pointed look, a silent conversation passing between them.

She heaves a sigh and relents. "Fine. But I'll be back tomorrow."

"Good," Aidan agrees. Aidan stands, crossing his arms over his chest as he faces me. "Take care of her or start running."

"Promise," I declare, holding his gaze, feeling like this is more of a first date instead of a ride home.

He gives me a stiff nod, then steps over to Alex, his large frame visibly softening as he takes her into his arms. "Thank you," she murmurs softly, hugging him back. He whispers something into her ear. She rolls her eyes, but nods in agreement as she moves out of his embrace. "Bye, Aidan."

"Bye. Love you."

She smirks. "I know." He chuckles, shaking his head. "Bye, Grant. I'll see you tomorrow."

"Thanks, Alex. Feel better." Grant waves. "See you in a few, Dec."

Alex grabs her purse from behind the desk while Aidan gets his keys, handing them to me with a look of warning. I nod and walk out the door, holding it for her.

We step out into the crisp fall air, the sun tucked behind the clouds and the trees just beginning to change color. "I can drive," she states.

"Yeah, but you're obviously not feeling well and your brother gave me the keys."

Huffing, she turns to me with a fire in her eyes. "I'm not incapacitated, I'm feeling better already."

"That's great but let me drive."

"You think you can just come here and take over?"

I arch my eyebrow in challenge. "I was already here. I live up the road and my family lives here. I'm definitely not trying to take over, but I am trying to take care of you when you obviously don't feel well. Is it too much to ask to let me?"

"Yes."

My eyes widen, surprised by her honesty. Knowing it's a short drive and I'll be stuck in the car with her either way, maybe this would be a good time not to argue. Grinding my jaw, I grunt, "Fine." Holding the keys out, I let them dangle from my fingers and she swiftly snaps them away.

"Smart man."

"I won't argue with you there."

She laughs, her eyes instantly bright with amusement, the sound sending shivers down my spine. "Just get in."

We do and soon she's pulling out of the parking lot and heading towards her brother's house. Taking a deep breath, I attempt to start simple. "So, how long are you planning on being here?"

She purses her lips making me wonder if she'll give me anything. "I'm not sure. I may be here for a while." She glances at me out of the corner of her eye, my stomach twisting at the thought.

"What brought you here besides your brother?" I probe, feeling like I'm pulling teeth to get anything out of her.

"How do you know it's anything besides him?"

Arching my eyebrow in challenge, I question, "Do you get a job every time you visit somewhere for a few days?"

Frowning, she glares out at the road and mutters, "It's complicated."

Heaving a sigh, I run my hand through my hair. "Is everything okay? Did you get fired from your job? Running from an ex? Just wanted to get away?"

Huffing a humorless laugh, she side eyes me and immediately focuses back on the road. "You sure are nosy."

"You're rigid, feisty as ever, and incredibly stubborn, but I feel the tension coming off you in waves." Her breathing picks up along with her fury. "I just want to help you, Alex. Is that so wrong?"

"You want to help, Declan?" she snaps, pursing her lips, her cheeks rosy with her own frustration.

"Of course, I do."

"Great. There's plenty for you to help with. I'm pregnant and it's yours."

Blood drains from my face, attempting to process her words. "What?"

She scoffs and shakes her head as if she's not expecting anything from me. "Nothing left to say?"

"I–"

"Just forget it. You don't owe me a damn thing," she claims as she parks her brother's car and jumps out, leaving it running. "Have a good life!"

The bang of the door closing startles me. "What the hell?" Turning off the car, I swipe the keys and jump out, chasing after her. "Alex, wait!"

Without looking back, she stalks into the house slamming the door behind her.

"Fuck me. What just happened?"

Chapter 8

Alex

Why did I blurt it out like that? What the hell was I thinking? Sighing, I shake my head. Guess it doesn't matter anymore.

Pounding on the front door ensues almost immediately. Closing my eyes, I take a deep breath and exhale slowly, attempting to ignore it, hoping he'll go away. Knowing that likely won't happen until the cops come or Aidan borrows someone's car to come check on me, I take one more deep breath before snapping, "I'm coming!"

Trudging towards the door, I open it and glance up at Declan, leaning with one hand on each side of the door frame, his head hanging low, giving me a tortured look. "Let me in to talk, please." I stare it him, unmoving. "At least give me a chance to process everything before you shut me out. I'm not going anywhere, Alex. There's no way I'm letting you walk away from me again."

Crossing my arms over my chest, I narrow my eyes, glaring. "And what do you think you could do about it?"

"Just give me a chance, Alex. Please," he pleads, his voice cracking.

Heaving a sigh, my shoulders sag and I stomp over to the couch. Slumping into it, I bury my face in my hands, a tear slipping out without my consent. Quickly, I wipe it away as I hear the door click shut and his approaching footsteps. The couch dips next to me, his masculine scent hitting my nostrils like a tsunami and making my stomach flip.

Stupid traitorous body!

"Listen," he begins, reaching for me. I flinch, scooting away. It's dangerous to be too close to this man.

I look up meeting his gaze, lifting my head high. "I'm sorry, Declan, but I don't know you."

He nods. "You're right. I don't know you either besides you're beautiful, independent, intelligent, and strong. Don't ever challenge you to pool or darts unless I want to risk getting my ass kicked. You stick a little bit of your tongue out when you're focusing really hard on something and you're a firecracker both in and out of the bedroom."

My cheeks turn a dark shade of red while chaos ensues in my gut, not sure if it's from him or the baby growing inside me. I shake my head in denial. "That doesn't mean you know me."

"And you're right again, but I would like to know you better, Alex."

"Because of the baby."

"No, because of you." I snort, blushing again, but refuse to break our gaze. "You don't have to believe me, but I wasn't happy when I woke up alone that morning."

"What? Disappointed you weren't getting morning sex?"

He huffs a laugh. "Yeah, but that wasn't why. I wanted to see you again."

"We said it was just for the night."

"Yeah, we did, but that doesn't mean I didn't feel a certain way. You surprised the hell outta me."

I shake my head at him. "Back up. This is too much. I came here to tell you that I was pregnant because I thought you had a right to know."

"I'm glad you did."

"But that doesn't mean I want to know you." He flinches visibly, but I push forward. "What happens if I don't keep the baby? You disappear?"

"No. That's not who I am." His face pales and he closes his eyes. I watch his Adam's apple bob up and down when he gulps hard before focusing back on me. "You don't want to keep the baby?"

"I didn't say that."

His jaw ticks. "I realize I have no right to decide what you do with your body, but I will help you through this. I'd like to get to know you better Alex, but no matter what happens between us, I will be by your side every step of the way. I'm loyal and protective of those I care about. It is your decision, but you should know, I want this baby."

I shake my head, my face showing nothing but disbelief. "You're not even going to question if it's really yours? Who else I was with in the past couple months?"

"Could it be someone else's?"

Scoffing, I retort, "No." He nods, pinching his lips tightly together. "But how can you just believe me like that?"

"I don't believe you would lie about something like this when you sought me out to tell me in the first place, especially when I know your brother well and I'll soon be related to his partner."

My mouth drops slightly open, not used to anyone but Aidan having any faith in me. "But..."

"If it makes you feel better, we can have a DNA test when the baby is born. I mean..." He winces and looks away, guilt weighing on me for letting him stew.

"I'm keeping the baby," I confess, watching him closely for his reaction.

Color returns to his cheeks as he breathes a sigh of relief.

"And if you want to be here for the baby, that's fine, but that doesn't mean anything for me and you."

He inches closer to me on the couch, holding my gaze. "I do want that, Alex. It doesn't matter that this took me by surprise, I know what I want and I don't shy away from my responsibilities."

My breath catches in my throat and I snap, "I'm no one's responsibility. Besides, you don't owe me anything and I definitely don't expect a single thing from you." Bitterness weighs on my tongue, no matter how much I try to hide it.

"That's not what I meant. I want to be there. If I have anything to say about it, I wouldn't have it any other way." Pausing he licks his lips, drawing my gaze. "Of course, you don't have to give me time with you, but I'm still asking. Please, give me a chance to know you better."

I shake my head, dragging my eyes back to his. "I don't know, Declan. I just wanted to tell you about the baby. A relationship is not what I was looking for."

A crooked smile curves his lips. "Sometimes things hit you from out of nowhere and knock you off your feet and other times you're able to grab onto it and hold on, enjoying the ride of your life. But if you don't reach out and take a chance, you only protect yourself from living." My stomach twists at his poetic words, knowing he's right. Doesn't mean it's not terrifying. Holding my gaze, he continues, "That's one of the things that drew me to you the night we met. You were relishing every moment and you weren't about to let anyone take that away from you."

Damn. I'm in so much trouble, but I try to shake it off. "Anyone can spout pretty words."

"They aren't just pretty if they're true."

I scoff. "Yeah, right. I'm sure you're the first man ever who's happy you knocked up your one-night stand, a woman you thought you'd never see again."

"But I'd hoped I would see you again."

My stomach churns. "I can't do this with you."

"What do you mean you can't do this?" His eyes widen and his body goes rigid. "Don't push me out of your life. Not now. Why would you even come here to tell me if you were going to shut me out?"

Disappointment crushes my chest, but I have no right to feel that way, especially when I know I'm provoking him with a false iron stake. "You really don't know me. I can't cut you out of my life if you were never mine in the first place."

"Alex–"

"I'm not shutting you out of anything, Declan. I don't feel good. I'm going to go lay down and you need to get my brother's car back to him."

He sighs, clenching his jaw. "Is there anything I can do for you?" My eyes narrow, but I don't bother responding. He needs to go, not to pretend that he cares about me. Pursing his lips, he prods, "Can I at least have your number?"

Opening my mouth, I hesitate for a moment, but as much as I hate to admit it, he's right–I have to be able to talk to him somehow. "Give me your phone."

Without question, he opens it and does as I ask. Quickly, I type in my own cell number and send myself a text before handing it back to him. His fingers brush mine as he wraps his hand around the phone, causing a bolt of electricity to shoot right through me.

"Happy?" I growl, irritated with my traitorous body as it stirs, overheating.

A crooked smile lights up his face. "Ecstatic."

I roll my eyes dramatically and trudge to the door, flinging it open, desperate for the cool air. "Great. Then, you can go."

His grin falls, but he nods, stepping into my space, his scent instantly enveloping me. My body tingles making me hold my breath. I'm not able to take much more of feeling him looking down at me, waiting for me to meet his gaze. My eyes drop to his mouth before lifting. Licking his lips, he claims, "Sure, this is unexpected, but that doesn't mean unwanted. We just have some things to learn to close the gaps." Tipping his head towards me, his lips graze my forehead. "And believe me, I can't wait to close every single one of those openings."

A gasp escapes my lips before I can stop it. He gives me that crooked grin, and pulls the door shut behind him before I have a chance to react.

I flop down onto the couch with a groan as thoughts of Declan take over my brain at the memory of his touch. A shiver runs down my spine. My body wants what it can't have–not if I want to survive. I can't get sucked into his world. It's not worth it. Right?

Besides, who knows how long he would even stick around? Maybe I won't have to worry about it for long. My hand falls to my churning stomach while my head screams at me that this could change everything. But I need to be the reason, not our circumstances. How would I ever know the truth?

Sighing, I close my eyes. Why am I even thinking about it? For a man like him, I would only ever be a baby mama.

I'm not someone to bring home to the family.

Chapter 9

Declan

After changing into gray sweatpants and a dark blue t-shirt, I flop down on my couch attempting to process what happened and what the fuck I do from here. I got my wish. Alex looked sexy as hell even though I could see in her eyes that she wasn't feeling well. But I never thought seeing her again would be like this.

Suddenly, my front door swings open, Ella walking in without an invitation. "Hi, big brother."

"Don't you knock?"

She laughs, shrugging. "Guess you shouldn't have told me where the key is."

"What are you doing here, Ella?" I ask, running my hand through my hair as I sit up.

"Grant said you were off when you came back to pick up your car. He told me you barely said a word." I quirk a brow, waiting for more of an explanation when I'm not even sure how to begin. "Thought I'd return your kindness and come check on you for once."

"I'm fine," I grumble, defensively.

She frowns. "Obviously not."

"No, Ella, I am, it's just..." I snap my mouth shut, clenching my jaw.

How do I communicate something I can't even process? Her eyes widen, prompting me for more. I stare at my sister, knowing I need to talk to someone, but I'm not ready for the entire family to know what's going on.

Then again, she can keep a secret. Besides, she would know I need to be the one to tell them. Heaving a sigh, I run my hand through my hair and claim, "I think it's time I collect on that favor you owe me."

She arches her eyebrows in question. "What favor are you collecting? You've done a lot for me."

My chest tightens, a smile tugging at my lips. "Remember when I didn't tell mom and dad anything about Grant moving in with you?"

Her eyes widen. "Oh, that. Then, this must be good."

I chuckle softly. "You could say that."

She pokes me in the stomach. "So, tell me! But remember–same warning you gave me–small town and all, it won't be long before everyone knows."

I shake my head, still stunned by the news. It definitely won't be a secret for long. Ella puts her water bottle to her lips and tips it back her gaze falling away from me making it easier to confess. "So, I'm going to be a father," I blurt out. Her head snaps back towards me, and she gasps, water spewing from her mouth and hitting me in the face and chest making me jump up. "Ella!" I exclaim, the moment another reminder of the night I met Alex.

"I'm sorry, but did you just say you're going to be a father?" she asks her eyes wide.

"I did." Grimacing I wipe my hand down my face and she starts laughing. "What the hell? Why are you laughing?"

"First, sorry for that." Frowning, she gestures to my face as I use my t-shirt to dry the rest. "But second, are you kidding? You put boxes of condoms in Finn's room all the time to make sure he uses them and lecture all three of us about protecting ourselves, and I'm pretty sure you threatened Grant at least on one occasion, but you don't follow your own rules?"

Narrowing my eyes, I cross my arms over my chest. "I always do, but apparently one of them didn't work."

Her face falls, going through an array of emotions from confusion to surprise and even hurt. "Oh. Sorry. How come I didn't even know you were dating anyone?"

"Because I'm not."

"Oh." She bites her lip in thought, slowly releasing it. "So, who's the mom? Do I know her?"

My hand runs through my hair and grips the back of my neck, not wanting her or anyone else to think less of Alex. I've never met a stronger woman. Just thinking of the way she handled herself in the bar with that asshole and again today with me. But Ella is the last person to judge anyone. I hold her gaze watching her close for her reaction and confess, "Aidan's sister, Alex."

Her eyes widen in shock. "Wait, Alex?" I nod in affirmation. "I don't understand."

"I'm not explaining about the birds and the bees, Ella."

Tilting her head, she narrows her eyes at me, grumbling, "Ha-ha. How do you even know her?"

Knowing what I'm about to reveal to my little sister and hoping it doesn't change the way she looks at me, I wince. "We met a little over a month ago a couple towns over."

"Hmm. But you said you haven't been dating anyone."

I shake my head. "No, we're not dating. Honestly, I didn't even know how to find her. Believe me, I tried. I sure as hell didn't have a clue she was Aidan's sister."

Ella frowns, obviously unhappy with me. I don't blame her, but I hate disappointing her. "Okay. So, how has she been feeling?"

"I'm not sure, but I don't think she's been feeling the best. She left the garage today because she got sick."

She rolls her eyes dramatically. "There's your answer Einstein. I thought you were supposed to be the smart one?" I give her a look, telling her I'm not impressed making her giggle. "Anyway, what happened when she told you?"

"Nothing. She tried to tell me she didn't need shit from me. But you know that doesn't work for me."

"Of course not. So, what have you done about it?"

I shrug. "I brought her home. Then, I left to go back to the office because she wanted to get some rest."

She rolls her eyes again. "That's not what I mean, Declan. What have you done to help her feel better?"

Cringing, I admit, "Nothing, I guess."

Ella narrows her eyes in disbelief. "Seriously? What the hell is wrong with you?"

"I just found out about it a couple hours ago."

"So what? You're home laying on your couch like you're feeling sorry for yourself when you could be doing something. This isn't you Dec, you're always the first one to be there. Annoyingly so. You know how to take care of her. I know that better than anyone. So, get off your ass and do something to help her. Show her you will be there for her and the baby."

"Like what? She kicked me out."

Crossing her arms over her chest, she gives me a look. "Has that ever stopped you before? Find a way to help her."

"I've never taken care of someone who's pregnant before."

"You had never taken care of someone who had non-Hodgkin's lymphoma before either, but you did."

"We had mom and dad," I feebly argue.

"So?" she prompts, arching her eyebrows in challenge. "When I got sick, you were just as much of a parent as mom and dad were to all three of us–you still are. You watched Char and Finn when I was in the hospital or mom and dad had to go to work. You have always been there for all of us, even when we don't want you to be." She smirks. "But we're all adults now; even Finn is graduating high school this year. It's time to take care of yourself, Dec. Alex will be a part of that, whether you want to be with her or not. So, figure it out fast because I guarantee she's just as scared and lost as you are right now–probably more."

Sighing, I shake my head. "How did you get so smart?"

She grins, bumping my shoulder. "I had a great teacher."

Chuckling, I loop my arm around my sister's neck and pull her to me. "Thanks, Ella."

Her arms wrap around my waist, giving me a quick squeeze. "You're welcome, big brother."

I kiss her on the top of the head before releasing her and sliding back. She tilts her head to the side, assessing me. "What?" I prompt, arching my eyebrow.

"I'm still surprised you needed a push with this. That's not like you. What's holding you back anyway?"

"Nothing."

"Do you like her?" she taunts, her voice sing-song like when we were kids.

A smile tugs at my lips. "Maybe."

"Oh, you do." She grins, her eyes sparkling.

"Ella," I warn.

"Come on. Tell me!"

"She's just different." I shrug. "I wanted to ask her out, but she left before I had a chance and now this. I have so many questions."

She nods in understanding, her gaze full of empathy. "And now you wonder if she'll believe you like her at all."

I pinch my lips tightly together and shrug as if the answer is obvious. "I'm not even sure where to begin. There's so much more to consider now."

"Dec, instead of analyzing everything like you do, act like you would if it were me or Char." My eyes narrow, glaring, but she rolls her eyes and waves me off.

"You know what I mean. You're making it harder than it needs to be. All you have to do is be your annoying self. She apparently likes you well enough."

"Gee, thanks."

She giggles, grinning proudly. "Happy to help."

I chuckle at her antics. "It's just–she's different." Heaving a sigh, I concede, "I know you're right, Ella, but I can't fuck this up."

"Shoot, I wasn't recording that. Give me a sec and say that again." She pulls out her phone, taps on the screen and holds it up, looking at me with a broad smile on her face.

"She's different?" I question, feigning ignorance.

"No, the other part."

"I can't fuck this up?" Smirking, I arch my eyebrow in challenge.

Heaving a sigh as if exasperated, she emphasizes, "No, the part where you said, you're right, Ella."

Shaking my head, I laugh. "There's not a chance in hell those words ever came out of my mouth."

As she gives me a playful shove, we both burst out laughing. Although I won't repeat it aloud, I know she's right.

Chapter 10

Alex

Knocking on the door becomes louder before I roll off the bed, grumbling, "I'm coming." It better not be Declan. It's only been a day!

Stomping towards the front door, I yank it open, my best friend, Sloane standing there dressed in blue jeans and a long-sleeved white blouse, flaring at the waist. She crosses her arms over her ample cleavage, narrowing her eyes. "Why the hell didn't you tell me you were home?"

"Sorry. I was going to, but I didn't have the chance."

Her blue eyes roam over me from head to toe before her eyebrows draw down in concern. "I call BS. There's something you didn't want to tell me." How the hell does she do that? "What's wrong?"

"How'd you know I was here?" I ask an obvious attempt at avoiding her question. Turning away, I trudge to the couch and sit in the corner, curling my legs up underneath me.

"I ran into Aidan at the hardware store, and he told me I should stop and see you." My eyebrows hit my hairline. She's a landscape architect, not usually the one you see at the hardware store. Waving off my surprise, she states, "I was there with Kelly. He had an idea for the house and wanted to pick up a few things."

"That makes sense, but what else can possibly be done to that house?" Her fiancé, Kelly, is an architect and bought an old house on the edge of town. Him and his construction team have been completely renovating it and Sloane is working on the landscaping. It was her dream job and the final product looks incredible.

"You'd be surprised, but this time it's just something for us."

"So secretive. Sounds like a sex room or something."

She huffs a laugh. "We don't need a room for that."

"Doesn't mean it wouldn't be fun."

"Stop avoiding!" She knows me well.

"Fine. I'm pregnant," I divulge, watching her closely, and waiting for her reaction. I'm not one to hide the facts. Feelings, sure, but not facts.

Sloane laughs, startling when her bright eyes take me in, realizing I'm not laughing along with her. "Wait. You're serious."

"Yup," I say, popping the p.

"Are you okay? How are you feeling?"

I scrunch up my nose in displeasure. "Not great, but I'm okay."

She sits down next to me, reaching for my hand and waits for me to speak. The small gesture gives me the comfort I crave, and I exhale slowly, relaxing into the couch. Just knowing she'll wait, as long as I want her to, is exactly what I need.

"When I was here last month, I stopped at a bar a couple towns over to release some stress before going back. I played some darts and some pool..." I shrug, a grin tugging at my lips. "Won a few dollars."

"Of course you did."

"This guy was being a sore loser because he kept losing to a girl."

Her eyebrows draw down in confusion. "Wait, what?"

Knowing what she's asking, I shake my head. "Not the guy I hooked up with, someone else. But the guy I hooked up with tried to come rescue me." I giggle at the memory, Sloane joining in knowing I like my independence.

"I wish I could've seen that."

"He was so damn hot, Sloane, my mouth was watering. I just wanted one night with a man like him."

Her brow furrows, puzzled. "What do you mean, with a man like him?"

Frowning, I shrug. "I mean he's not only hot and great in bed, but he was funny and sweet. Plus, he seemed to have his shit together. But I'm not the kind of woman a man like him brings home to meet the parents. I'm the good for one night kind of woman for someone like him."

"Why would you say that? That's not true. You're amazing–"

"Sloane, I didn't say that so you would give me a pep talk. I love you girl, but it's okay. I know who I am."

She shakes her head in denial. "Alex–"

"Anyway," I interrupt, knowing she'll keep defending me if I don't stop her, "we had an incredible night." I pause, humming in appreciation at the memory. "Mmm... The sex was so good, Sloane. He did this thing with his tongue."

She laughs. "Okay, so a superhero in bed."

A smile tugs at my lips. "Definitely. But I left the next morning before he woke up. And now," I hold my free arm out for emphasis, "here we are."

"Okay, do you know who he is?"

My cheeks heat and my gaze drops to my lap, suddenly nervous. "Um, yeah."

She squeezes my hand, prompting me to continue. "Are you going to share?"

"Remember that driver's license I sent you in case something happened to me?"

"Yes! But I never really looked at it." She reaches for her phone, scrolling back through our messages, but I don't wait for her to find it.

Closing my eyes, I confess, "It's Declan Howard."

She gasps and my eyes fly open. "Declan? He's hot, Alex."

"I'm well aware."

She laughs. "I thought for sure you were going to tell me someone older."

I smirk. "He is older."

Waving me off, she insists, "You know what I mean. You always had a thing for older men." Because they were safe and kept my emotions completely out of it. "And he's such a nice guy."

"You know him?" I ask, suddenly wanting to know as much as I can.

Shrugging, she concedes, "Not really, but I know who he is. His whole family has always been really nice. I see him with his family a lot and everyone who's ever mentioned them always has such good things to say about them."

"He has a big family?" I can't imagine what that's like.

"Yeah, two sisters and a brother, but I think he's the oldest." Pausing, she cocks her brow in challenge. "Shouldn't you be talking to him about this stuff?"

"Sure, I guess. But telling him I'm pregnant and he's going to be a father was enough drama for me for one day."

"I imagine. How'd it go?"

"As good as it can when you confess you're eternally connected to one of your one night stands."

"He'll do the right thing."

Shaking my head, I claim, "It doesn't matter what he does. He needed to know the truth because I'm keeping this baby. Whatever he decides to do is up to him. I'm not expecting anything from him, but I won't stand in the way of him being in the baby's life either."

"That doesn't mean he won't want to be there." My stomach clenches wondering if her words hold any truth. "Besides, having a sexy, sweet man who's that good with his tongue close by couldn't be a bad thing."

Grateful for her deflection, I smirk. "It's not just his tongue. He..."

"Okay, okay," she interrupts, laughing.

My grin falters, a lump forming in my throat as the truth slams back into me. "That's not the problem. It's the sweet and around all the time that I don't know if I can handle."

Her eyes fill with empathy and understanding. "I'm here for anything you need."

Giving her a sad smile, I mumble, "I know. Thank you."

"I love you, Alex."

"I love you, too, Sloane."

Leaning in, she wraps her arms around me, giving me a squeeze. My head falls to her shoulder as I hug her back, a few tears spilling over onto my cheeks and dampening her shirt.

"It will be okay."

"I know," I whisper, hoping she's right. Next to Aidan, she's one of the only ones I trust in this world.

Pushing away, I wipe my tears and ask, "So now that I'm sick, want to bring me some tacos?"

Her head falls back in laughter before her gaze falls back to mine. "I would be happy to. I'm pretty hungry myself."

"You don't have plans with Kelly for dinner?"

"No. I told him I'd be eating with you tonight unless you kicked me out. You know I don't get to see you nearly enough."

"About that..."

"What?" she questions, dragging out the word as if she knows I'm about to reveal something big.

"Well, with Aidan here and this," I gesture to my stomach, "I'm going to be spending a lot more time here in Genesis Beach."

"What do you mean by a lot more time?"

"I kinda moved in with my brother and started working for him at G & A Cycles."

"Yes!" She squeals in excitement making me jump. "It's about damn time you come back to us!"

A smile curves my lips grateful someone besides my brother is happy to have me here in town. With them by my side, I know I can do this.

Now I just have to figure out how to keep my hands off that sexy man who knocked me up.

Or do I? I've always been good about keeping my feelings at bay, especially when it comes to men.

Why would they start to surface now?

Chapter 11

Declan

Wednesday afternoon, I sit at my desk and text Alex, checking to see how she's feeling. Unfortunately, she's still giving me nothing, but a simple, "Fine, thanks."

After two days of this, I'm almost desperate to see her, at least to know she's okay. Maybe Ella's right and I should try what I do with my siblings and just show up. I've been hesitant to do that until now, but texting alone isn't going to do shit. I'm done waiting. I'm trying to respect her wishes, but how the hell am I supposed to help her and get to know her better if she's not giving me an opportunity to do it?

Sighing, I send another text.

I could bring dinner and dessert to you.

Last night, TV didn't hold my attention, and I couldn't sit still. I made chocolate chip cookies to keep my mind off her and avoid going to my parents. There's no way I can keep something like this from them for too long, so being there with Alex on my mind would be a bad idea. I'm not ready to have that conversation–not yet. I need some time with Alex before I tell them what's going on.

Alex

Thanks, but Aidan will be here, so I don't think it's a good idea.

Dropping my cell on my desk, I clench my jaw, done waiting. Surprising her seems to be my only option. I push myself to get as much done as possible, so I'm able to extend my lunch. Leaving the office, I stop at the store for a few things before heading over to G & A Cycles. Tossing my black suit jacket in the car, I hope she doesn't hide like I'm sure she did last time.

Grabbing a fall mix of flowers in one hand and a bag with chicken noodle soup, saltines, and my homemade chocolate chip cookies in the other, I stride into the shop my eyes immediately landing on Alex sitting behind the desk, her violet hair hanging loose over her shoulders, staring at the computer.

Lifting her gaze, she greets, "Hi, how–Declan."

Grinning wide, I hold up the things in my hands. "Hey, Alex. Since you've been so busy and you haven't been feeling well, I thought I'd bring some things to you."

Her hazel eyes widen in surprise. "Oh."

"These are for you." I hand her the flowers, and a shy smile curves her lips showing me a glimpse behind her walls, catching me off-guard, my breath hitching in my throat. Seeing even a spark of her raw and vulnerable is enough to bring me to my knees. Damn, she's beautiful. In that moment, my determination to get to know everything about her brick by brick isn't just a desire, it becomes cemented inside me.

"Thank you. You didn't have to do that."

Clearing my throat, I claim, "No, but I wanted to."

"Well, I appreciate it."

Holding up the other bag, I offer, "I brought you something to eat, if you're hungry."

She frowns. "I haven't been able to eat much."

Nodding, I elaborate, "I thought chicken noodle soup, and saltines might help."

Her eyes flash. "It might. Thanks."

"You're welcome."

I hand her the bag, and she opens it peering inside. "Chocolate chip cookies too?" Grasping one she takes a bite, closing her eyes and moaning in appreciation, the sound going straight to my cock. "These are so good. I could live on these."

Chuckling, I shuffle, stuffing my hands in my black suit pants. "That could be arranged if you agree to go out with me."

She startles, her eyes going wide. "I'd settle for you telling me where you got them."

My face heats as I admit, "I made them."

Her Adam's apple bobs up and down, swallowing the bite in her mouth while she stares at me in surprise. "I'm impressed. A man of many talents."

Giving her a crooked smile, I say, "I needed something to help convince you to see me again." Undoubtedly, I sound a little desperate but I don't give a fuck.

Her lips twitch and she arches her eyebrows in challenge. "Are you trying to bribe me?"

"Is it working?"

"A little bit." Her admission brings a broad smile to my face.

Aidan steps out of his office. "Hey, Alex, what time do you need to head out?" He pauses, glancing in my direction. "Hey."

I nod in acknowledgement, my curiosity piqued.

She blushes, her cheeks turning a beautiful shade of pink. "Um, in a few minutes."

"Where are you going?"

Her eyes flicker to mine and swiftly veer away, leaving me on edge before she even speaks. "I have a doctor's appointment."

My heart plummets into the pit of my stomach and I take a deep breath, exhaling slowly, determined not to react. "About the baby?"

"Yeah." She nods.

Her confirmation is like a slap in the face. Was she even going to fucking tell me? I get that we're not together, but that's not what this is about. Maybe making my feelings known will make a difference.

Straightening, I remain calm and request, "Can I come?"

Her eyes widen and her mouth falls slightly open. "You want to come with me to the doctor's office?"

Her reaction leaves me unsettled. What kind of assholes has she been dating? I realize we were supposed to only be one night, but even then, that would never be me. "Of course. I wasn't kidding when I said I wanted to be involved."

"But that doesn't mean–"

"It does to me," I interrupt, crossing my arms and holding her stare. I've never been more serious.

Aidan's lips curve up, but he swiftly wipes it away before suggesting, "That makes it easier. Then, you can ride with Declan, and I'll keep working." He looks at me, asking, "Is that okay with you?"

"Absolutely." I nod in satisfaction.

"Aid," she begins, likely preparing to argue.

"I'll see you later."

She pushes the flowers at her brother. "Fine. Do something with these."

Smirking, he nods. "No problem."

Pinching her lips into a thin line, she pulls the cookies out of the bag and slips the soup and crackers into the refrigerator behind her. "I'll save it for lunch tomorrow."

"What about now?"

She smiles. "I've got cookies."

Chuckling, I open the door for her, and we walk towards my car as I dial my assistant. She answers on the first ring, "Mr. Howard?"

"Something came up and I need you to cancel the rest of my afternoon. I'll finish the Jenkins proposal from home later and get it over to them first thing in the morning at the latest," I inform her, the tapping on her computer heard in the background.

"Got it. Anything else?"

At least I know she'll do what I need. She's an incredible assistant and always has my back at the office. "No, thanks. Have a good night."

Once we're buckled into my car, I glance at her and ask, "Where are we headed?"

"The Ob/Gyn over in Jefferson, Dr. Sherman. Are you sure you have time to drive over there and stay for the appointment?"

"I would make time, besides it's not that far."

"Okay."

"Alex, I want to be there for you and the baby." She gives me a slightly skeptical look but remains silent, staring out the window as I drive. "Are you okay?"

She shrugs, admitting, "Just a little nervous. This is all new to me."

"All the more reason to let me be by your side. I know we need to get to know each other better Alex, and I'm definitely no expert when it comes to this, but I will do everything I can to help. And if there's something you need, just ask."

"Like an orgasm to release some tension?"

My dick jumps and I shift, smirking. "Abso-fucking-lutely!"

Finally, she smiles back at me, giving me the same sexy smirk I remember from our first meeting. "Well, then, maybe we'll have to negotiate after my appointment." She licks her lips and I clench my jaw. This may literally be the hardest appointment I've ever gone through.

Holding back a groan, I park and jump out, jogging around to open her door. Reaching down, I offer her my hand. "Alex."

Quirking her brow, she asks, "Do you do that every time?"

"Do what?"

"Open doors and stuff?"

I shrug. "Yeah, it's how I was raised."

"Well, at least one of us has manners," she whispers, frowning as she takes my hand.

It's not long before they call, "Alexa Schoeller?

"I thought Alex was short for Alexandra."

Turning her head, she narrows her eyes in warning. "No, but you better not tell a soul it's anything but Alex, my brother gives me enough shit."

"Got it," I concede, a laugh escaping before I can stop it, but I quickly cover it up.

"I can still kick you out," she threatens.

Nodding, I plead, "Please don't, but how did I not know that was your name?" She glares at me, and I put my hands up in surrender. "Okay, but it is a beautiful name."

Ignoring me, she follows the nurse to the back with me right behind her. The nurse starts with the basics before we step into a small, sterile room. "Remove your clothes from the waist down, including your underwear and cover yourself with this," she advises, handing her a crisp white sheet before stepping out of the room.

"Do you want me to leave while you get comfortable?"

She scoffs. "There's no getting comfortable in here and you've already seen it all. Well, sort of."

"Did you forget what seeing you naked does to me?"

She gives me a crooked smile, her eyes sparkling. "Definitely not. But here?"

"Pretty much anywhere as long as it's you," I confess, turning.

She laughs, the light sound going straight through me.

"Okay, I'm done changing."

A knock at the door follows, interrupting us. The doctor steps into the room, her voice soft, soothing. "Hi, Alexa, I'm Dr. Sherman."

I quirk a brow at her, but she just shakes her head. "Hi, but it's Alex."

"Okay, Alex. And I do have the confirmation that you're pregnant. Congratulations."

"Thank you."

"Are you the father?"

My stomach twists as I nod, her question jolting me. "Yes, I'm Declan."

"Nice meeting you both. I'm going to start with an internal exam and then we'll use the wand for an internal sonogram." She gestures to a small computer on a cart with some extra attachments. "With that we can take some measurements and listen for the baby's heartbeat. It looks like you're almost eight weeks along so it shouldn't be a problem." She glances between the two of us. "Do you have any questions?"

"No," we both respond, although I don't have a clue what she's talking about.

Standing near Alex's head, I listen and watch, Alex appearing more uncomfortable than anything. "Are you okay?" I ask.

She grimaces, but nods, contradicting herself.

Reflexively, my hand glides down her arm, intertwining our fingers and squeezing gently, attempting to ease her anxiety.

"Okay, now we just need to find the heartbeat." Inserting the wand inside her vagina, she moves it around until we hear a rapid thumping making both of us gasp. "There it is." Dr. Sherman smiles.

Looking around the room, my chest tightens as if I'll find the source of the beautiful sound bouncing off the walls. Squeezing Alex's hand a little tighter, I glance down at her. Her eyes fill with tears, but she looks away, not meeting my gaze. This doesn't feel real. I imagine this isn't easy for Alex, sharing something like this with a relative stranger; ones who spent one incredible night together. That's exactly where we are now.

At the bar, she instantly caught my attention, already letting me know she was something special. The last thing I want is for her to remain a stranger. What she doesn't know is I won't stop until I change that.

I only hope she'll let me in.

Chapter 12

Alex

My heart pounds erratically, racing just as fast as the sound of our baby's. Our baby. Mine and Declan's. How did this happen? Internally, I roll my eyes at myself. Instead of asking myself questions I already know the answers to I need to focus on the here and now. But it's not easy.

Everything about this moment feels surreal–the sound, the look on Declan's face as he reaches for my hand, the warm comfort he exudes standing next to me. This isn't my life, but everything about this reality–excluding Declan by my side–is my life now. The rapid heartbeat echoing in the room is proof. And I refuse to let this baby feel anything less than unconditional love.

The rest of the appointment goes by in a blur and before I know it I'm sitting in Declan's car staring out the window.

"Are you okay?" he asks, pulling me out of my stupor.

Forcing a cheeky smile, I glance at him. "Why wouldn't I be?"

"You kind of have a lot going on." He chuckles softly, the low rumble giving me goose bumps. Damn this man. "I want to know how you're feeling, Alex. I want you to be able to talk to me, trust me."

A humorless laugh escapes before I can stop it. "It's kind of hard to trust someone you barely know."

"You're right. So, please, let me get to know you better. That night, you already got to me–"

I scoff, interrupting, "What happened between us that night is called lust."

He nods. "Sure, but I've felt lust before and with you, everything was more explosive, intense, intriguing. You may not believe me, but I wanted to find you after you left. The problem was you didn't make it easy."

I pinch my lips together in thought, wondering if it's true or if he's just spouting bullshit like most men I know. Either way, I guess it doesn't matter at this point. I should at least get to know him since he wants to be a part of this baby's life. If I'm going to have to spend time with him no matter how we feel about each other, might as well make it enjoyable, but I need to set boundaries.

"You're right, I don't believe you." He winces and I amend, "At least I don't right now, but you can't be mad at me for doing what we agreed to."

"True. And I'm not mad, but that doesn't mean I didn't change my mind. I wanted to see you again and I'm sure as hell glad you're here."

"Sure, even considering?"

"Especially now."

Sighing, I concede, "So, what do you suggest?"

He shrugs. "Come over for dinner tonight, I'll cook."

I arch my eyebrow in challenge. "That could be dangerous and I'm not just talking about you cooking."

Chuckling, he claims, "That's only if you want it to be and you don't have to worry about my cooking. I can handle myself in a kitchen."

My stomach twists. Why the hell does that make him even more sexy? An image of him in the kitchen wearing only an apron with a spatula in hand comes to mind and I swiftly shake the thought from my head. Sort of. Oh, who am I kidding? My thoughts are turning dirtier by the second as I picture Declan on his knees eating me for dinner. Clearing my throat, I challenge, "And what happens if I want to cross that line."

"You won't hear me arguing." The corners of his lips curve up in amusement. Fuck me. This is a bad idea, especially with my mindset. Can't he be a little more difficult? Taking my silence for hesitation, he continues, "I'm only asking you to come over and have dinner with me, Alex. Let's start there."

"Fine. Dinner."

He grins. "Fantastic."

Damn. What did I just agree to? He pulls out of the parking lot before I have a chance to change my mind. Smart man. Grabbing my phone, I send a quick text to Aidan.

> I'm going to Declan's to talk. I won't be home for dinner.

Aidan

> Ok. Call me if you need me.

> I will. Thanks.

It's not long before we pull up to his house, the same one I thought I'd never see again and it's even more beautiful and intimidating when I'm not desperate to jump him or escape. But the moment I step through the door, I find it more comfortable than I remember. Then again, I don't think I took much time to look around, my focus solely on him.

"What kinds of things do you like to eat?" he asks, giving me a crooked smile.

My face scrunches up in displeasure at the thought of food. "I don't know. No fish because I don't know which ones I'm not supposed to eat and no turkey."

"Is that what made you sick when I brought lunch at the beginning of the week? Turkey?"

"Yeah, I think so."

"So, no turkey. What about chicken fajitas?"

"That sounds good—I think."

He grins, goosebumps erupting on my skin once again. "Why don't you come sit at the counter and I'll get started."

My core heats as my dirty thoughts rush back to me and I bite back a groan. Keeping myself busy is likely the best idea. "I can help."

"But I promised to make you dinner. Let me do this for you."

Reluctant, I ask, "Are you sure?" I suck my bottom lip between my teeth, drawing his gaze, his eyes flaring.

He groans and licks his lips. "Not sure if I'll be able to do anything if you keep doing things like that."

My cheeks heat, but I look away, wondering if I could ever be more than that to a man like Declan. The idea of a life with a happy family has been eternally out of reach for me since my mom died.

Shoving my mom out of my head, I emphasize, "I can be useful."

He smirks and steps towards me. "Oh, I know you can." Placing his hands on my hips, he looks into my eyes and licks his lips before lifting me and setting me on the counter. A soft squeak in surprise slips from my mouth. Planting one hand on each side of me, he leans close, inhaling deeply, making me quiver. "Let me do this for you. Please."

My mouth falls slightly open, and my breathing picks up its pace as I look into his pleading, heated gaze. "Okay," I murmur, my voice barely a whisper. Before he backs away, I weave my fingers into his hair, and tug him towards me, sealing my mouth over his.

He groans, my tongue instantly taking advantage and slipping into his mouth, exploring, and probing for more as he meets me lick for lick. Tilting my head, I deepen our kiss. His hands slide to my thighs, gripping tightly, and making my panties wet. Every touch, every kiss only spurs me on, but he has other ideas. Slowing our kiss, he moans, extracting himself from my embrace, but staying in my space, so I can still feel his warm breath on my cheek. "You're my kind of wine, firecracker, but I really do want to get to know you and if we keep this up, I'll get reacquainted with the parts I already know and will happily worship them."

Arching my eyebrow, I challenge, "And that's a bad thing?"

"Fuck, no, but I want to know everything else about you too."

My cheeks flush. Tearing my gaze away, I swing my legs to calm my nerves, causing him to take a step back. Grabbing that as my opportunity to escape, I take a deep breath, and jump off the counter, his hand instantly reaching out and steadying me. "Then, let me help with dinner. I can't sit still if all you want to do is talk."

Chuckling, he claims, "I want to do a helluva lot more than that darlin'–" Halting my footsteps, I give him a look and he smirks, correcting himself. "I mean Alex. But I have to ask, you didn't flinch at firecracker, but darlin…"

"Firecracker has more power behind it. But I've been called darlin' by too many people who likely couldn't remember my name. I will never be anyone's darlin."

He winces, swiftly covering it up. "Thanks for sharing. You won't hear that from me again."

"Would you look at that, a man who listens," I taunt, grinning playfully.

Leaning towards me, he lightly brushes his lips across mine and pulls away all too quickly. "So, since you insist on helping me with dinner, how about cutting some peppers?" he asks, offering me a knife.

I take it, my hand brushing his. Giving him a cheeky grin, I attempt to lighten the mood, the air thick with sexual tension. "And he even trusts me with his weapon."

His head falls back in laughter, the sight hitting me hard in the chest a moment after I realize what I said. My cheeks heat, but I wiggle my eyebrows suggestively, owning my words.

It's not long before we fall into comfortable conversation, chatting about foods we love and our cooking abilities as we prepare dinner side by side.

The moment we sit down together at his kitchen table, he looks at me, holding my gaze. "Thank you for having dinner with me."

"I'm happy to be here."

Reaching for my fajita, I take a bite, moaning in appreciation. "This is delicious Declan," I mumble around my food, covering my mouth.

He clears his throat. "Thanks, but you helped."

I shrug in response. "So, what do you like to do for fun besides pick up women in bars and try to rescue them when they don't need it?"

The sound of his laughter runs through me bringing a genuine smile to my face. Taking another bite of my fajita, I stare at this beautiful man already enjoying my time with him.

Hopefully, not more than I should.

Chapter 13

Declan

A soft smile touches my lips while I watch Alex, curling her legs up underneath her as she makes herself comfortable on my couch. Tipping her head back, she lets it fall against the back of the cushions, her eyes blinking shut. Damn, she's beautiful. Even with her eyes closed, sitting quietly, she lights up the room in a way I didn't realize it needed.

It's been years since I've had a relationship that lasted more than a few weeks with my family being my priority. But now that I'm at the point of wanting more from a woman, and not just from anyone, but from her—where do I even begin? I'm not sure what we want from each other aligns. There's no doubt in my mind we have chemistry. Right now, I want her again so bad, my entire body is vibrating with need, but I can't approach this—her like I do my other *relationships*. Alex needs to be cherished and treated like a queen. But it's obvious she's hesitant and I don't want to spook her either.

The first thing I need to do is tell the rest of my family before they find out from someone else. Ella's right, this is a small town and although I live just outside Genesis Beach, everyone knows me, knows my family and their need to butt in becomes infectious. My stomach ties into knots at the possibility of my parents finding out through the grapevine. That's the last thing I want. They don't deserve that. But this is not a conversation I can have over the phone.

Unfortunately, I don't want my time with Alex to come to an end, yet tonight. I'll just need to make sure I talk to my parents tomorrow, then I'll bring Alex over to meet them. That is if she'll go with me, but I can't worry about that yet. I'll broach the subject when the time comes and start to think of ways I might convince her to meet them.

"Are you going to stare at me all night like a creeper or are you going to come over and sit next to me like a real man?"

A laugh escapes before I can stop it. I love how feisty she can be. "Just admiring the view."

Turning her head towards me, she quirks her eyebrow. "Sounds a little bit like a creeper to me, but if I let you do that from over here, will you give me some of that water in your hand?"

Chuckling, I stride towards her. "Anything you need, firecracker." I lower myself next to her, handing her the glass as she lifts her gaze, meeting mine.

Her tongue juts out, licking her lips before taking a large gulp. Her tongue slips out once again, my eyes tracking every single movement. "Thank you."

Giving her a small nod in acknowledgement, I keep my eyes pinned on her and ask, "How are you feeling?"

"Fine. Just tired."

"Do you want me to take you home?"

"Only if you want to."

Her non-committal answer reminds me of my sister, one of the reasons why I'm constantly worried. But my concern has proven to be valid in the past. How will I know when I need to worry with Alex? Or when she isn't honest with me to spare my feelings or concern? "Look, Alex, you need to be honest with me about how you're feeling and tell me what you need from me at all times. I don't know you well enough to read your mind."

"Okay." Her lips twitch in amusement.

I elaborate, attempting to explain myself. "My sister used to try to hide when she was sick because she didn't want to worry anyone."

"I can understand that."

Is that what you're doing? I question myself.

But instead of asking her, I give her a reason why being left in the dark about what's going on haunts me. "Right, but the last time she did that, I found her nearly unconscious on the floor and ended up rushing her to the hospital." She gasps. "Things can change in an instant. It's why I have their initials tattooed on my chest. They're important to me. I've never been so scared," I admit, leaving myself vulnerable, but I need her to understand the magnitude of how hard that day hit me, even if I don't reveal everything right now.

"You don't have to worry about me. And besides, I'm not family."

Flinching, I shake my head, her response rubbing me the wrong way, although it's true. "You may not understand this or feel the same, but I already care what happens to you."

"Because of this baby."

"No, because of you. I meant it when I said I wanted to find you again after that night, I just didn't know where to begin."

"Look, Declan, I told you I'd give you a chance to get to know me better now that I'm pregnant, you don't need to keep trying to butter me up." She shrugs. "Besides, you already know you can get me between your sheets if you play nice."

Her response makes me cringe. Why doesn't she get it? Does she really not want to give me more? Or let me see who she is? What's inside her head and her heart?

"What if I want more than that?"

"Well, you've already got it," she claims, smirking, and gently patting her belly with both hands.

Exhaling harshly, I run my hand through my hair and gripping the back of my neck, attempting not to show my frustration. She has to know that's not what I'm talking about, but she seems skittish. I'm afraid if I push too hard, she's going to run away before I have any chance with her at all.

Redirecting, I ask, "Where did you and Aidan grow up?

She stiffens and shifts, sitting up straight. Narrowing her gaze, she snaps, "We moved around a lot."

Suddenly, I feel like I'm looking at a caged animal about to pounce or flee, but I don't have any idea where to go or what to do to stop it. Cautiously, I respond, "Okay, I get that. I have a lot of friends who had one or both parents in the military growing up." The look on her face tells me that's not it. "No matter the reasons, I can imagine it can't be easy to be moving so much, especially when it comes to friends." She huffs in indifference. "You and your brother seem pretty close."

"We are." She frowns, eyeing me dubiously.

"I'm close with my brother and sisters too," I say hoping it will help her open up, even if only a little. "You know Ella, but I'm not sure if you know our younger sister, Charlotte, or the youngest of all of us, my brother, Finn."

"Just Ella. She came to see Grant a couple times when I was here visiting, plus Aidan brought me with him to go out for dinner with them last time I came here to visit." Pressing her lips firmly together, she looks away, but I don't miss the melancholy look in her eyes before she turns. Opening my mouth to press for more, she shakes her head, stopping me and I snap my mouth closed. "Listen, Declan, I really am tired, maybe driving me back to my brother's house is a good idea. Would you mind?"

Taking a moment to assess her, I give her a tight nod, pissed at myself and curious to what prompted her sudden urge to leave. Are there certain topics that are off limits? It's not like we talked much about our families before. But family isn't something I'll ever take off the table when it comes to getting to know someone; it's too important to me. Family always comes first. If her situation is different than mine, that's okay, but we still need to, at the very least, have a conversation about it.

I watch her closely, searching for a reason for her to stay, but my mind keeps coming up blank, distracted with my thoughts going in so many different directions and my cock begging for me to get her back in my bed. Maybe it's best if she goes home tonight; I know I can't force it, that will only end in disaster.

And I can see her tomorrow. "If that's what you want, of course I will."

"Thank you. I think that's a good idea." Feigning a yawn, she claims, "I'm barely able to keep my eyes open."

I force a smile, my insides churning. How the fuck am I already starting to fall for this woman?

There's no way in hell I can tell her that if this is how she reacts to simple questions. I just might be screwed and not the kind I'm used to when it comes to women. Guess this is my payback for all my prior indiscretions. I need to figure out a way for her to give me a chance to not only get to know her, but to be a part of her life as more.

Maybe I will make it to my parents tonight after all. The sooner I get this conversation over with, the better.

Chapter 14

Alex

Desperate to break the silence, even on the short ride, I try to find neutral ground. "So," I begin, dragging out the word, "what do you do for a living?"

He flinches before swiftly schooling his features and hiding it. "I'm mostly a project manager at a marketing firm."

"Mostly?"

"Well, I'm also the boss for most of them, the director of the project management team, so I end up doing a lot more than just marketing."

My eyes narrow, assessing his stiff posture, his thumbs drumming on the steering wheel and his square jaw clenched. "You don't like your job much, do you?"

His eyes widen in surprise. He opens his mouth to respond, but then snaps it shut and heaves a sigh, his body sagging. "Sure, I like it, but it's more complicated than that."

Enjoying the focus on him, I arch my eyebrow and prod, "Sounds to me like you have something to share."

He nods. "You're right."

"Well, I thought you wanted to get to know each other."

"I do, Alex, but that's not something that's easy for me to talk about."

"Really? And you think everything is so easy for me?"

"That's not what I mean." He groans in frustration, his hands wringing the steering wheel. Keeping my lips pinched tightly together, I watch him and wait. How does he expect me to share if he's not willing to do the same?

A few minutes later he pulls in front of my brother's house and parks his car. Turning in his seat, he faces me, his eyes getting a look of determination. "Fuck it. It's not like it's a secret, but it is a lot. I guess it will be easier to just get it over with."

"Okay," I mumble, dragging out the word.

"You know my sister, Ella." I nod. "Well, she was in and out of the hospital for most of my life. She had Non-Hodgkin's lymphoma."

My mouth falls slightly open, a soft gasp escaping. I'm not sure what I expected him to say, but it wasn't this. "Is she okay?"

"She is now, but she's been in and out of remission and it's hard to let go of the fear that something will happen again."

"The day you found her and brought her to the hospital?"

He nods. "We thought it had come back. Luckily, we were wrong, but even then, she needed help."

"She has Grant now."

He huffs a humorless laugh, "Yeah, she has Grant now and I know she loves him. But my point is, my head tends to go to the worst case scenarios, so I need you to be honest with me when it comes to your health, what you're feeling, or what you're thinking. Please."

His eyes flash, giving into some of his pain, allowing me to see it–see him–open and vulnerable making my stomach twist. Reluctantly, I nod, wondering if I'm agreeing to something I won't be able to handle.

"Okay, Declan, I can do that for you."

"Thank you."

"You're welcome. Now you want to tell me what that has to do with what you do for a living?" I ask, suddenly recalling my original question.

He shrugs. "I couldn't leave."

"What?"

"I got into my dream school, Yale, with an incredible offer." My eyes widen, impressed, while he shakes his head. "But I couldn't go. I couldn't leave my family when they needed me the most."

"Dec..."

"I've spent most of my life helping out with my family. Either I'd be watching Ella so my mom and dad could take Finn to one of his football games or Charlotte to one of her shows." Pausing, his lips tug up and he glances at me, his pride evident. "When I wasn't watching Ella, I'd be the one watching the two of them at home or taking either of them to their shit. Finn is a fantastic football player, and now with Grant's help, he's gotten even better. He has scouts coming to watch his games all the time. And Char, she is incredibly talented. It's like nothing I've ever seen when she's on stage. She's one of those they call a triple threat–she can sing, dance, and act. It will be amazing to see where they all end up."

He sighs, running his hand through his hair. "Anyway, at the time, I couldn't leave any of them. If I did, there was no way I would've ever made it through because the stress of not knowing if they were okay might've killed me. But now, even Ella has moved on. She met Grant, finished school, and she has a job she loves. All three of my siblings are doing what they want to do and I'm not only happy for them, but I want it for all three of them. While they followed their dreams, I went to college nearby and got a job at the closest marketing firm I could find to home."

"So, you gave up your dreams to protect them and help with theirs."

Remaining silent, he looks out the windshield, staring at the dark street. His silence an admission although it's obvious he refuses to garner any regret.

"Aidan and I would do anything for each other too," I say, wanting to give him a piece of me, without sharing too much.

Turning back to me, he gives me a sad smile. "Good."

Reaching towards him, my hand cups his cheek and he leans into my touch, the small action squeezing my heart. Closing the distance between us, he brushes his lips across mine, kissing me soft and slow. My lips tingle, and goosebumps spread across my body as I kiss him back, instantly heated. His fingers find the back of my neck and he holds me to him. Tilting his head, he deepens our kiss, maintaining the tortuously slow pace. His kiss is packed with everything I could ever want and everything I've been trying to avoid–care, devotion, loyalty, heat and promise–making my head spin.

Breaking our kiss, my forehead rests on his, both of us gasping for breath. "So, how are you feeling?" I ask, my lips twitching as I attempt to lighten the mood.

His head falls back in laughter, the sound rolling over me like a raging fire. "You sure you don't want to turn around and come back to my place?" he asks grinning mischievously.

I smirk, but his phone beeps, interrupting us. Snatching it, he looks down at the screen, his brow furrowing. "Everything okay?" I ask, hesitant.

Scowling at his phone, he grumbles, "Um, yeah–it will be anyway. I'm sorry, but I have to go."

Faltering at his one-eighty, I sit back in my seat. "Oh, okay."

He shakes his head. "Sorry, Alex. It's Charlotte–my sister."

I shrug like it doesn't matter. "It's fine."

"I'll text you later?"

"No big deal. I'm probably going to bed early." Gathering my things, I scramble to get out of the car. Starting up the path, I give him a wave over my head, not looking back. His pounding footsteps on the front walk swiftly creep up behind me.

"Alex, wait. I'm walking you to your door. I just need to go pick up my sister."

"No worries," I claim, forcing a smile as I turn to face him. *It doesn't matter, Alex. Stop acting like a jealous bitch. You're not even in a relationship with the man, at least not a romantic one.* And now I'm talking to myself while he likely decides whether or not to take me at face value.

Hesitantly, he nods in acceptance changing the subject as we reach the door. "I'm glad we got a chance to talk."

"Me too, Declan. Have a good night," I say flippantly, reaching for the door.

His hand on mine stops my forward momentum. My gaze drops to where we touch, rising as he slowly glides his fingers up my arm, to my jaw, gently tilting my head to meet his gaze. Stepping closer to me, he cradles my face in his hands and looks into my eyes as if he sees into my soul making it difficult to breathe.

"I mean it, Alex. Thank you."

A chill runs down my spine, and I hold my breath in both anticipation and fear, unsure what I truly want. But before I can think too much, his lips brush against mine, kissing me tenderly and unhurriedly. My heart races, and a soft gasp escapes my lips, his tongue slipping inside to meet mine. He pulls back all too soon and the rawness consuming my chest dissipates leaving me off-kilter.

"Bye, Declan."

Swiftly, I slip inside my brother's house trying not to overthink the way he held me and the way his lips moved against mine, but it's hard not to. Especially when he kissed me like he cared, like I was a treasure, and he would do anything for me. I can't trust that feeling; it's too perfect. Anything good won't last; not for me. Aidan is the only one I trust that I know will stick around.

But what about this baby? Involuntarily, I flinch. Will I be enough to protect this innocent life?

"Good, you're home."

I jump, my hand falling to my chest attempting to calm my racing heartbeat. "Shit, Aidan, don't sneak up on me like that."

Arching his eyebrows, he taunts, "Didn't think I needed to with how much you tell me my footsteps sound like a stampede."

"Guess you've been practicing."

He snorts and shakes his head. "Sure, that's it. How'd it go with Declan?"

I shrug. "Fine. Not what I expected. He wants to be involved."

He tilts his head to the side, assessing me. "With the baby, you, or both?"

Heaving a sigh, I ignore his question, trudging towards his spare bedroom. "Goodnight, Aid."

"Doesn't surprise me."

"What?" I ask, spinning on my heel to face him.

"Him wanting you or wanting to be involved. He's a good guy, Alex."

His words hit their mark. Coming out of anyone else's mouth, I would've laughed it off, but coming from Aidan, I can't help but trust his words. The question is, what do they really mean when it comes to me? "I'll see you in the morning."

"Goodnight," he mumbles, disappearing back into his room, knowing he gave me even more to think about.

What do I do?

Chapter 15

Declan

After leaving the office, I stop home to change into faded blue jeans and a simple dark green T-shirt before heading to my parents. Hopefully, no one else will be home. Knowing Finn should be at practice and Char and Ella normally don't stop in the middle of the week unless there's something going on eases my concern. It's not that I don't want to tell Char and Finn, but I want to have a conversation with my parents first. As it is, I hope they're not hurt if they find out Ella knew before them.

I pull into the driveway and take a deep breath as I step out of my car, my eyes roaming over the house I grew up in—a large white colonial on just under an acre of land with a wraparound front porch. The white wicker furniture adorned with cherry red cushions bring me a small comfort. I can do this.

My feet drag as I trudge towards the front door. Steeling myself, I push it open and step into the foyer, calling out, "Mom? Dad?"

"Declan, is that you? We're in the kitchen," my mom replies, her voice echoing off the wood floors.

"Hi," I greet them as I step into the room, finding the two of them with empty plates sitting at the same end of the large oak table. My mom has her blonde hair hanging loose over her shoulders, contrasting her navy top. She started dying her hair a long time ago to cover the gray from the stress of the four of us–likely mostly from Ella's illness. I glance at my dad, his light brown hair and blue eyes mirroring my own. The only physical trait of my mom I acquired was her smile, but I'll take it. "Please, don't get up."

"It's good to see you," my mom says.

Both my parents smile at me as I make my way to them, kissing my mom on the top of her head before I sit down next to her, hoping that's the right move. I'm not sure who I want to look at when I start talking, nervous about how they might react.

"What are you doing here?" my dad asks.

"Everything okay?" my mom questions at the same time. Her brows furrow and her tired gaze turns wary, prompting me to comfort her before her imagination runs wild. We've all been through enough without any added weight.

"Yeah, it's fine. Everything is okay," I insist, laying a comforting hand on her back. Her body relaxes only slightly. "I just have something I wanted you both to know."

My mom holds her breath, while my dad stiffens, waiting, anticipating the worst even with my insistence. Who could blame them after being in and out of the hospital with Ella for most of her young life? Hopefully, this will be a good thing, even before they have a chance to meet Alex.

Knowing they won't relax until I tell them my news and feeling like there's no easy way into this conversation, I blurt it out. "You're going to be grandparents."

A soft gasp escapes my mom's lips, her hand falling to her chest to calm her racing heartbeat. "Is Ella pregnant? Why isn't she the one telling us? Is she okay? We should get over there right away." She pushes her chair back, the legs screeching against the wood floors as she abruptly stands.

Reaching out, I grab her hand and gently squeeze. "Mom, no. Ella is fine. This is about me. I'm going to be a dad." I gulp over the sudden lump in my throat. Voicing the words aloud hits me like a tsunami.

Her mouth falls slightly open. Slowly, she lowers herself back in her seat, keeping her eyes on me. "You?"

I nod, glancing at my dad out of the corner of my eye, his hands tightly clasped in front of him. Clearing my throat, I reveal, "I found out a couple days ago, but I needed some time to process it myself."

"You're not dating anyone," my dad states—not questions.

"Her name is Alex. We met a couple months ago. You know Grant's partner at G & A Cycles? Aidan?" They both nod in affirmation, their confusion evident by the looks in their eyes. "Alex is his sister. She recently moved in with him and she started working at the front desk at their shop."

"Oh," my mother murmurs, a smile slowly tugging at her lips. "I'm going to be a grandma?"

Relief slams into me at her question knowing they aren't going to ask how we met. Admitting to my parents that I've been having one-night stands was not exactly on the list of things I ever wanted to do in my life.

"Yeah," I confirm, my own grin lighting up my face.

She pulls me into a warm embrace. "That's wonderful news. I'm so happy for you, sweetheart. When are we going to meet Alex? I can't believe we haven't seen her around town. Or maybe we have..."

Exhaling slowly, my body relaxes, and I sit back in the chair. I knew they would be supportive, but that didn't make it any easier. It's still scary as hell confessing something like this to them, especially when they believe I'm single and they have certain expectations. But they can't possibly believe I've been celibate all this time. I'm just not going to think about that, likely mirroring their own stance.

"Maybe." I shrug. "Either way, I'm working on it. I wanted to tell you first. And besides, coming to meet the whole family at once can be intimidating.

I don't want to overwhelm her and scare her away by throwing her into our chaos."

My mom frowns. "You say that like it's a bad thing."

"You know that's not what I mean."

"Is it just her and Aidan?"

"Yeah." I nod, suddenly curious about what it was like for her growing up.

"You have to bring her over, Declan. What's been keeping you?" she asks, narrowing her eyes but not expecting a response. "So, if you met a couple months ago, this has to be new. How has she been feeling? When is she due?"

"Tired, nauseous, but okay I think."

"Ginger helps with the nausea, and it will pass–eventually. Well, it did for me anyway." She purses her lips in thought.

"I'm not exactly sure when she's due. Maybe this summer?"

"You didn't get a due date?"

"No, we did." My mind drifts to the doctor's appointment, trying to remember what they said, but I was still in shock.

"Declan, you need to pay more attention. These details are important."

I wince. "I'll find out." The silence from my dad leaves me uneasy. I chance a glance in his direction and catch him watching me, his hands no longer clenched. "Dad?"

"I'm going to assume this wasn't planned since we've never even met the girl. Am I right?"

"Yeah, but Alex is–"

"Are you happy?"

"Of course, I am. Maybe the timing is different than I expected, but I'm excited. We may not be together, but–"

"You're not together?" my mom interrupts.

I flinch, hating the truth. "Not exactly."

"But you like her," she comments, always perceptive.

"Mom..."

With a wave of her hand, she brushes me off. "Declan, it's fine. You're almost thirty. No matter how you feel about her, we want to meet her. She will be a part of our family whether you're together or not now that our grandchild is on the way. We want her to feel welcome and we will do everything we can to help with that."

"Thanks, Mom." Leaning towards her, I wrap my arms around her, giving her a hug. She whispers in my ear, "And Declan, you two will figure it out when you're ready."

Shaking my head, I pull back, ready to argue. She can't have expectations, no matter what I want. "Mom..."

She laughs. "I'm teasing."

"Your mom is right."

Looking at my dad, I arch my eyebrow in challenge. "About what?"

"Most things." He smirks, my mom giggling softly. "But this time I'm talking about Alex. She will be part of our family in some way now, no matter what happens with the two of you. We want to meet her. I'm sure your brother and sisters will want to meet her too if they don't know her already."

"Ella knows her, from Grant."

"Did you tell Ella?"

"Yeah, but I haven't told Char or Finn."

"Maybe we should call a family dinner?" mom suggests.

"Let him share his way," dad insists, giving my mom a look.

I offer him a grateful smile. "I'll talk to them and then we can make a plan for y'all to meet her."

My mom grins, excitement shining in her eyes. "Soon, Declan. Please, I can't wait too long."

Dad and I laugh, knowing I'll be lucky if something doesn't slip if I don't let them know tonight. "When will Finn be home?"

As if on cue, we hear the front door open and close, footsteps approaching. "Hey, Dec. What are you doing here?" my younger brother asks as he steps into the kitchen, his hair a shade lighter than mine wet from a shower. He's taller than me at just over six feet–he seems to keep growing. But like me, he mostly takes after our dad.

"You sound so happy to see me," I mutter, sarcasm thick on my tongue.

"Too tired to care."

"Tough practice?" dad asks, unmoving.

"Yeah. Coach added a few new plays and had us running them constantly. Jace is coming over later to study and go over them together to make sure we're ready for tomorrow." Sometimes I still have to remind myself when he says Coach, he's talking about Grant.

"Could I talk to you first?"

He arches his eyebrows and nods, hesitant. "Sure."

"I thought we could video call Ella and Char too?" I'd rather get this all over at once and I don't want Char or Finn to feel bad that Ella already knows.

His eyes narrow and his body goes rigid. "Everything okay?"

Finally feeling like everything will work out, I give him a reassuring smile. "It's good–really good."

Nodding, he breathes a sigh of relief, returning my grin. "Then, let me put my stuff away and I'll meet you in the other room to call them."

"Okay. Thanks." He walks out of the room and toward the stairs as I look back at both my parents. "Thank you for being so understanding."

My dad huffs a laugh. "What did you think would happen?" I shrug. "Now if we would've had this conversation when you were Finn's age, it would've been a much different conversation."

"Don't put that out there," my mom states, shaking her head. "But we're happy for you, Declan and we can't wait to see our beautiful grandbaby."

"Thanks, Mom." Bending down, I wrap my arms around her and give her a hug before walking around the table and doing the same with my dad. "Thanks, Dad."

"Congratulations, Son."

Chapter 16

Alex

My eyes blink open, staring at the ceiling. Like nearly every morning since I met the man, Declan is the first thing that crosses my mind before I shove out of bed and rush to the bathroom, my belly in chaos. After purging nothing but stomach acid, I take a few deep breaths, wiping my sweaty brow. I hate being nauseous. Hopefully, I'll get over this phase soon.

Sighing, I stumble towards the kitchen on unsteady feet. Aidan glances up from his breakfast plate the moment I step into the room, his eyebrows instantly drawing down in concern.

"Are you alright?"

Forcing a small smile, I nod. "I look that bad, huh?" He gives me a look. "Yeah, I'm fine, Aid. Just tired and a little nauseous. But as long as you didn't make any turkey, I should be all right."

"Nope. But I made scrambled eggs, bacon and toast. Grab yourself a plate of food and come sit down."

"I don't know if I can eat anything," I complain, frowning.

"You can and you will. Besides, you'll feel better when you do."

"Like you're an expert," I grumble, rolling my eyes in annoyance, but do as he says, taking the seat across from him.

"Did you sleep okay?" he asks, his eyes narrowed, but I only shrug in response. "Are you still stewing over what to do about Declan?"

My shoulders sag. "Yeah, but I'm just thinking."

"About what?"

Scrunching up my nose in irritation, I admit, "You're right. I didn't sleep well." He remains quiet, continuing to eat and waiting for me to elaborate. "I woke up in the middle of the night after having a dream about mom."

His jaw clenches before he forces himself to relax, always the protective big brother before worrying about himself. Looking me in the eyes, he studies my face. "I thought the nightmares were gone."

I scoff. "Apparently they just disappeared temporarily."

"Have you been having them for a while?"

Shrugging, I confess, "No. The first time they reappeared was right before I found out I was pregnant, and now they haven't stopped." He winces, probably coming to the same conclusion I'd drawn—for now, they're here to stay. Hopefully they will vanish once the baby comes. In the meantime, I'm dealing with it the best I can. "But luckily, they aren't every night. Unfortunately, they have been happening more often."

"Maybe you should see a therapist again."

"Or maybe I can talk to my favorite brother instead."

"Alex, I'm serious. You–"

"So am I. I don't want to go back to therapy right now, or ever if I can help it, but especially if this is only temporary." He gives me a look in warning. It's the same look that makes my skin itch, wanting to rebel, but he's not dad. "It's not that I'm not dealing with it, Aidan. I promise. But thinking about therapy and diving back into the past feels like the last thing I should be doing when I have the future to think about. Right now, I need to focus on me and this baby and figure out what I'm going to do, Aid. Drudging up the past will only weigh me down. I'm managing just fine–for now, but I promise if it gets to that point, I will go back. Okay?" I challenge, arching my eyebrows in defiance. I'm more than aware how much it has helped me.

He glares at me from across the table and eventually stands with his plate, grunting his defeat. Swiftly, he prepares another plate of food and strides over setting the plate down in front of me. Planting one hand on the table and his other on the chair, he stares at me, waiting for me to give him my full attention. "I'm trusting you with this. You sure as hell better keep that promise."

"I will," I affirm, confidently, holding his stare.

Reluctantly, he nods in acceptance before giving me some space and thankfully changing the subject. "Interested in going to the high school football game tonight?"

"A high school game?"

"Yeah, Grant is the coach, and his future brother-in-law is the quarterback. He has an incredible arm." I frown, wondering if he's talking about Declan's brother, but I'm not about to ask. "Football is a big deal around here, Alex. I'll get you to come sooner or later. This year's team is really good. They're undefeated."

"I'll think about it."

"That's good enough for me." He stands at the sink, rinsing his dishes and carefully placing them in the dishwasher. "I'm going to jump in the shower and get ready for work. We'll take off for the garage in like thirty minutes."

"I'll be ready."

A moment before he steps out of the room, he halts, glancing over his shoulder in my direction without meeting my gaze. I shovel a bite of food in my mouth, waiting impatiently, my curiosity piqued by his hesitation. "Oh, don't forget, we have that thing to go to tomorrow at Grant's house."

"What thing?" I question, choking down my food. My stomach turns once again, this time with a different kind of unease, already knowing I'm not going to like whatever nonsense he's about to spew.

"Ella and Grant invited us over for a barbecue."

My mouth drops open in surprise. I sure as hell didn't know anything about it. Clenching my jaw, I toss my fork down on the table, the clanging echoing between us showing my frustration. "You never told me, Aid."

Spinning back towards me, he gives me an apologetic smile. "Oh, sorry. I thought I mentioned it. But we're still going. And besides, I think it would be good for you to meet some people."

I scoff knowing exactly why he didn't tell me until now. I'm almost surprised he didn't wait until we were in his car on our way. "Some people? You mean Declan's family?" He doesn't answer, patiently waiting only succeeding in further infuriating me. "You can't tell me what to do. I'm not going," I retort without even taking a second to think about it.

My chest tightens. Why wouldn't Declan invite me? He sure as hell texted me enough this week, giving him ample occasions to broach the subject. I thought he wanted us to spend time together and get to know each other. This seems like a great opportunity to do that, but maybe he doesn't mean it like that. Maybe he doesn't want me at a family get together. I know it's not just family but isn't that even more of a reason to invite me. My head spins and I clench my jaw, holding back all my exasperation and anger.

"Yeah, you are," he insists, his eyes sad, resigned, although I'm not sure if it's because of me or for me. Either way, I don't like it. "Grant is my partner. I already told them we will both be there."

"Aid–"

"Leave it alone, Alex," he demands, his firm tone leaving no room for argument. "You can stay home tonight, but you're coming tomorrow, even if I have to drag you there kicking and screaming." Especially now–his implied words remain unsaid. But I know my brother. He's making a statement, showing how proud he is of me at the same time giving Declan a warning. Aidan won't let anyone fuck with me under any circumstances.

Right now, I can't help but hate him and love him for it. I'm not sure if I can do this. I frown, grumbling sarcastically, "That sounds fair."

Chuckling, he adds, "Never said it was, but my promise to you is that I will be there with you if you need anything."

"Anything?" I arch my eyebrows in challenge.

He laughs. "Well, for you, I'll make sure to have an appropriate list so I can get out of there with my balls intact."

I snort, making him laugh harder. "Believe me, I would never go anywhere near your balls."

"Damn straight."

"And please, don't ever mention them again when I'm anywhere within earshot." Sticking out my tongue, I make a face at him. Laughing, he stalks out of the room without another word.

"Ugh," I groan, taking a small bite out of the toast, attempting to settle my stomach. What has Aidan gotten me into? Or more accurately, I'll admit I put myself here, but that doesn't mean I want any of this. Do I?

My phone beeps with a text and I swipe it off the table, Declan lighting up the screen.

Declan

> My brother has a football game tonight. I've been meaning to ask you, but I'd love it if you would come with me.

He wants me to go to the game. I need to get out of my head and stop assuming the worst. But what if he's there with a bunch of people I don't know? I don't want it to be uncomfortable for any of us. Maybe I will go with Aidan and meet him there.

> We were just talking about the game. I'll come with my brother and meet you there. Ok?

Declan

> Sounds good. I'm looking forward to seeing you.

Chapter 17

Declan

Stuffing my hands in my jeans pockets, I sit on the cold metal bench at my old high school. Most of the town is here. Everyone cheers the team on with my brother, Finn as the quarterback and his best friend, Jace, his number one receiver. Standing at any of these home games is one of the times you truly realize just how small Genesis Beach really is with Ella sitting next to me and most of the people I grew up knowing scattered around the bleachers, waving in greeting.

There's a chill in the air, but the energy remains vibrant, pulsating with excitement as the red and white uniforms of the boys run onto the field, ready for what they believe will be another win as the crowd goes wild.

My phone vibrates in my pocket, and I pull it out, glancing at the screen, smiling at the sight of Alex.

Alex

Running late, but we're on our way.

Awesome. We're towards the front in the center of the bleachers. See you soon.

Alex

Ok.

Ella elbows me in the stomach, getting my attention. I look at her, arching my eyebrows and she asks, "What's got you smiling so big?"

"Alex is on her way. I wasn't sure if she would really come."

"It can be intimidating," Matt, Grant's brother states, joining the conversation with his wife Amy on his other side. It's almost surreal how much alike they look, except Grant's got a few years on him. "There is a hell of a lot of people here and all of you know each other."

We laugh and I nod. "True. I thought you guys were from a small town?"

He smirks. "Yeah, but this isn't my town."

We laugh and I turn back to my sister, lowering my voice so only she hears. "By the way, Ella, can we just focus on easy stuff tonight? She doesn't know I already told all of you about the baby and I'd really like that to come from me."

"Of course. It will probably be too loud here anyway to have a good conversation."

"Thanks. Where are mom and dad?" I ask, glancing around.

Ella points to the back of the bleachers, all the way at the top, and my eyes follow. Both my parents stand underneath the call booth, leaning against the boards talking with Jace's mom, dad and girlfriend, Lynn, along with some of the other parents from the team. "With the other parents. Besides, you know dad gets too anxious to sit and he can't stand the whole game unless he's in the back or on the sidelines."

"Both Grant and Finn wouldn't like that."

She laughs. "You got that right. Oh, don't let me forget, Char asked that we text her updates during the game."

"You won't forget, but okay."

"Aidan is here," Matt announces, interrupting us, waving in his direction.

Turning my head, I spot Alex walking in front of her brother immediately, her violet hair hanging in loose waves around her shoulders. She's wearing a slightly cropped black sweater and ripped jeans looking hot as hell. Her eyes lock with mine and she smiles, moving in our direction.

Aidan greets us, sitting in front of Matt and Amy, but my gaze never waivers from Alex. "Hi," she says, surprising me when her voice comes out soft, timid, unsure, the opposite of the woman I've gotten to know. But I'm determined to help her feel comfortable, I want her to know she made the right decision in coming tonight. At least, I believe she did.

"Hi, Alex. You look absolutely beautiful," I tell her, leaning down and giving her a chaste kiss.

She blushes a deep shade of red. "Thanks."

I scoot over to make room for her, my hand reaching for hers and intertwining our fingers. "I'm glad you came."

"Me too, but I admit, I don't know much about football, so you're going to have to help me keep up with what's going on."

"Don't know much or don't know anything."

"I probably know the very basics." I nod in acknowledgement. "Which one is your brother?"

Tipping my head towards hers, I point to the center of the field. "He's number 4, the one that just threw the ball." Jace catches the pass, completing a first down. "Way to go, Finn! Good job, Jace!"

Matt and Amy scoot over, introducing themselves to Alex. "We've heard a lot about you," Matt informs her.

"All good things," Amy adds.

"Yes, I've heard about both of you as well. It's good to finally be here at the same time and meet y'all," Alex answers as the game draws our attention.

Finn steps back with the ball in hand and Jace begins running on the sideline turning his head and watching for the ball, his opponent a step behind. Reaching up he snatches the ball out of the air, pulling it down to his chest and pushes, running faster. We all slowly stand, the clapping and screaming getting louder and completely erupting a moment before he crosses the line into the end zone.

"Touchdown!" We all cheer, the excitement and energy from the crowd coming alive.

It's not long before it's halftime and the score is 13-0 after a missed extra point from our team's kicker. Everyone claps and stomps their feet on the metal bleachers, the sound echoing all around us. "Save our seats," Ella requests. "We're going to get some popcorn. Want anything?"

"Yeah, would you mind grabbing an extra popcorn and two waters?" I request.

"No problem," Ella agrees, descending the bleachers with Amy and Matt right behind her.

I look at Alex and ask, "So, what do you think?"

"Your brother is really good. I'm having a lot of fun. Thanks for inviting me," she states, tilting her head to the side, assessing me as if she's looking for something, but I'm not sure what.

I nod, pulling her close. "Good."

"Hey, Dec," Laine calls as he walks down the bleachers, approaching us with a broad smile. He stops in front of me and shakes my hand, giving me a firm pat on the back with the other. "Your brother is on fire tonight."

"Yeah, he is."

He glances down at Alex, arching his eyebrows in question and holds out his hand. "Hi, I'm Laine, this asshole's best friend."

She laughs. "I'm Alex. Nice to meet you, Laine."

"Alex," he repeats, his smile growing, recognition registering on his face as his eyes flick to me. "It's great to finally meet you. I hope he's treating you right."

She doesn't get a chance to answer as Julie and Gina walk by, Julie spotting me and halting in her footsteps while Gina says hi to Laine. "Declan! It's so good to see you." Unexpectedly, she throws her arms around me as if she hasn't seen me in years, knocking me off balance. It's likely she's had a few drinks. "Finn is doing amazing! Is Ella here?"

I laugh, amused. "Yes, Ella is here. She just went to get some popcorn, but she should be right back."

She releases me and looks at Alex, her eyes widening in surprise. "Oh, hi, I'm Julie," she holds out her hand towards Alex.

Stiff, Alex takes it. "Alex."

My gaze goes back and forth between the two, my pleasure growing seeing Alex's jealous demeanor. Is it strange I like it? "Alex is my girlfriend," I state, my eyes glued to Alex, watching her reaction. Her eyes fly to me, but she doesn't confirm or deny my words. "And Julie is a good friend of Ella's. She's a nurse at the hospital," I add, watching Alex's face instantly soften. "It's good to see you, Julie."

"You too, Dec, and it was nice meeting you, Alex."

Alex smiles. "You too."

She walks away with her friend and Laine chuckles, leaning towards me. "I'm pretty sure you shocked the hell out of her." He glances at Alex revealing, "First time he's ever said those words." He stands tall and waves. "I'm going to catch up with them. I'll see you guys later. Say hi to Ella."

I wave, still focused on Alex, desperate to know what she's thinking. "Alex–"

"So, I'm your girlfriend now? Don't you think I should have a say?"

"You definitely should, but I didn't know how to introduce you."

"What about, *Alex is a friend of mine?* Or even *a good friend of mine?* It would be a stretch but it would work."

My lips curve up, giving her a mischievous smile. "Maybe I was just projecting. You know, like wishful thinking."

"You're trouble, Dec."

"You inspire me."

She scoffs, then laughs. "What am I going to do with you?"

"Go with me to Mackie's after the game."

"Isn't that one of the restaurants on the water?"

"It is, but it's casual. Great view, good food. We would have a good time, and it would give us more time to talk because if I bring you home, I'm not making any promises."

Her face heats and she sucks her bottom lip between her teeth, releasing it slowly, knowing it tortures me. "Okay. We can do that."

I grin. "That's a yes?"

"Don't make me regret it," she taunts just as Ella returns with Grant's brother and sister-in-law, all of them holding drinks and snacks.

Chapter 18

Alex

We sit down at a small table near a window, overlooking an expansive porch wrapping around the large, square, cedar shake building and out to the ocean. Each window is adorned with aqua blue shutters, folded back to take in and enjoy the beautiful view. The restaurant is slightly raised on massive stilts to assist with keeping it safe from erosion and storms, especially hurricanes. Long ramps leading up to the building sit on the parking lot side, as well as the back with a set of stairs located on both sides of the front, or the side facing the water, providing easy access to the beach.

The square bar in the middle of the restaurant appears to be made of a reclaimed wood, similar to the floors, with high top tables surrounding it and shorter, wider ones interspersed between. Tall booths with the same treated wood as the bar sit along the walls by the windows on the sides and smaller tables in the front overlooking the ocean.

"You're right, this place has a great vibe."

"I'm glad you like it. How's your mahi-mahi?"

"Delicious, thank you."

"Wish I could take credit." He grins, his eyes sparkling, giving me a look that makes my heart race and my body heat.

I giggle. "I'm really glad I got the chance to see your brother play tonight. The crowd goes crazy."

"Of course, it's always better when they're winning. Hopefully they can stay undefeated this year. I'd love for you to come to another game, or if I'm honest, every game."

My face heats, a smile tugging at my lips. "I'll think about it."

"Better than a no."

Looking around, I attempt to reign in my thoughts. Spotting pool tables and dartboards in the back, a slow smile spreads across my face. Turning back to Declan, I question playfully, "Up for a game?"

He chuckles, the sounds going right through me. "Playing a game with you can be dangerous. I've seen it and it doesn't end well."

"For you it did."

His head falls back in laughter. Damn, I love his laugh. "Yes, it did. So, what do you propose?"

"Pool, darts, either, both..." I quirk a brow.

"We can do that."

"But let's make it interesting." I smirk.

"Interesting for you can be trouble. I know better than to bet against you." His lips twitch up in amusement.

"Afraid?" I taunt, leaning on my forearms, pushing towards him.

His eyes flash with heat igniting my own desire. "Smart."

"Then, what if we make it that whoever loses has to do something of the winner's choice for the other person as long as it's reasonable."

He stares at me thinking. "What kind of parameters would we have on that?"

"What? Don't want to do my laundry for the next year? Or bring me food whenever I want?"

"That's what you'd want?" He quirks his brow.

"I'm not sure, I'd have to think about it."

"So, I don't have to decide right now?"

"No, we can decide later."

He pauses, staring at me in thought. Leaning forward, he gives me his crooked smile causing my heart to skip a beat. "Alright, Alex. I'm in," he says, giving me what I want, but suddenly I'm questioning if I just sealed my own fate. Too late now.

"Shake on it."

"I've got a better idea." He grins, his eyes glinting with mischief.

Standing, he leans over the table, his fingers weaving into my hair as he tilts my face up to meet him. He pauses for a moment to give me a chance to refuse him, but he should know by now that's not about to happen. I reach for his wrist as he presses his lips to mine, soft and slow, heating me to my core. His tongue sweeps inside my mouth, tangling with mine for a quick taste. I have to remind myself we're in a crowded restaurant. He pulls back, looking down at me, his eyes dilated.

"Now that's the way to make a bet." I laugh, trying to shake off my desire.

A few minutes later, we finish our dinner, and he pays the bill before we make our way to the back, grabbing the only open pool table. "Best of three different games?" I suggest, hoping I can get it done in two.

"You got it, darlin," he drawls, poking me.

My eyes narrow. "Did you forget I don't like anyone calling me darlin?" I ask, already knowing the answer.

"Sorry about that." We both grab cues and chalk them. "Are we starting with 8-Ball?" he asks, referring to a common pool game.

"Sure. Flip for who breaks?"

"Your choice."

I arch my eyebrows in surprise, but I'm not about to argue. "I'll break."

He nods and strides around the pool table racking the balls and setting the cue ball down for me ready to shoot. I make my way around the table and line up the shot to break. A stripe ball falls in a corner pocket, and I continue, dropping three more stripes before missing and Declan takes over. My eyes follow him around the table, watching his muscles ripple as he attempts to get the perfect shot. He drops four balls before missing, leaving me on edge. He's good.

"You're turn." He grins, stepping in front of me and giving me a chaste kiss.

"Thanks," I murmur, trying to block out my body's reaction to something so simple and focus. Walking around the table, I maintain control, dropping the remainder of the stripes, then calling the 8-ball pocket and sinking it easily. "Yes!" I grin, my confidence returning.

"Great job," Declan states, kissing me again and making me laugh.

"I like the way you lose."

He shrugs. "I'm going to kiss you every chance I've got."

Blushing, I giggle as he presses his lips to mine once again and I nudge him back. "Do you know how to play 9-ball?"

"The one where you have to drop the balls in number order?"

"Yup," I confirm, my stomach flipping. He knows way too much about pool, but I only need to win one more.

The second game goes quickly, Declan completely controlling the table. I narrow my gaze. He laughs, shrugging. "Lucky. So, what's our last game?"

"One pocket, where we each get one corner pocket that we're allowed to sink our balls, and any balls you hit that drop in a different pocket, you lose a point."

"Got it. Your turn."

I end my turn with two points, Declan doing the same before it's my turn again. I'm about to take my shot when a beautiful woman in a Mackie's shirt bounces over, grinning at Declan. "Hi, Dec. James told me you were here."

"Hannah." He smiles giving her a hug. "How are you? It's been a while."

"I'm good, but busy," she gestures behind her. "Just wanted to say hi, but please say hi to Ella for me. Tell her to call. We miss her around here."

"I will." She gives Declan another quick hug making my stomach turn and offers me a small wave before turning back towards the restaurant. Why didn't he introduce me?

Clearing my throat, I attempt to push away my unease to no avail. My ball bounces off the cushion and falls in on the opposite side, making me lose a point. Declan arches his eyebrows but doesn't say anything. Unfortunately, he keeps his focus and ends the game. "Sweet."

Frowning, I grumble, "I thought you weren't any good."

He smirks. "I didn't say that. I said I know better than to bet against you."

"Apparently that didn't do me any good."

He chuckles pulling me to him and giving me a chaste kiss. "We'd kick ass playing partners."

"We would." A slow smile spreads across my face as we put everything away. "So, what do you want for winning?" I ask, hoping to get whatever it is over with.

"I'm not sure. I think I'm going to have to hold onto that win for a little while. But I promise, I'll come up with something good."

My face falls. "That's what I'm afraid of."

Laughing, he wraps his arm around me, my stomach churning once again. "Are you ready to go?" I nod and he waves at the bartender before we walk outside. He opens the car door for me, and I slip inside. I've never dated a guy that's kind of old fashioned with manners and chivalry, but I have to admit, I like it. In contrast, my dating history is more of a string of short-term hookups.

I buckle my seatbelt, my stomach churning again. Focusing on a spot on the dashboard, I breathe in through my nose and out through my mouth, trying to take some calming breaths. "Oh, no," I quietly mumble, the nausea not going away.

"Are you all right, Alex?" Declan glances at me out of the corner of his eye.

"Um, I don't know. I'm just really nauseous all of a sudden. Can you take me back to my brother's house?"

"Of course." I feel his eyes on me every chance he gets, but I focus on remaining calm and keeping the contents of my stomach where they should be. Reaching out, he gives my leg a gentle squeeze. "We're here."

He jumps out, opening my door and helping me out as I pry my eyes open, slightly dizzy. "Thanks," I mumble grasping his arm, using him as my support as we walk to the door. He helps me inside, my brother not yet home, but I'm desperate for him to leave; I need some space.

"You sure you'll be okay?" he asks, his eyebrows drawn down in concern.

"Yes, I'll be fine and Aidan is on his way home."

"Can you text me when he gets home anyway?" he asks, reminding me what he revealed about his sister.

"Of course, and thank you, Declan. Tonight was fun."

"Thanks for coming out with me."

I nod, and he leans in, brushing his lips across mine. Putting my hand on his chest, I gently push him back. "I'm sorry, Dec, but you have to go. I need to go lay down."

"Goodnight, Alex. Text me later and let me know you're okay," he requests, his eyes full of concern.

"Okay. Goodnight."

He slips out and I lock the door behind him, wondering why after such a great night I didn't even get an invite from him to tomorrow's barbecue. Maybe tonight didn't go as well as I thought. This is the reason I don't date.

Well, one of them anyway.

Chapter 19

Declan

Debating inside my own head is getting old quick, but I can't stop second guessing myself. Should I invite Alex to come to my sister's or should I wait for next time? It's kind of last minute at this point and I don't want her to think I didn't want her to be there, but I honestly completely forgot about asking her last night and giving her an invite now feels like she's an afterthought when she's anything but.

Springing my family on her doesn't seem like the best idea either, especially when I just told them about the baby. I want a chance for them to process everything and the opportunity for me to talk to her first, but I also question if waiting is the right thing, especially when I should've asked her last night. I'm such a dick.

"Ugh," I groan, running my hand through my hair in aggravation. I've never had such a hard time making a simple decision, but I'm so out of my element when it comes to Alex. I don't know why I'm questioning it in the first place. Probably because I need this to go well–I want to do everything I can to do right by Alex and I feel like I've already messed up.

I haven't been able to get her out of my head. How her sweet floral scent contradicts her feisty spirit, the way her velvety skin pebbles under my fingertips, and the taste of her lips drives me wild. Kissing her soft, full lips until I can no longer breathe, having her hot, wet and ready for me on my kitchen counter, and making her fall apart with my tongue pushes me to the brink. I'm hard again just thinking about doing it again and everything else I crave to do to every inch of her body. I readjust, trying to get comfortable.

There's no doubt in my mind that our chemistry is combustible, and her confidence is pure fire–one of the sexiest things about her, but sometimes it feels like a front, desperate to showcase her independence in front of everyone–Aidan the only exception.

Dinner was great last night, but how do I get her to really open up and give me a chance? It feels like she's on the precipice, but I'm already hanging over the edge, clinging to the hope there could be more.

Grabbing my phone, I text my best friend for the third time, desperate for some useful advice.

What the fuck am I supposed to do?

My phone rings almost instantly. Swiping to answer, the sound of Laine's laughter in my ear makes me glare at the phone, even though he can't see me. Obviously, he's enjoying watching me stew in my turmoil. "I've never seen you like this before. Relationships are different than a hookup, Dec."

"No shit, that's why I've been texting you. I thought you were supposed to be good at this."

"Me?" He scoffs. "I'm not the one who spent their whole life taking care of my brother and sisters."

"That's different."

"Only when it comes to sex and if that's your problem, maybe that's why you've never had more than a hookup."

"Fuck you, Laine. I'm serious. Help me out."

"You like her."

"Of course, I do. You know I've wanted to find her since the night I met her."

Chuckling, he mumbles, "Who would've thought, Declan actually wants more from a woman?"

"Forget it. I'll figure it out."

"Look, I get it, but what you need to do is simple, Dec, call her," he declares, emphasizing each word. "Or text. It doesn't fucking matter. Just stop sitting on your hands with your thumb up your ass and do something about it."

"Hope you don't talk to the kids at the center with that mouth." Laine is the one who got my sister involved with Breaking Cycles in the first place and I'm incredibly grateful for it. She loves being able to help kids who are going through the wringer. I glance at the time, reading 4:37pm. "Shit, I'm going to be late. I gotta go."

"Alright. See you later Dec. You've got this."

"Thanks. Catch you later."

Disconnecting, I send a quick text to Alex.

How are you feeling? Wondering if you were busy later? I'd love to see you.

Her response is almost immediate.

Alex

Fine. But I have plans.

I clench my jaw, her curt response irritating me, but I have no right to feel that way. Alex is not mine. She has plans. What kind of plans? Get over it. Move on. She'd tell you if she wanted you to know.

What about tomorrow?

Alex

Maybe. I'll let you know.

She'll let me know. I take a deep breath and exhale slowly. I'm not built for this shit. She's going to push me over the edge.

Shoving my phone in my pocket, I grab my keys and wallet, striding out the front door knowing my sister is expecting me. I'm already behind and I don't like anyone to worry.

About an hour later, I walk up to Ella and Grant's house on the beach and knock on their front door holding flowers and a case of beer. The door swings open, Ella smiling brightly. "Declan, you're finally here. Did you get lost?"

"Yeah, sorry I'm late, but I brought you flowers." I hold out a colorful fall bouquet to her, including two sunflowers.

Smiling, she takes them and steps back as I walk inside. "Thank you." She gestures to the bottles I'm holding. "The beer too, or is that all for you?"

"I'm driving, so no, but I sure as hell could use one." I follow her into the kitchen and set the case on the counter. Ripping the package open, I grab one and pop the top, tipping my head back for a drink.

"We have a couch or plenty of ways to get you home if you want a couple beers, Dec. You okay?"

"Yeah, fine. Where is everyone?"

"Out back. I came in to grab the salt and pepper for Finn."

"Then, let's go," I say, forcing a smile. Looping my arm around my sister's neck, I urge her towards the back door.

"Okay," she agrees, dragging out the word.

We step outside, the scent of the saltwater filling the air. The tall seagrass blows in the breeze, with a path of golden sand leading to the dark blue waters just beyond; the backdrop of her backyard. I glance around the space, spotting my siblings and some other familiar faces.

"Hey y'all."

I wave towards the group, my gaze landing on Grant's assistant coach for Finn's football team alongside Aidan. Standing with his arms crossed over his large, tattooed body, his eyes narrow on me. Hiding behind him, I catch a glimpse of purple. My heart sinks.

"Shit," I mumble under my breath. "I'm an asshole."

Ella arches her eyebrows at me. "I'm going to assume by that you mean you're an idiot and you didn't bother mentioning today to her." I grimace in response. "That's what I thought when she got here without you. You know, Dec, for a smart man, you are really trying hard to mess this up."

"Ella–"

"Don't bother, Dec. Go talk to her. Apologize and make sure she's comfortable here. Introduce her to the rest of the family."

Feeling like a chastised child, at the same time, knowing she's right, I nod. "All right. I'm going."

"Good. And Dec?"

"Yeah?"

She pauses, waiting until I look her in the eyes. When I do, her voice goes soft. "You've looked out for me for a long time, but not only do I have Grant, but I'm okay." Pausing, she takes a step closer, her eyes drilling into mine. "And I'm going to be okay. It's time you start focusing on yourself and your future."

My chest tightens. "Thanks," I begin, my voice cracking, the emotion that slams into me with the truth in her words overwhelming.

Before I can say anything else, Grant steps over to us, giving Ella a chaste kiss. "Matt took over the grill for a few minutes," he informs her before glancing in my direction, his lips twitching up in amusement. "Hey, Dec. Nice of you to make it."

"Hey, Grant," I mumble, holding my beer up in greeting.

Alex finally steps around her brother in fitted black jeans and a dark purple tank top, showing off her ink and every sweet curve of her body causing my breath to hitch. Everything around me goes silent. The ocean instantly fades into the background as she turns, laughing, her eyes sparkling. Her bright smile is aimed at another man nearly blinding me, causing my heart to stutter.

"Ah, excuse me. There's someone I need to go talk to," I say, not bothering to listen to their responses, my attention solely consumed with Alex.

Chapter 20

Alex

"Stop fidgeting," Aidan urges, placing a comforting hand on my back.

"I can't help it. You know I didn't want to come."

"Yeah, you did," he claims, smirking.

The door swings open before I get the chance to retort, Ella smiling at us. "Aidan, Alex, it's so good to see y'all."

"It's good to see you too," Aidan claims and leans down, giving her a hug in greeting. "Thanks for having us."

"Yes, thank you," I add as she gives me a hug.

Releasing me, she moves back, and we step inside. The living room is on our left and the kitchen sits behind it with a sliding glass door leading to their backyard, the ocean just visible from here. I love the calm, beachy vibe. Turning, Ella calls, "Grant, Aidan and Alex are here."

"This is so beautiful."

"Thank you." She smiles. "It's my haven."

Moments later, Grant walks into the room from the short hallway on the left side of the living room. He moves behind Ella and wraps one arm around her, placing a kiss on the top of her head before he even glances towards Aidan and me with a wide grin. "Thanks for coming." He holds out his hand for Aidan and shakes it, before giving me a one-armed hug, his other arm never straying from Ella. It's sweet.

"Wanna head out back? Everyone is here except for Declan."

Her words bring me both relief and a little bit of nerves at the same time. I assumed he would be here. "Oh."

She gives me a comforting smile as she steps out from under Grant's arm and links her arm through mine. "He will be here though." My eyebrows draw down, my doubts creeping further in making her laugh. "I promise he's a really good guy, but he can be an idiot sometimes."

"What? I don't..." I shake my head, not even sure what I was about to say when I'm not sure what she knows.

We step out onto the back deck, my eyes widening at the gorgeous view, the sky streaked with reds, oranges, and yellows where it meets the blues of the sea. I'm momentarily mesmerized by the whites of the waves cresting as they smoothly roll into the shore. "Wow. This is spectacular."

"I agree. It's a little choppy today, but do you like to paddle board?" Ella asks, pulling me away from the view.

"Um, I've never tried it, but I would love to."

"Normally it's pretty calm here in the mornings. It's my favorite time to go if you ever want to come with me. I'd be happy to show you how and I have an extra board."

"Thank you, Ella. I'd like that."

"Good. Before you leave let's plan a time." I nod in agreement.

A familiar man with broad shoulders, dark brown hair, emerald eyes and visible tattoos on his arms walks towards us holding the hand of a beautiful petite blonde woman. It takes me a moment but then it hits me that I met them at the game last night; Grant's brother and his wife. "Aidan, good to see you," he greets my brother with a wide smile, holding out his hand. They shake and give each other a firm pat on the back.

Aidan glances at me, grinning wide. "Y'all, this is my little sister, Alex."

"We met last night at the game. Did you forget already? And I'm not that little."

Aidan shrugs and Amy laughs. "I get that all the time."

"Come on, let me introduce you to everyone," Ella urges, gently tugging on my arm.

Aidan nods. "While you do that with Ella, I have to go say hi to someone, if y'all will excuse me." He steps away before I get a chance to respond.

My heart pounds erratically in my chest, suddenly anxious. This was a bad idea. I shouldn't be here with Declan's family without him. "Um..."

"My brother and sister are dying to meet you."

"Ella, where can I find the salt and pepper? It's not on the counter," a boy calls from doorway, appearing to be a much younger and a little bit taller version of Declan.

"I'm coming," she calls and turns back to me. "That's my younger brother, Finn. I'll be right back." That explains it. He looks much different when he's not wearing a football uniform. I watch as she spins on her heel, striding towards the house, leaving me feeling out of place.

Forcing a smile, I make my way over to Aidan, finding him talking to a guy that it takes me a moment to recognize. He's tall with broad shoulders, short black hair and brown skin. My gaze is drawn to his inked sleeve covering his right arm and peeking out of the top of his black t-shirt. Dragging my eyes up to his chiseled jaw covered in scruff, I meet his golden gaze. "Nice ink."

"Thanks." He grins, his eyes swiftly skimming up and down my body. He's good looking, but he doesn't ignite my blood or bring my body to life like Declan can. Damn him—get out of my head. "Looks like we both got more color since the last time I saw you."

My eyes widen. "Ryder!"

His eyes flash with heat. Laughing, he pulls me into his arms, my hand falling to his chest. Now, him, I can handle. No feelings. No pressure. No complications. Except there will be a constant complication with me now.

"You didn't forget about me, did you?" he growls low in challenge, arching his eyebrow.

"No, but you have to admit, you look a little different than the last time I saw you."

Releasing me, he shrugs, smirking. "We both do, but it's damn good to see you, Alex."

"So, how do you know my sister?" Aidan inquires, his eyes narrowed on Ryder making my head fall back in laughter. He knows I can handle myself but that doesn't make him any less protective.

Placing my hand on Aidan's forearm, I insist, "Stand down, big brother. Ryder and I were in the same foster home briefly. He's one of the good ones." Glancing at Ryder's arched eyebrow, I advise, "And Aidan is my biological brother. He's the one who fought for me."

Both men nod in acceptance, their shoulders relaxing.

Ryder stares at me and shakes his head in disbelief. "I really can't believe you're here."

"I feel the same. It's surreal seeing you here. How do you know Grant and Ella?" I ask.

"I coach the boys high school team with Grant. Well, I'm his assistant and I teach U.S. History there." He points to Finn as he steps outside. "I had Finn in class last year, but I don't work with the quarterbacks too often. He's one of those kids who's a natural with both; sports and academics."

"Huh," I mumble, taking it all in.

"Surprised?"

"No. Should I be?"

He gives me a crooked grin. "Looks like I'm the one who's taken aback. We need to catch up. Go out with me."

"Dude," Aidan grumbles irritably, making both of us laugh.

"She's taken," Declan declares, interrupting, placing a possessive hand on the small of my back.

A sound of disbelief exits my mouth. "Liar." My body heats at his touch and my eyes narrow. I'm not mad, but he knows I don't want a hero. Ignoring Aidan and Ryder, I spin towards Declan, still glaring. "Declan, surprised to see you here."

"This is my sister's house," he states in explanation.

"And?" I prompt, arching my eyebrow in challenge.

He clenches his jaw prompting me to squeeze my legs together. How is that hot? "I want you to meet my family."

I scoff. "You sure about that?"

Taking a deep breath, he steps closer to me. "Positive."

"Then maybe you should've thought about that before and actually invited me," I retort, emphasizing invited. Spinning on my heel, I stride straight for the cooler and flip it open. I frown, realizing I can't grab what I really want. Reluctantly, I reach for a bottle of water, wishing it were wine. Too bad I don't have that touch.

I feel his body heat behind me making mine tingle before he says a word. "I'm sorry, but I really would like you to meet them."

"I'm going to the bathroom," I grumble, ignoring him. I slip inside, with Declan following right behind me.

"Alex, stop, please."

"Why?" I challenge, spinning around to face him.

"Because my family is important to me and so are you."

"You don't know me. Stop pretending like you're happy about this. You obviously didn't want me here to meet your family," I argue, a fresh wave of betrayal rolling through me when I have no right to feel that way.

"That's not true."

"Really?" I scoff. "Then, why didn't you tell me about it?"

"Because I didn't want this. Do you know what I spent the last couple days doing besides working?" He steps into my space, making it difficult to breathe, so I just shake my head in response. "I told my parents about you and the baby. They're thrilled and can't wait to meet you. They know we're not together, but they also know I'm very interested and I want more." My eyes widen in surprise. "That's right, I want more," he reiterates, emphasizing each word. "Then, after I told them, Finn came home and we got on a call with Ella and Charlotte so I could tell all of them at the same time. Although, I talked to Ella the first day you told me."

"You did?"

He nods. "Yeah, I did. But I wasn't sure about asking you to come today before I had a chance to talk to you."

"About what?"

"What you were okay sharing with everyone, and what you didn't want people to know. I wanted to make sure you were comfortable with me telling my family since we didn't exactly talk about that. It was important to me, but we didn't touch on that and that's not fair to you. I started questioning what I should have revealed."

"Dec, it's fine," I murmur, overwhelmed with his thoughtfulness and realizing how wrong my first impression was about this man. Honestly, I probably knew, but admitting it to myself is an entirely different level because that would mean he's right and it might be time to give him a chance. I'm not sure if I'm ready for something like that–a relationship–and this isn't one I can mess up and completely walk away from.

"Alex, my family wants to get to know you whether we're together or not but give me a chance–a chance for us to really get to know each other. I know I keep saying it, but I mean it. I want this with you, whatever it's going to be. Why not spend more time with me outside the bedroom?"

Smirking, I claim, "Well, that's not really adding any boundaries."

He huffs a laugh, the deep sound rumbling through my body and sending a shiver down my spine. "True. But what could it hurt? We can shape our boundaries in any direction we want to make it so it's right for us. Just me and you–no one else."

My head begins spinning multiple scenarios of how this could turn out; the good, the bad and the ugly. I suck my lower lip between my teeth, deep in thought and groan in frustration. "I don't know, Dec."

I glance in his direction, his eyes flaring with heat and his jaw clenched. "You're driving me crazy, worrying your lip and those sounds..."

"Sorry." My face heats, blushing.

Reaching up, he runs his fingers tenderly down my cheek before dropping his hand back in his lap. "Don't apologize, especially for that." Heaving a sigh, he asks, "Look, I know you can't deny that we have chemistry, but are you not interested? If that's the case, I'll back off. I don't want to, but I will for you. Just know that either way, I still want to be involved."

I shake my head, blurting out the words before I can stop myself, "I am interested."

"Okay," he mumbles, dragging out the word. "Do you want to see other people? Like Ryder?" He visibly flinches at his own question causing my stomach to churn. "Is that it? I know we aren't..."

"No, that's not it," I interrupt, not wanting him to even tread into any territory where we start to define something before we have any idea what it is we're trying to figure out. But no matter how much I don't want to, even I can admit it's there. "It's just not easy for me. Let's leave it at that–for now."

He nods slowly. "Okay. I can do that."

"So," I begin, desperate to shift the subject away from my past, and dip into dangerous territory, "why didn't you want Ryder to ask me out?"

A low growl falls from his lips making me giggle. I don't giggle, but apparently it's become common for me when I'm around Declan. "You know why."

Arching my eyebrows in challenge, I poke the bear. "Do I? It's not like you're bothering to *show me* I shouldn't hook up with other men. Pretending I'm taken doesn't count."

"I think I've made it perfectly clear what I want."

Unmoving, I stare at him, defiant. I'm not sure what I need, but I'm confident it's more.

Chapter 21

Declan

For fuck's sake. She's taunting me.

In seconds, I'm on her, not able to hold myself back. Pushing her up against my sister's kitchen counter and sealing my mouth to hers, I devour her, thankful she kisses me back with her own pent up passion. One hand weaves into her hair, the other wrapping around her back holding her tight to me. Turning my head, I deepen the kiss. I moan into her mouth, my tongue tangling with hers, fighting for dominance.

My body ignites as she wraps her legs around my waist, rubbing herself against my hard cock. Tearing my lips away from hers, I lick and kiss my way down her neck and along her collarbone, eliciting a soft moan from her lips. I groan, slipping my hand from her hair and gliding down her side. Sliding my hand between us, I palm her breast, my thumb running over her already pert nipple.

"Dec," she whimpers, urging me on. She digs her fingers into my back dragging them down to my ass and squeezing, dragging us closer.

"Come home with me," I rasp, pleading–no, demanding. She doesn't answer before I'm kissing her again.

A low chuckle sounds from behind me making me halt but keeping Alex close. "Seriously, Dec? Couldn't wait?"

"Walk away, Finn," I order, hearing his laughter as he makes his way towards the bathroom.

Slowly, Alex lowers her legs, rubbing against me on her way down. "Oops," she mumbles, amusement clear in her voice.

I pull back, looking down at her, chuckling at her mischievous grin. "That's my brother. He's seventeen."

"That explains it." She laughs. "I saw him before you got here. You can tell you're related, but he's taller."

My eyes narrow. "But I'm way hotter."

She laughs again. "To me? I should hope so, he's a minor and you're–old."

"Ouch. Back to the old shit."

She shrugs. "Just telling it how it is."

Grinning, I press my lips to hers. Leaning back, I look down at her. She has no clue how much I love her feistiness. "You have no idea what you do to me."

Smirking, she cups me, making me gasp. "Oh, I have a little idea."

"There's nothing little about me."

She giggles, conceding. "True. I'll give you that."

Taking a deep breath, I attempt to calm myself down so I can walk outside with Alex and introduce her to my siblings. "So, can I assume that coming here today was what your plans entailed?"

"Maybe."

"Come home with me after this."

She hesitates, but I'm not sure if she's just being playful or if she's really unsure and I don't like it. "I don't know."

"Alex, you know we would have fun, and I want to spend more time with you without my family, your brother, or anyone else."

"You mean Ryder?"

A growl escapes. "Definitely without him."

Clearly amused at my jealousy, she laughs, just as my brother strides back into the room.

"All good?" he asks.

I step back and turn, narrowing my eyes at him. "Don't be an asshole. Finn, I'd like you to meet Alex."

"It's nice to meet you, Alex," he mumbles, stepping towards her, his lips still twitching in amusement.

She laughs. "You too, Finn. I saw your game the other night. You're a great football player."

"Yeah?" He straightens, his gaze swinging to me and back to her. "I guess I'm alright."

"You're so much more than alright," I emphasize, making my pride for my brother apparent.

"Thanks, Dec."

"It's the truth."

He smiles, his cheeks reddening. "I'm going to head back outside. You guys coming? Or are you going to risk getting caught by mom and dad?"

Alex groans, blushing. I flick his ear and he stumbles out the door laughing. "I'm sorry, Alex."

"I didn't know your parents were here."

"They aren't. Finn is being a dick, but that was meant for me. You're just part of the collateral."

"Oh, he's going to be trouble."

"Going to be?" I scoff. "He already is."

She giggles, the sound going right through me. "You're telling me he takes after his big brother."

I smirk, shrugging. "So, you never answered me before."

"About what?" she asks, feigning innocence.

"Come home with me later. I can bring you back to your brother's whenever you want but come home with me."

My gaze falls to her lips as her tongue juts out, licking them, drawing me in. But I can't kiss her again if I'm not leaving with her now. "And then what happens?" she asks, her voice coming out breathy.

My heartbeat picks up its pace. "We'll talk, maybe watch a movie, and definitely do more of this." Lightly, I brush my lips over hers, barely holding myself back from doing more.

Alex quickly makes me lose all my senses. The soft flowery scent mixed with touch of vanilla, her heated breath on my skin, her soft curves, the sound of her voice, her sweet and salty taste that's uniquely her.

I need to be strong, keeping it light while I'm in Ella and Grant's home with so many people around. "But only if that's what you want."

"What do you think I want?"

"I will never assume, Alex, especially when it comes to you."

She tilts her head to the side, assessing me. "Alright, Declan. I'll come hang out with you after this. But–"

"There's a but?"

She grins, the look she gives me going straight to my groin. "Absolutely." She pauses, gathering herself and her smile falters before she forces it back, showing me a glimpse of her vulnerability underneath. "So, if we do this, where do we start?"

An easy smile curves my lips as I exhale in relief.

"Do you want to come meet my other sister?"

She nods. "Okay."

Sliding my hand down, I grab hers, entangling our fingers together. Lifting it to my mouth, I brush my lips across the tattoo on her wrist and drop it back down between us. She glances down at where we're linked before looking back at me, a tentative smile curving her lips.

"Are you ready?" She nods, giving my hand a squeeze.

We walk outside together and approach Charlotte, her boyfriend Kane by her side. I clench my jaw, trying to get my emotions under control. When the fuck did he get here? He must've come through the gate. I can't stand the guy, but Char insists he's a good guy and treats her right. I have my doubts, but what can I do unless I find out otherwise.

One thing is guaranteed: I will be watching him like a hawk.

"You okay?" Alex whispers in my ear.

"Her boyfriend," I murmur, giving her a warning at the same time wanting to be open with her.

"Got it."

"Hey, Char," I say from behind her. She spins towards me, her blonde hair flying as she throws her arms around me, giving me a hug. "Glad you're here," I tell her, returning her hug. She's been so busy with her new theater group, I feel like we barely see her. Mostly, I blame Kane. It's like he wants all of her time, but we're a close family after all we've been through. That doesn't work with us.

"Hi, Dec. I've missed you!" She pulls back, glancing at Alex and squeals. Releasing me, she throws her arms around Alex, taking her by surprise. "You must be Alex. I'm so excited to meet you!"

After a moment, she returns her hug, a genuine smile tugging at her lips. "That's me. It's so great meeting you, Charlotte."

"Please, call me Char and this is my boyfriend, Kane."

My sister starts chatting with Alex a mile a minute, while my focus goes to Kane, a possessive hand on her hip. His cell phone rings, and he pulls it out, glancing at the screen. "I have to take this," he states, stepping away.

I clench my jaw, glaring at his back hating how he never makes her a priority. Char glances at me and forces a smile. "He's on call today."

Scoffing, I challenge, "For the theater?"

Flinching, she shakes her head and heaves a sigh. "Don't go there, Dec," she says, almost pleading.

"You deserve better," I insist, my fingers twitching, desperate to protect her.

Clenching her fists at her sides, she glares at me as if I'm the problem. "I'm not doing this with you right now."

Knowing we have an audience and this conversation is getting us nowhere, I take a deep breath, silently seething. "Fine. We'll talk about it later."

She shakes her head and Alex tries to redirect the conversation. "So, Char, tell me about the show you're doing," she requests. I give her a grateful smile, already looking forward to leaving.

Chapter 22

Alex

Kicking off my shoes, I curl up on the couch, sinking into it. Closing my eyes, I wait for Declan. I'm suddenly completely exhausted. Today has been unexpected to say the least. Walking into Grant and Ella's today, I was ready to go back on my word to my brother and make sure Aidan would never have children. But everyone was so welcoming. Then when Declan showed up, his possessiveness both pissed me off and turned me on. Good thing I'm not shy because I seem to do the same to him.

But sitting here, relaxing with him in his home, gets me back in my head and I'm struggling to reach the surface. What is it about him that I don't want to stay away from? It's almost like I can't, but that's ridiculous. I've never had a problem before, so why now?

The couch cushions bounce lightly beside me. Blinking my eyes open, Declan's pale blue eyes meet mine causing a lump to form in my throat, but I quickly gulp it down. "Opening my eyes to find you looking at me is kinda disturbing."

He laughs, his eyes sparkling, making my heart skip a beat. "I brought you some water. Thought you might be thirsty." He gestures to a glass on the coffee table in front of us. His head tilts to the side, assessing me. "Are you alright? You look exhausted."

"Gee, thanks," I grumble, glowering.

"You know what I mean. It's been a long day and you have more than most to take care of." His gaze drops to my belly and swiftly back to my face. "You know, it's okay for you to be tired and to rest." Reaching out, he tucks a loose strand of hair behind my ear. "Let me take care of you."

My head tells me this is a bad idea, but everything else inside me is screaming at me like a banshee to say yes, *you can do anything you want.*

Instead, I compromise, settling myself into the crook of his arm, my head resting on his shoulder. He pulls me close, his lips brushing over the top of my head, eliciting a soft sigh of pleasure from my lips. My face heats, but there's no way I'd dare look in his direction.

I don't remember the last time anyone besides my brother took care of me. It's nice. His fingers run gently through my hair, the motion soothing and making me melt further into him, relishing the feeling of being safe, cared for, and protected while he's here. I can't imagine a feeling like this could last forever.

"Can we watch a movie?" I ask, desperate for something to yank me from the fantasy trying to take root in my head.

"Sure. Do you have something in mind?"

"Not really, just something with a lot of action."

"My kind of woman," he declares, confident. My stupid heart stutters in my chest making my breath catch in my throat, but I remain frozen, refusing to alert him of my growing feelings or fears.

Grabbing the remote, he begins flipping through his streaming services before settling on a police movie that has a little of everything: action, comedy, and romance. "How does this one sound? I've heard it's good."

"Sure, that's fine."

His phone rings, interrupting us. He glances at the screen, mumbling, "I'm sorry, I have to take this." He runs his finger across the screen to answer. "Hi, Char." He stiffens and sits up straight, leaning away from me. "Are you okay?" He pauses, standing. "I'm coming to get you." He slips his shoes on. "Yes, I am, Char. Tell me where you are." Grabbing his keys by the door, he glances at me, clenching his jaw. "Fine. I'll do it right away. Text me when you get back to your place and you better fucking call me in the morning."

He disconnects the call and starts tapping away on his phone. "Is Charlotte okay?" I ask.

"Not really, but she will be."

"What happened?"

He finishes what he's doing on his phone and tosses it on the coffee table in frustration. "She got in a fight with her asshole of a boyfriend and he left her at a bar. Her phone isn't connecting to any of her ride apps and she didn't bring her purse. I just ordered her ride because she said she would walk home if I came to get her. She didn't want the people she works with to see me pick her up after dickhead left her."

"I'm sorry."

"Thanks." Grabbing the remote, he presses play and as the circle spins, loading the movie, he whispers, "I'm really glad you were there today."

"Yeah?"

"Absolutely," he confirms, staring straight ahead. "My family is extremely important to me if you can't tell." He huffs a laugh and runs his hand through his hair. "I'd do anything for them."

"That's obvious."

"We've been through so much with Ella being sick for so long, we all took care of each other. But since I'm the oldest, I was ultimately the one responsible. Sometimes I feel like I'm their parent more than their brother. I love my mom and dad, but there were four of us and only two of them. They did their best, but with all the time they spent at the hospital or at doctor's appointments and trying to keep their jobs, my mom eventually quit, but it still wasn't enough. They had to depend on me a lot. The only good thing it did was it brought all of us really close."

"I know what you mean. I feel that way about Aidan." The words are out of my mouth before I can stop them.

"You two seem close."

"We are. Aidan basically raised me. My mom died unexpectedly when we were kids and my dad had a hard time with life after that. I was ten when it happened." My heart thrashes against my ribcage, my brain catching up with the words spilling out of my mouth like word vomit.

What the hell am I thinking?

"I'm so sorry, Alex. Damn, I'm so sorry." His sincere apology squeezes my chest so tight I can barely breathe. His hand cups my cheek, urging me to look at him, but I know I can't handle that. My chest feels like it's wide open, gaping, and hemorrhaging. I'm left weak and vulnerable to the taking. I can't do that. There's no way I'm going to let this feeling overtake me, consume me. So, I do what I know will stop it.

My gaze falls to his mouth as I pull myself up and straddle him. Focusing on the man beneath me, I run my thumb over his full lips. Cradling his face in my hands, I close my eyes and kiss him soft and slow. But I need more. Tilting my head, I press into him, deepening our kiss. My tongue juts out, tangling with his, licking, kissing, exploring.

His hands begin to roam my body, my skin pebbling beneath his touch. Reaching down, he grasps the hem of my tank top and lifts, my breasts spilling out as he pulls it over my head. "Fuck, no bra," he states in awe as his mouth closes over my breast.

"It was built into the tank," I murmur, breathless. Focusing on his tongue swirling around my nipple, my back arches towards him while I dig my fingers into the hard muscles of his shoulders, desperate for him. A guttural moan leaves my lips as he sucks me into his mouth, releasing my breast with a pop to take the other one into his mouth, giving it the same treatment.

Heat pools low in my belly. My hips move automatically, grinding over him. Suddenly he stands, flipping me onto my back. Unbuttoning my jeans, he tugs them down, dropping them onto the floor, my panties soon following. I'm so wet and ready.

He looks down on me in appreciation. "Damn, Alex, you're so fucking gorgeous."

I blush. Shaking it off, I insist, "You have too many clothes on."

"No, I'm going to have a snack first."

"Declan," I whimper at the thought. "At least your shirt, please. I want to feel your skin." Reaching one hand behind his back, he pulls his shirt over his head, doing as I asked. My eyes widen, relishing the view. "Mmm, thank you."

He kneels on the couch beside my feet as I watch his every move, wondering what he'll do next. Crawling up my body, he places kisses on my ankle, my knee, my inner thigh. "Ah…"

Inhaling deeply, he hums as he exhales just over my sex, but he doesn't touch me. Looping his arm under my knee, he takes my leg with him, and continues moving up. He takes his time, pressing his lips to my belly, the side of my breast, and the spot on the apex of my neck that drives me wild just before his lips crash into mine, hard and demanding.

My entire body tingles with anticipation, his jeans rubbing against my clit. Turning my head, I tear my lips away from his, begging for more. "Declan, please."

Propping himself up on his elbows, my leg still between us, he looks down at me, his eyes a deep blue like the ocean but all fire, for me. Giving me a salacious grin, he mumbles, "I like you this way."

I try to glare at him, but I can't. Every time either of us moves, another wave of desire washes through me. Sliding back, he slips my leg over his shoulder before lifting my other leg and doing the same. Grasping my hips, he settles himself in front of my pussy and sticks his tongue out flat against me, licking me slow, but firm. "You're fucking soaked for me," he moans in appreciation.

My head falls back, and I cry out as he does it again, sucking my clit between his teeth. He slips his tongue inside me, followed by his thumb, quickly pushing me to the edge. "I'm not going to last."

My words spur him on, and he works his tongue faster over my folds to my clit. His thumb drives in and out of me when I feel his pinky at my back entrance. I want to argue, but I'm too primed and breathless to care. Just after he pushes it inside, I scream his name, "Declan," completely falling apart. My body spasms, almost violently, as he continues to lick up my juices.

His low chuckle brings me back to reality. "Damn, that was hot."

I gasp for breath, looking down at the man worshipping me and wondering how I got here. "If I had any sense, I wouldn't have let you do that."

"You sure about that? You came so hard. Watching you fall apart was more than worth the risk of retaliation."

"Mmm," I moan. "It's always the ones you don't expect that take you by surprise in the bedroom."

"Speaking of bedroom–" he stands, lifting me and holding me tight to him. My legs automatically wrap around him. "It's time to bring you to mine where I can properly fuck you." I giggle. "And you meant to say I'm the only one who has ever surprised you in that department." He wiggles his eyebrows suggestively making me laugh harder.

"Whatever you say, cowboy," I mumble, knowing it will rile him up. I'm not about to tell him he's right, although he is. I've never had an orgasm that hard in my life and I just might kill to have that again.

Chapter 23

Declan

Striding into my bedroom with purpose, I toss Alex onto the bed making her squeal in surprise. My footsteps stagger and my body boils as I watch her naked body bounce on my bed. Gritting my teeth, I demand, "Don't go anywhere," before forcing myself to turn towards my bathroom.

"Wasn't planning on it," she replies, flopping back on the bed, a content smile on her face.

I wash my hands and splash some water on my face, relishing the mouthwatering taste of her on my tongue. I'm so hard thinking about being inside her, my balls begin turning blue. Time to find a condom and fix that. I bought a new box the other day, it should be under my sink. Yanking the cabinet open, my eyes search the contents, but it's not there. Frantically, I look through every drawer and cabinet in my bathroom, coming up empty.

Fucking Finn. "Shit," I mumble under my breath.

Propping herself up on her elbows, she looks at me, her eyebrows drawn down in concern. "What's wrong?"

Damn she looks delectable and now I'm fucked, unfortunately, not literally. Heaving a sigh, I inform her, "I'm out of condoms."

"Oh." She sucks her bottom lip between her teeth, releasing it slowly, causing my eyes to flare. She has to know what that does to me by now. "Does it really matter?"

My eyes widen. Cautiously, I step towards her, almost afraid if I move too fast, she'll run. "What are you asking, Alex?"

"I'm already pregnant and I'm clean. I got checked after we were together that night and I haven't been with anyone else since."

She's right, but I'm shocked she's even suggesting it. Going bareback seems so much more personal, intimate, yet she still seems to deny our connection is real. "I got checked out then too and I haven't been with anyone else since either," I confirm, but she should know... "I've never gone without one."

"Neither have I," she reveals, her admission doing more than messing with my dick. "But what better time to go without than with the woman you already knocked up?" She smirks, attempting to break the crackle in the atmosphere between us. Slowly, I take a step towards her. Suddenly, holding up a hand, she stops me. "Don't come any closer until those damn jeans come off."

Chuckling, I oblige, my black boxer briefs going along with them. She licks her lips as I stalk towards her, ready to devour my prey. Reaching between us, she wraps her hand around my thick shaft. I groan, my hips arching towards her hand as she pumps once, twice. Grunting, I push back, removing her hand. "This is already going to be quicker than I'd like."

"That's okay, you already have proven your worth." I grin. She always has a comeback, glad this one was for me. "And besides, I know from experience, you're even better when you come back for seconds and thirds."

Needing to touch her, I grab her wrist, bringing it to my lips, my tongue jutting out and licking her tattoo. "That first night, you licked your wrist right here just before you took that tequila shot. My tongue has been wanting to use that as a starting point ever since."

"Mmm," she mumbles, her eyes hooded.

"It looks like a Celtic love knot," I observe, tracing it with my tongue.

"It is. It's for my family," she reveals taking me by surprise. It's rare she shares something that personal so willingly. Her eyes widen as if just realizing what she exposed and I feel her heart rate quicken in panic. Her words only confirm it. "I need you, Declan. If you're not going to do it, let me ride you."

My eyes flare, letting it go and focusing on the moment. "Oh, you will, but not this time." I look down into her eyes, my jaw clenching at the thought, but I can tell she's using our chemistry as a distraction. The look in her eyes tells me she needs it–needs me, whether she admits it or not. Taking action, I climb over her, circling my pelvis at her entrance. She attempts to arch her hips towards me, but I grasp her hips, holding her firmly in place and pinning her to the bed.

"Ready?" I ask, trying to maintain my control.

"Yes!" she insists impatiently, prompting me to lose all control. With one quick thrust, I fill her up, her scream turning to one of pleasure as I plunge deep inside her. The feel of me bare rubbing against her swollen, heated walls is almost too much. My body feels like it's on fire about to combust and I haven't even moved yet.

"Dec," she urges breathlessly.

"Give me a second," I rasp, my voice a deep, low hum vibrating over her skin eliciting goosebumps. "You feel so fucking good. Hot, wet, tight–perfect."

"Please," she begs, squeezing my cock inside her, urging me on.

"Damn, woman," I grumble, my hips no longer able to remain still.

She huffs a laugh and I instantly swallow it up with a hungry kiss. My tongue sweeps inside, tangling with hers. I feel her hands roaming over my body, feeling every ridge and digging in as if desperate to get closer. Our bodies begin moving together in a perfect rhythm, the only sounds the slap of our skin, our heavy breathing, and moans of pure pleasure.

Lifting her right leg, she wraps it around me, urging me impossibly closer. The new angle does the trick hitting her in what seems to be just the right spot every time I thrust into her. Every little sound, touch, and slide of my dick in and out of her, ignites a fire inside me. I need her to come before I fucking lose it.

"Dec, I'm gonna come," she moans as if on cue.

Her words are exactly what I needed to hear. I drive into her harder and faster, stirring the growing tingling sensation deep inside me, desperate to explode. "I need you to come, Alex. I want to feel you squeeze my cock. Come for me!"

"Yes!" She screams, her body obeying, convulsing around me, squeezing me as if begging me to fall over the edge with her.

With a grunt, I plunge inside, my movements becoming erratic while I feel her body tremor from aftershocks around my cock. With one last push, I still, shooting my seed inside her, eliciting another aftershock, her pussy squeezing my cock once again. When I'm empty, I collapse partly on top of her, remaining inside her warmth as I catch my breath.

Prying my eyes open, I reluctantly slip from inside her, and stretch out my body next to hers, keeping her close. Glancing at Alex, a smirk tugs at my lips. "Give me an hour and I'll be ready for round two."

She giggles. "We'll see, cowboy."

A low growl falls from my lips as I stand, taking her with me. She sure knows how to push me. "Maybe we'll start the next round now. Time to get cleaned up."

I turn on the shower, waiting a moment for it to warm up before I step inside with her. Slowly, she lowers her feet to the ground. Holding on, I steady her. "Whoa," she whispers.

"You okay?" I ask, my eyebrows drawing down in concern.

"Yeah, I'm fine."

Her words do the opposite of easing my worry. Knowing she won't want me to take care of her, I don't give her a choice and change the direction of our shower, so that's all it is. Picking her up, I tenderly, press my lips to hers, moving us under the spray as I kiss her deeper. She flinches slightly, but her lips continue to move over mine. When I know we're both wet, I spin her around, placing her back to my front. I reach for the shampoo and squeeze some into my hands. Weaving my fingers into her hair, I massage her scalp, the soap quickly foaming while her body relaxes in my arms.

"Ready to rinse?" I ask softly. She nods sliding under the spray.

While she's busy, I squirt some body wash into my hands and onto a washcloth, taking my time running both over every inch of her body, struggling to keep my focus on taking care of her with my dick coming back to life.

As the soap disappears down the drain, my lips brush against her silky skin, trailing over her tattoos on her shoulder, her arm, her back and the snake on her thigh. I move back to get a better look, my fingers replacing my lips.

The colorful art appears connected. Her body tenses, my fingers running over a beautiful angel with long red hair, crying blood red tears down to a small garden of lilies. It shows the intricate web of roots underground and the beautiful flowers above in pink, yellow, and white. It's gorgeous, but I've never seen anything like it. I wonder if it has anything to do with her mom. Her body's reaction tells me it's not something she's ready to talk about. Hopefully she will be comfortable enough to open up to me, eventually.

Turning in my arms, she looks up at me, her look pleading, vulnerable, taking me by surprise, but she swiftly shutters it closed. Keeping her eyes pinned on me, she squeezes soap into her hand and focuses solely on my cock.

"Alex," I say in warning.

"Yes?" she asks, a devilish look shining in her eyes.

In one swift movement, I pick her up as if she weighs nothing and pin her against the wall with my body. She wiggles in my arms arching towards me, but I hold tight, turning off the water. Wrapping her in a towel, I carry her to my bed and tuck her under the covers. "I can walk you know," she grumbles.

"I know, but I like you close." I press my lips against hers and pull back. "I'm going to finish cleaning up."

"Then, why'd we get out?"

"I'll be right back," I insist. "You're too distracting." Giving her a wink, I smirk and head towards the bathroom.

I'm such an idiot. She's pregnant.

She should be taking it easy and I'm planning how I can claim her in every inch of my house. Yeah, she's pushing me, but she's also using me as a distraction, that much is obvious. Or maybe she's trying to divert my attention from getting closer to her. Either way, I need to put her first, even if she's not doing it for herself.

I rush through my shower as promised and climb into bed behind her, pulling her back to my front—a perfect fit.

Damn, I'm in so much trouble.

Chapter 24

Alex

Lying in bed, I press my lips into a thin line as my gaze roams over all the hard ridges and valleys of this beautiful man while his eyes are closed. I don't move, not wanting the moment to end. But I'm exhausted feeling like I just ran a marathon.

I'm not sure what tonight means, but the way he cared for me felt unlike any other man I've ever been with. He's pushing it, involving more of me than I'm ready to give, or maybe I am. I guess I'll keep trying to take it as it comes.

"Please tell me you're not thinking about leaving," he mumbles without opening his eyes. "I want you to stay."

My heart lurches, his words playing like a symphony, desperate to be heard, but I push my shoulders back and shove it down. I'm not ready to dig into my building emotions for this man. For now, I'm better off ignoring it. "No, I'm staying tonight. I just wanted to send a text to my brother, so he wouldn't worry."

"Good."

Sighing, I roll back over and curl up into the same spot he tucked me into before, feeling safe and cared for in his warm embrace. The feeling is completely foreign to me, making me wonder how long it will last. Closing my eyes, I try to relax and pray for a dreamless sleep. Having one of my bad dreams is the last thing I need tonight.

"Can I come with you, Mom?" I ask, looking up at her, my eyes pleading. She's tall and beautiful with long red hair, bright green eyes and the kind of smile that makes everyone want to be around her.

Glancing down at me, she smiles. "Of course. I have to go to the pharmacy to pick up the medicine for dad. Afterwards, we'll pick up your brother from practice and maybe we can grab a pizza for dinner."

"Yes!" I fist pump the air.

She laughs. "Come on, let's go."

"Dale, we'll be back in an hour," Mom calls into the living room. "Alexa is coming with me."

"Okay. I love you both. Drive safe," he replies, his voice hoarse from being under the weather.

"Love you too, Dad."

"I love you, honey. Text if you think of anything else you would like me to pick up for you and try to get some rest," she reiterates just before we walk out the door.

We settle into the car and my mom pulls out, driving towards town. "Are you trying to procrastinate your homework?"

Grimacing, I nod. "Yeah, I guess. I just hate math."

My mom laughs. "You know, dad and I will be happy as long as you try to do your best in school."

I roll my eyes dramatically. "I do try hard."

She nods in acknowledgement, turning into the parking lot at the pharmacy. "I know, Alexa. I just don't want to see you give up."

"Mom, I promise I won't. I just wanted a break."

"Well, okay, a break I think we can do." She grins. "Come on, let's get the medicine for dad."

"Okay." I climb out of the car and follow my mom into the pharmacy, trudging to the back of the store. She walks up to the counter, giving the pharmacist my dad's name and date of birth.

"It's almost ready Diana. Have a seat."

"Thank you."

"Mom, can I have some candy?" I ask, my gaze scanning the colorful display of sweets in front of the counter.

"Not today."

I frown and cross my arms over my chest. My mom's hand falls to my back as we step to the side. A man dressed in a gray suit stumbles as he steps up to the counter. His hair is sticking up in all directions as if he were tugging on the ends. "I need to refill my prescription for Oxycodone," he states, handing the pharmacist a piece of paper with his hands trembling.

Like the pharmacist did with mom, he asks for his information and types it into his computer. Looking up he frowns, answering, "I'm sorry, but your prescription is expired. You'll have to contact your doctor, or if you'd like, I can contact them for you," he offers.

He shakes his head vehemently. "No, I can't wait for that. I have to get back to work. Can't you get it done now?"

"I'm sorry, Sir."

The man flinches. "I don't want to hear I'm sorry, I want to see you going to your cabinets and getting me my medicine."

"I can't do that. You'll have to come back."

The man slams his hands on the counter, knocking over a display and making me jump. My mom reaches for me and shuffles me behind her as she cautiously takes a step backwards. "Give me my medicine now!"

"Sir, I'm asking you to leave."

"No, not until...not until you help me," he stammers, his voice rising with every syllable he mutters.

"I'm calling security," he warns, his voice shaking, while my mom takes another slow step backwards.

His face turns red, and his eyes go wide as he yanks a gun from underneath his jacket, pointing it at the pharmacist. "Give me my fucking medicine!"

My mom gasps, taking several quick steps backwards. The man spins around, pointing the gun on us and screams, "Don't you fucking move!"

"Okay, okay," my mom says, her voice shaking. "Just don't hurt my little girl." Tears stream down my face as I cling to my mom's waist, peeking out from behind her at the man, afraid of what he might do.

"Stay where I can see you." He points towards the end of the counter and takes a step back, so he has all three of us in his line of sight at the same time. "Now get me my medicine, then I'll leave."

The pharmacist glances in our direction and then back at the man in front of him. "Okay, okay. Just don't hurt anyone."

He doesn't respond, but holds the gun on the pharmacist, his hand quaking and continues glancing back and forth, trying to keep his eyes on all of us.

Sirens are heard in the background, the man suddenly turning white then red in seconds. "Did you do that? Did you fucking call the police?"

"No, no," he stammers, "I didn't do anything."

The sirens continue to get louder. "You did! You fucking did!" A loud pop sounds, echoing in my ears.

I scream, squeezing my mom tighter with my tears coming faster. "Mommy," I cry, frozen, terrified.

"Shit. Why did he make me do that?" The man looks at my mom in a panic as the sirens ring louder. "I can't go to jail. This isn't my fault."

My mom shakes her head. "No. Please, no!"

Another pop sounds and my mom crumbles to the ground. Everything around me goes silent except the ear-piercing sounds of my own terror and grief. I scream at the top of my lungs, dropping down beside her. "Mommy! Mom, no! Mommy, please!" I cling to her as blood pools around us, drenching our clothes. "Mommy! Please, we have to go home. Mom!" Screaming and crying, I hug her tight as chaos ensues around us, the police arriving too many precious moments too late. "Mommy, please! We have to go get Aidan. Get up, please. Mommy, please! Mom!"

In the next second hands wrap around me, tugging me away from her. "No! Mommy! I kick and scream, reaching for her and trying to get away. "I need to help her! Please, help her. Mom! Get up. We have to go. Mommy, please! Someone help me! My mom needs help. Mom, please."

Something pokes me in the arm and my body weakens, going limp as uncontrollable sobs completely take over. "No. Please, no."

"Alex, it's okay. I'm right here. It's okay." Declan's deep voice whispers in my ear giving me unexpected tranquility as he holds me close. My legs are pinned protectively between his and my arms are crossed in front of my chest while he holds me firmly in his embrace, attempting to console and calm me. My rapid heartbeat begins to slow, my body taut with fear starts to relax. "You're okay. I've got you." He kisses me on the top of my head and begins loosening his protective embrace.

But as reality slams into me, I'd rather do anything except look him in the eyes and see his pity reflected back at me. I just endured my worst nightmare while sleeping in his bed.

Why did it have to be this way?

Chapter 25

Declan

Small tremors beside me drag me from my slumber. Groggy, I pry my eyes open, squinting around my darkened room, quickly realizing the sun is not yet up. Shaking continues beside me, and I look at the beautiful woman, restless beside me. I scoot closer, thinking she's cold, but find her skin is warm to my touch.

"Alex?" Gently, I rub her arm, but she doesn't seem to know I'm here.

She begins to stir, quietly muttering, her words all unintelligible. "Alex, it's me, Declan. Are you okay?" I think she's having a nightmare. My thoughts are confirmed as tears fall from her eyes, at the same time she's sealing them shut as if trying to build a barrier between her and her personal terrors.

Powerless, my heart hammers in my chest. Delicately, my hands and lips roam over her skin, brushing her hands, her arms, her shoulders, her neck, her face, trying to calm her, wake her, but it's not working–nothing seems to help. "Alex, it's okay. You're okay. I'm here," I continue attempting to soothe her, but it's not working. My heart hammers against my ribcage, a helpless panic growing inside me.

What should I do?

Her tears fall faster, and I try again, desperate. "Alex, baby, please open your eyes. It's okay. You're all right." But my words and actions seem to have the opposite effect of my intentions. She begins squirming, kicking and screaming, growing more violent, more distressed and shattering my fucking heart. "Alex, please. You're okay."

She nails me in my shin and in my ribs. Crossing her arms in front of her I tighten my arms, holding her firm and close to my chest, her back to my front and then I move my leg up and over, hoping she doesn't nail me in the balls before I have a chance to wrap my legs around hers. Squeezing tight, I pin her to me.

Her muttering slows but her crying intensifies causing my entire body to ache for her. Pressing my face to her cheek, I whisper in her ear, trying to remain calm and strong for her. "Alex, it's okay. I'm right here. It's okay." Pausing, I take a deep breath, getting my own emotions under control at seeing her this way. "You're okay. I've got you. You're safe." I kiss the top of her head and repeat the same words over, and over again until I feel her body calm and her sobs subside.

Cautiously, I loosen my hold, relaxing my muscles, but continue to hold her in my arms. Reaching up, she wipes away her tears and sniffles but doesn't look at me or say a word. Anxious for her to speak, to tell me she's okay, I prod, "Are you alright?" She nods, her head barely moving. "Do you want to talk about it?"

"No. There's nothing to talk about," she rasps, her voice hoarse.

"Alex–"

She snaps, "I said no, Declan."

"Okay, whatever you want." I nod, pinching my lips tightly together, clueless as to how to help and eager to do so. She scared the shit out of me. I've never seen someone have the kind of nightmare that awakens your worst memories and brings them to life so violently; the kind of trauma that you come up fighting with every part of you in hopes of coming out on the other side with a different ending. This woman is so fucking strong. I just wish she didn't have to be, but I want to do everything I can to help get her through.

Now I just need her to let me.

"Maybe you should drink some water. It will be good for your throat. I'll be right back." Swiftly climbing out of bed, I rush to get a glass of water, and return, finding her sitting up with her knees pulled up to her chest as if protecting herself from everything outside her bubble when I return. "Here," I offer.

She takes a sip of the water and licks her lips, setting the cup on the nightstand. "Thank you."

"You're welcome." I sit back down on the bed, wrapping my arm around her. My hand automatically reaches for hers and slides to her wrist, rubbing soothing circles over her tattoo. Her body slowly releases the tension as she sinks back into me, resting her head against my chest.

Heaving a sigh, without looking at me, she quietly admits, "My dream, it was about my mom."

My heart squeezes, agonizing over her pain, vibrating off her in waves. The worst part is I know there's nothing I can do except what I'm already doing. Unfortunately, it doesn't feel like it's nearly enough. "I'm so sorry."

"And before you ask, I saw a therapist for years."

"But you don't anymore."

"No, but I promised my brother I would go back if I needed to, so I'll think about it." She finally lifts her head and looks at me, her eyes red and puffy and the fire that usually shines bright in them absent. "Right now, I think I just need to get some more sleep. I'm completely exhausted. You wore me out," she claims, giving me a sad smile.

I flinch, aware she's trying to change the subject, but my guilt resurfaces despite her intentions. "I'm sorry, Alex. I overdid it with you."

She rears back as if I slapped her. "Like hell, you did. Is that why you didn't fuck me in the shower?"

"No," I claim, knowing she hit the nail on the head. "But Alex, you just said you're exhausted, and I do want to take care of you."

"I already told you, I can take care of myself, Declan. I've been doing it for years. You're doing the needless hero thing again."

Shaking my head, I deny, "No. I'm more than aware you can take care of yourself, but there's nothing wrong with me wanting to be there for you too."

She scoffs. "That's not the same thing and you know it. Don't you dare start holding back with me, Dec, or I'll find someone who won't," she threatens, feigning confidence, but this time I see right through it.

My eyes narrow and I exhale slowly, getting my emotions under control. The thought of her with another man pisses me the fuck off, but she's pushing me with a purpose and I'm not about to walk away that easily. Playing along, I give her the reprieve she desires. She's been through enough tonight. "Don't you fucking dare."

"Why not? We're not anything more than a brief past and future coparents." She flinches at her own words, swiftly trying to hide it.

I clench my jaw. What the fuck? Too far. "Look, Alex, I don't know what will happen with us, but no matter where we end up, I can tell you we are and will be a helluva lot more than coparents. I get that it's complicated, but I like you," I emphasize each word. "I really like spending time with you, and I love you in my bed. But mostly, I'm absolutely not sharing you with anyone."

"Don't I have to agree?"

"Are you telling me you don't?" I ask, arching my eyebrow in challenge. When she remains silent, I grind my teeth and push a little further. "So, you're saying I should go find another woman to fuck?"

She winces and looks away. Taking a deep breath, she squares her shoulders and meets my gaze. "No."

"You have to give me more than that. What do you mean, Alex?"

"I'm saying–" She scrunches her nose up adorably in frustration. "I'm saying that I don't share either."

My lips twitch up in amusement at the same time, internally I breathe a sigh of relief. She narrows her eyes at me, making me chuckle. "Good. Glad we got that settled." I lift her wrist to my lips and kiss her tattoo.

"And I guess I kinda like you too."

My heart skips a beat. Fuck, I'm in so much trouble. "Kinda?"

"That's all you're getting for now."

Grinning wide, I proclaim, "I'll take it." I press my lips to her temple. "Come on, you... I mean, we need some sleep."

Thankfully she listens. She scoots back down in the bed, and I happily go with her, keeping my arm cradled protectively around her as she lets her head rest on my chest. "Thank you, Dec," she murmurs, her voice barely a whisper.

My eyes remain on her as she easily falls back asleep. Unfortunately, I'm not so lucky. I can't stop thinking about her nightmare. If she hadn't had one in a while, why now? Is it me? The pregnancy? Either way, I don't want her to have to deal with anything like that again. Something so traumatic, so violent makes me wonder how her mom died. There's definitely more she's not telling me. Without the whole story, how do I protect her?

Helplessly watching her trapped in that dark place was not only terrifying, but it hurt like I was being stabbed repeatedly with the dull end of a knife, and I didn't do anything but watch it happen. If it caused me that much pain, what the fuck did it do to her?

Unfortunately, she made it obvious she didn't want to talk about it. But she can't leave me in the dark on this forever. I just want to help her.

Why is that wrong?

Chapter 26

Alex

The sound of Declan's heartbeat kept me calm, and relaxed, so I was able to get some sleep without any more bad dreams. I can't believe I had the nightmare about my mom with Dec to witness it. But he's still here. He didn't kick me out or let me push him away. I'm so used to Aidan being the only person I depend on when it comes to our past, that having someone else in my corner feels surreal. I don't know what to do with it.

Now, as I look around the bedroom, without him in it, I almost question if any of it even happened. Sighing, I stretch and walk over to his dresser, pulling out a black t-shirt and tugging it over my head. Pulling it to my nose, I close my eyes and inhale deeply, relishing the woodsy scent of him.

Making my way downstairs, I find him in the kitchen on his cell phone. "Maybe you should think about getting another job." He turns, leaning back against the counter and spotting me, giving me a crooked smile. "I know it's not easy, but just consider it, please." He pauses, his eyes roaming up and down my body as I lean against the counter. "Well, if you refuse to break up with him, at least think about another job." He closes his eyes momentarily, his body sagging as he exhales. "Thanks, Char. Love you." He sets his phone down and sighs, giving a shake of his head as if the conversation will go with it. "Hi."

"Good morning."

He smirks. "It's afternoon. You slept most of the day."

My mouth drops slightly open in surprise. "What? I should call my brother."

"I texted him to let him know."

Not sure what to think of that, I walk around the island and sit at the counter. "Th—thanks," I stammer.

Stepping towards me, he apologizes, "I'm sorry if I overstepped, but I thought you needed the sleep."

Nodding, I change the subject. "Your sister okay?"

He shrugs, frowning. "She made up with him."

"I'm sorry to hear that. It's obvious you don't like the guy, but don't you think she can handle herself?"

"If she could, she wouldn't be with him," he grumbles. "I'm sorry, that's not fair. But I just wish she wouldn't give him so many chances."

"Do you try to take on all your family problems?"

"I just want to be there for them. And I'd also like to be there for you if you'd let me," he claims stepping closer and brushes his lips across my temple. "I like you in my shirt," he murmurs, his hands skimming my sides and trailing down to my legs, finding my bare skin, eliciting goosebumps. Tilting his head, he kisses my skin, moving down my neck, finding the spot that drives me wild.

"Mmm," I moan in pleasure. My hands slide up his arms and over his shoulders, wrapping around his neck. He barely brushes his lips over mine when my stomach growls, loudly interrupting us.

Pulling back, he chuckles, looking down at me. "Are you hungry?"

Frowning, I admit, "Yeah."

He laughs louder at my reaction, the sound going right through me. "It is late, I should feed you. I just made a sandwich. I'd be happy to make you one if that's alright. I have ham, chicken..."

The sound of his voice fades in the background as the smell of turkey hits me suddenly turning my stomach. Stumbling out of the chair, I push past him and run for the bathroom. I make it to the toilet just before I heave the remnants of nothing but stomach acid into the bowl.

"Ugh," I groan, overheated. Wiping my brow, I step up to the sink, leaning on the white porcelain.

Declan appears behind me in the doorway, his eyebrows drawn down in concern. "Here," he offers, holding out a washcloth, a toothbrush and toothpaste. "I thought you might want this. I keep extra toothbrushes for my siblings. They tend to stop by unannounced and stay for as long as they like."

"Thanks," I mumble, grateful. Taking everything from him, our fingers brush and I'm suddenly completely overwhelmed. I'm feeling too much. "Um, do you mind? I need a minute," I say with my hand on the door.

"Of course. I'll be in the kitchen."

He walks away and I shut the door, swiftly cleaning up and pulling myself together. I'm grateful he's not focusing on what happened last night, but I'm also struggling to just shrug it off. How much should I share with him? Attempting to shake off my doubts, I roll my shoulders back and stride out of the bathroom in search of my clothes from yesterday, but they're nowhere to be found.

"Dec?" I call and he steps out of the kitchen.

"Everything okay?"

"Yeah, I was just looking for my clothes."

His hand falls to the back of his neck, giving me a crooked smile. "I just threw everything in the wash. I read the directions on the tags, I promise."

"Oh." My shoulders drop, feeling irrationally defeated. "Do you have some sweatpants or something I can borrow?"

"Sure," he mumbles dragging out the word. He jogs upstairs and brings down a pair of gray sweats. "I think these are Ella's. They'll probably fit you better."

"Thanks." Immediately I tug them on and slip on my shoes.

His hand reaches out, grasping mine, stopping my frantic movements. "Alex," he pauses, waiting until I meet his piercing gaze. "Is something wrong?"

I shake my head, gulping down the lump in my throat. "No, I just gotta go. I have a lot of things I have to get done today and I've already slept most of the day away." My explanation sounds fake even to my ears.

He clenches his jaw and nods, giving me a sad smile. "Okay. I'm not going to push you, but I want to know what lives in your nightmares. I can't help if you don't talk to me."

Gulping down the lump in my throat, I nod. "I'm just not ready."

"All right. Then, I'll get my keys and give you a ride."

The weight pushing down on me rises from my chest. "Thank you," I murmur, feeling like I'm able to breathe again.

A few minutes later we get in his car and make the short drive to my brothers. As he's pulling up to the house, he informs me, "I'll bring your clothes over after work tomorrow if that's all right?"

"Don't worry about it. I'll get them later."

He winces, and parks the car, turning to me and reaching for my hand. "Look, Alex, I'm not sure what's going on, but please know you can talk to me." I nod, not able to admit anything at the moment. "When's your next doctor's appointment?"

"I think in like three weeks. They only want to see me every four weeks until like 28 weeks or something."

"Okay," he mumbles dragging out the word. "You know with everything that happened the other day, I don't remember hearing anything about a due date."

"June 12th," I confirm, keeping my answers short, eager to escape and at the same time, fall right back into his arms.

A small smile tugs at his lips. "Thanks."

Lifting my hand to his lips, he kisses my tattoo sending shivers down my spine. I need to get out of his car before I ask him to take me back to his place. "Thanks for the ride, Dec. I'll text you later."

He huffs a laugh as if he doesn't believe me, but at the moment, I'm not sure if he's right or not. I scramble out of the car and practically run for the door before he decides to follow me. Pushing through the front door, I step inside, closing the door behind me and lean against it with a heavy sigh, but the anxious feeling only increases instead of disappearing like I thought it would.

Aidan stands looking at me with wide eyes and a glass in his hand. He sets it down, inquiring, "Everything okay?"

Instead of answering, I burst into tears and run to my brother, burying my face in his chest. He wraps his arms protectively around me.

"What the fuck did he do? I'll fucking kill him."

"He didn't do anything wrong, Aidan. I think he did everything right."

"What are you talking about?"

"I'm feeling way too much. I think I'm falling for him, Aid, and I'm scared."

His hold loosens and his body relaxes. "You're going to be all right, Alex. But honestly, I'm not surprised."

Pushing back, I look up at him through my blurry, tear-filled eyes. "You're not?" He shakes his head. Gulping, I confess, "I had the dream about mom."

"What? Are you okay?"

"He helped me through it. I didn't tell him what happened, but he was there for me. He keeps trying to take care of me and I have no idea what to do with that. He even did my laundry."

Aidan laughs. "And you're complaining?"

"What do I do, Aid?"

"You do what's right for you. Whatever you're feeling Alex, it's okay to feel, but it's not okay to do nothing about it."

Frowning, I challenge, "How would you know? You're always single."

He glowers at me but doesn't answer. "Don't wait too long and miss your chance at happiness, Alex. You deserve to be happy more than anyone I know."

"But what if it doesn't work out? We still have the baby. Or if something happens to one of us?"

"You can't think like that. Mom wouldn't want you to live like that and you know it." I wince, knowing he's right. "And besides, Declan is the real deal. Whether you're together or not, he will be there for you. I'm sure of it because if he's not, he knows I'd kill him." He smirks, but I can't break out a smile, not yet.

"How do I know if he likes me for me and not because I'm pregnant?"

He sighs, pulling me into another hug and kissing me on the top of the head. "Every time you like someone you're taking a chance. But saying that, the way he looked at you at Grant's yesterday? I'd say he's not just into you, but it was blatantly obvious he was interested. In fact, I was pretending I didn't have a fucking clue what he was thinking anytime his eyes were on you."

I huff a laugh. "Yeah, you probably don't want to know what I've been thinking either."

He clenches his jaw. "Do you really have to fucking go there?" I laugh harder and he sighs, shaking his head. "Anyway, from what I've learned about Declan, he's not the kind of man to say one thing and mean another. Maybe you should consider giving the guy a break."

I squeeze my brother a little tighter. "Thanks, Aidan. I don't know what I'd do without you."

"Alexa, the same goes for you."

"I'm not quite sure how to help you with that," the speaker sounds.

Shoving him away, I playfully smack him in the arm. "Hey! You said you were going to change that."

He chuckles, holding up his arms in surrender. "I did, I just changed it back the next day."

"Aidan," I say his name in warning. A smile tugs at my lips making me look anything but intimidating, only causing him to laugh harder.

Chapter 27

Declan

Today has been a Monday, from hell.

Between picking up the slack because we still don't have a replacement for the incompetent asshole I fired and Alex ignoring all my calls and texts since I dropped her off at her brother's place, I'm more than irritable. The moment I get home from the office, I change into jeans and a T-shirt, knowing there's no way I'm getting to the gym today. Grabbing Alex's clothes, I put them in a bag to bring to her. She told me not to worry about them today, but I don't want her to have to think about it. Besides, I'm afraid if I wait too long, she'll have completely closed herself off to me and I'm not about to let that happen if there's something I can do about it.

Reaching for my phone, I text her one more time, hoping she'll answer, but no such luck.

It was obvious she was freaking out yesterday. It felt like anything I said would only make it worse, so I gave her the space she asked for. Now my silence is fucking killing me thinking I may have made a mistake since she's apparently not talking to me. It's only been a little over twenty-four hours, but I'm anxious as hell.

I toss her clothes in the car and drive to Aidan's. Without alerting her that I'm coming, hopefully she won't have time to run or be too pissed at me. Guess I'll find out. I park my car in front of Aidan's house and knock on the front door.

It swings open, and Aidan stands in the doorway, grinning. "Declan. Perfect timing. I'm headed out to meet a friend. Alex is laying on the couch and I just ordered her a pizza. Make sure she eats."

My eyebrows draw down in confusion. "I could swear I didn't tell anyone I was coming."

He chuckles. "Probably not. She's being stubborn. It's good to see you here."

"Hmm. Thanks. You said make sure she eats. Has she not been?"

"She hasn't been feeling the best today but then asked for pizza. There will be more than enough for you too."

"I thought you were leaving?" Alex calls from the other room.

Turning his head, he calls, "I am. See ya later." He holds out his arm and gestures for me to walk inside. "Good luck." He chuckles.

"Thanks, I think."

He waves, striding for his motorcycle.

I close the door behind me, a little thrown off by Aidan's welcome and hoping I'm not walking into a lion's den. "Hey, Alex."

She screams, throwing a pillow at me as she spins towards me making me laugh. "What are you doing here? You can't just barge into someone's house."

"Aidan let me in."

"Ugh, traitor." She drops back onto the couch and stretches out her legs.

"I brought your clothes." I hold up the bag.

"Thanks. You can just leave them by the door."

I set them down and cautiously approach her, sitting down by her feet. "Are you feeling okay?"

"I'm fine."

"That's not what I heard."

"Fucking Aidan."

"He's out for a while, so you have plenty of time to tell me why you're ignoring me and for me to make sure you're all right while I watch you eat some pizza."

"How did you...forget it."

"Let's talk and after you eat, if you're doing okay, and you want me to leave, you can kick me out. Does that work for you?"

"Sure, but I never said I wanted to kick you out. It's just been a lot. My social battery completely ran out on top of everything else." I just needed to be alone. "I'm sorry I wasn't answering you. I know it's no excuse, but I guess I fell into old habits and just shut everyone out. It wasn't intentional. But even I see it in myself. I'm sorry, Declan."

Her words take me by surprise. "Wow. That's not what I was expecting."

"What were you expecting?"

I shrug. "A little more begging on my part." I pick up her feet and set them in my lap, rubbing them.

"If you begging means you rubbing my feet, keep doing that and don't stop."

I chuckle, doing as she requests. "You know, I've been doing some research and it's normal for you to be more emotional when you're pregnant."

"Yeah, I've heard that."

"Nightmares are common too."

She winces, but I keep rubbing her feet, hoping to ease her tension. "I'm really sorry about that."

"Please don't apologize for having bad dreams. It happens to everyone, but I want you to know I'm here for you when you're ready to talk about it."

"Thanks."

My lips twitch. "No matter what, I'd be happy to hold you anytime you want."

She arches her eyebrows in challenge. "So, you want me to call you in the middle of the night?"

"I'd be here in a heartbeat," I affirm, looking into her eyes, needing her to know the truth in my words.

"Do you ever feel like something is too good to be true?"

"Absolutely, but it's always worth taking the shot to grab hold of the good. There's too much bad shit in this world."

"I guess we can both understand that." She frowns.

The doorbell rings. "I'll get it," I offer, setting her feet on the couch and striding towards the door.

"That's probably the pizza," she murmurs.

I open the door, a large pizza box and another smaller one on top of it sits on the front porch. Grabbing it, I shut the door and carry it into the living room. "I'll get plates and napkins."

"Thank you and if you want something to drink, grab it. I have water already."

I search through the cabinets and find the plates and napkins, filling a glass of water for myself and bringing it all into the other room. "What kind of pizza did you get?"

"Sausage and peppers and some garlic knots," she reveals, taking a plate from me, a slice already in her hand. "Mmm," she moans in appreciation making my dick twitch. "This is orgasmic."

"Mmm...please don't say that when you don't feel well."

Her lips curve up in a mischievous smile. "It's the truth."

Reaching for a slice, while my eyes remain on her, I try changing the subject. "Aidan said you haven't been feeling well today."

She frowns. "Yeah, not the best. He brought me home from work within the first hour, but I'm recovering."

"Well, I'm glad you're feeling better, but remember that I want to know how you're doing, especially if you're not feeling well."

"It seems silly to bother you at work with something like this."

"Hearing from you, no matter the reason, makes my day better. And you never know, maybe there would be something I could do to help."

She huffs a laugh. "Yeah, right."

My phone beeps with a text from Finn to Ella, Char and me. "It's my brother," I mumble checking to see if it's important and grin at his message.

Finn

Ella probably already knows, but a scout from James Baxter University is coming to the game on Friday for another look at me, Jace and Kyle.

Ella

Congratulations, Finn! Grant told me you had something to tell me, but he didn't share what. I'm so happy for you! You'll be great on Friday!

Char

That's fantastic, Finn! Is that in South Carolina?

Finn

Yup, only a few hours drive.

Awesome! I'm proud of you Finn!

Finn

Thanks y'all. I'm nervous, but excited.

You've got this! We'll all be there cheering you on.

"Sorry. Finn just got some good news." I slip my phone back in my pocket, focusing on the beautiful woman in front of me.

"No worries. I'm sorry I'm not the best company tonight."

I smirk. "Your company is perfect. Thanks for having me for dinner."

"Apparently, I didn't have much choice."

"Like I said, if you want me to go, I'll leave, but I would like to stay. I promise, I'll be a perfect gentleman."

"You?" She arches her eyebrows in challenge, but her lips twitch, not able to hide her amusement. "You've been almost too much of a gentleman lately."

I huff a laugh. "Let's get you feeling better. Then I promise I'll be as un-gentlemanly as you'll let me. But you should know, when you're around, *that* Declan is always just under the surface."

She grins and finishes eating, curling into me. I exhale a content sigh. Having her here in my arms feels perfect. She has my heart racing, my stomach churning, and my body overheating for so many reasons and I want to explore every single one of them.

"I'm glad you're here and I promise I'll be better with communicating."

Chapter 28

Declan

Commercials where someone gets hurt in a ridiculous situation make me laugh hard. Like those insurance commercials.

Just commercials? What about in TV shows or movies?

Yes, those too, but at my first sleepover, we were watching a really funny movie and I laughed so hard I peed a little. Now, I'm careful when and where I watch comedies.

My head falls back in laughter. Alex has more than kept her promise with communication. Every day this week she has sent me random messages throughout the day, some serious while ones like these make me laugh. I fucking love it and attempt to give her the same back—serious and playful.

I've spent so much time watching those movies. They've been a great escape for me and my siblings throughout the years, as well as when I hang out with a friend, like Laine. But let me know if I should invest in some puppy pads just in case.

Alex

What a gentleman.

That's me. How are you feeling?

Alex

Better. Guess I just needed some sleep. I heard your brother's game went great last night.

It did, but I missed you. I'll pick you up in an hour.

Alex

I'll be ready.

A smile curves my lips, happy the week is over, and I finally get to spend some time with Alex. I don't care what we do, but I want her to have fun.

I drive over to Aidan's and park. I'm not even out of the car before Alex comes bounding down the front walkway with a broad smile on her face. She's wearing ripped jeans and a form-fitting purple, V-neck, long-sleeved shirt.

"Hi, Dec," she greets me, as she slips into the passenger seat.

Reaching for her, my hand slides under her chin, tilting her head towards mine. Leaning over the console, I press my lips to hers, kissing her soft and slow, savoring her sweet taste and tender touch. Tilting my head, I deepen the kiss, my tongue sweeping into hers for a better taste. She moans into my mouth, the vibration going right through me and heating me to my core. Slowing the kiss before I take it too far, I reluctantly pull back. "Damn, I missed you. You look absolutely gorgeous, Alex."

She huffs a laugh and arches her eyebrows in challenge. "Seriously? In this?"

"Yeah. You can make anything look sexy, beautiful, breathtaking..."

"Now you're just spouting synonyms."

I chuckle. "Sure, but it's true."

"Whatever you say."

"Well, I could prove it to you if you'd like." I smirk, a mischievous glint shining in my eyes.

She giggles. "That's okay, I'll believe you."

"Damn," I grumble making her laugh harder.

"So, what are we doing today?" she asks.

I sit back behind the wheel and start the car, grinning. "I guess you're about to find out."

"Did I ever tell you I don't like surprises?"

"You're just getting the wrong kind of surprises." Reaching over, I grasp her hand, intertwining our fingers and driving with my left hand. "It's just a short drive, so you won't have to wait long."

Pursing her lips, she sits back, relaxing as she looks out the window. A few minutes later, we pull into the marina, and I park the car and get out, pulling out a tote from the back seat. I make my way around the car as Alex shuts her door behind her, looking around. "What are we doing here?"

"Going on a boat ride. I thought we could take a ride along the coast, see some of the fall foliage. It's just starting, but it's always a great view from the water."

"That sounds perfect. But I didn't know you had a boat."

Smirking, I admit, "I don't. Laine let me borrow his. It's an old 25-foot center console with a head underneath." I point down the dock where we'll find his slip.

"Old?"

Chuckling, I attempt to ease her anxiety. "Don't worry, he takes good care of it. It's perfectly safe." I tip my head down, brushing my lips over hers. "I promise I won't let anything happen to you."

We easily find his boat and I help her climb aboard, stepping onto the forward seating. "It's nice," she says, looking around the boat in appreciation. The boat appears clean and almost new.

"I brought water and snacks," I tell her, setting the bag inside a compartment to keep it from ending up in the ocean or covering the boat before we back out.

Without me even asking, Alex easily releases the lines when I'm ready. "You seem to know what you're doing."

She nods and slides in next to me behind the console. "Yeah. My dad used to take us out on the water a lot before everything. My aunt and uncle had a boat, and let my dad use it whenever he wanted. So, in the summer, we went on a lot of family beach days, or we'd go fishing. I always enjoyed it."

"How long has it been?"

Shrugging, she admits, "I'm not sure. It's just muscle memory at this point. I don't remember a lot, but lines are easy coming off. Although, going on, I think I remember how to do it, but I might need a little more direction."

With one hand on the wheel, my free arm goes around her waist, my hand resting on her hip as I steer us down the canal lined with beautiful homes set back from the water and their own personal docks. "I can help if you need it, but something tells me you'll be fine. Sounds like those days were a lot of fun."

"Yeah." She heaves a sigh. "Until it wasn't."

"I'm sorry."

Frowning, she changes the subject, focusing on our surroundings. "You're right. Look at the coast."

Bright reds, oranges, and yellows blur among the greens on the trees behind the sandy shores as far as we can see. "Still a lot left to turn, but it is incredible."

"Yeah," she mumbles reverently. "This was a good idea, Dec."

"I'm glad you think so."

We keep the conversation light for a while, pointing out different things we see, asking simple questions and relishing our time together.

"What's your favorite color?"

"Green."

"Most men say blue. I'm impressed. Mine's purple."

Smirking, I say, "Would never have guessed." She shivers next to me. "Cold?"

"A little."

"We can turn back, it will still take us a while. I brought sweatshirts in case too. They're in the tote if you want to grab one."

"Thanks." Stepping away, she grabs my blue save the ocean sweatshirt and slips it over her head. My stomach twists into knots. Seeing her in my clothes does something to me every single time.

"Want a water or some...chips?"

"I'll take a water." She brings me a bottle, her own in hand, and leans against me once again. "Thanks."

"Did you spend a lot of time on the water when you were young?" she asks.

"Yeah, I guess as much as we could. We learned to take advantage of the time we have, so when Ella was healthy, those were the times we did things like this. But I spent a lot of time with Laine when I wasn't with my family and he's the one who taught me everything I know about boats."

My head spins, trying to decide how to ask so she'll talk to me. It's obvious why she changed the subject before, but she brought it back to the past. Does that mean she might answer my questions? I'll never know if I don't try. "Were you able to keep boating after you lost your mom?"

Flinching, she turns, glaring at me. Fuck. "Is that your plan? Take me out into the middle of the water and ask me hard questions until I answer?"

"No." I chuckle, attempting to lighten the mood.

"I'm a good swimmer, Dec. It won't work."

"I'm sure you are, but I don't need you to show me today. It's a little chilly for swimming. If there's something you don't want to answer, don't. But I like how much you've opened up recently. I'm enjoying getting to know you better, Alex. I want to know everything about you, the good, the bad and even the stuff you think is mundane. And I'll be happy to share whatever you want to know about me and probably some things you'll wish you never knew."

Pressing her lips into a thin line, she nods. Letting her head fall back, she closes her eyes, tipping her face up towards the sun. A slow smile curls her lips, the sunlight shimmering against her flushed cheeks, her hair–she's breathtaking. "Okay," she murmurs softly.

I press my lips into the crook of her neck, not able to hold back, my tongue jutting out and licking her silky skin. Goosebumps erupt on her skin, disappearing under her shirt, bringing a smile to my face. "I'm glad you're here," I tell her again, needing her to hear the truth in my words.

"You're trouble," she mumbles, her hand falling to my thigh and squeezing damn close to my twitching cock. "Your legs are solid muscle." She laughs, her hand sliding between my legs, cupping my balls and gliding up my hard length.

"Fuck, I think you have that backwards. I'm not the one trying to get us in an accident."

"You're moving slow." She looks around us before focusing back on me. "There's literally no one out here. It's not like it's summer and hot out. Let me take care of you for once."

I'm not sure if she's trying to avoid the conversation, but a single touch from her along with her request has me hard, my dick pressing against the zipper of my jeans begging to let her do her thing. I pull out of the canal just as she undoes my jeans, her hand reaching in and grasping my thick cock. "Fuck, Alex."

"You focus on the water," she insists.

Gulping, I attempt to do as I'm told when the only thing I can think about is the woman holding me tight in her hands, stroking me up and down. I steer the boat to a quieter cove as she tugs my jeans down a little lower and drops down to her knees, the sight so much better than anything I've imagined. "Holy shit, Alex."

Sticking her tongue out, she licks me from base to tip, her tongue swirling over the precum. Her hands wrap around me, stroking me up and down. She licks around my tip just before she opens her mouth and sucks me into her hot, wet mouth, hitting the back of her throat, her hand working where her mouth can't reach. Her other hand moves around me, squeezing my ass and pulling me closer while she licks me and sucks harder.

The vibration of her low moan shoots white hot fire throughout my body while I fight my impending orgasm. One hand grips the steering wheel so hard, my knuckles are turning white, while my other hand weaves into her hair as she sucks me hard, hallowing out her cheeks.

"Alex," I groan in warning. "I'm gonna come."

Instead of retracting, she swirls her tongue faster, sucks me harder and holds me firm. "Mmm," she hums over my cock, doing me in. A feeling deep in my core blazes, bursting like an erupting volcano. My head falls back as I pump into her mouth while she eagerly laps up every single drop of my release. She lets me go with a pop, looking up at me with a satisfied smile.

"Damn woman. I think you broke me for all other blowjobs."

She laughs, the sound going straight to my heart. I tug my jeans up over my ass. Reaching for her, I cup her face in my hand as she stands, looking into my eyes.

"So much for my surprise."

We laugh and she leans into me, my arm going around her once again as I put the boat back into gear, steering us back along the coast towards the marina.

Chapter 29

Alex

“Thanks for coming to hand out candy with me. You look sexy as hell in that costume.” His eyes slide up and down my body, his mouth tugging up at the corners. I’m dressed in a purple mini dress with matching heels and headband, and a lime green scarf around my neck, resembling one of my favorite cartoon characters from when I was a kid.

“Mmm,” he mumbles, brushing his lips against mine.

I grin, loving the way he’s looking at me. “Thanks. Where’s yours?”

“This is it,” he claims, holding out his hands, dressed in a football jersey with his name on the back and faded blue jeans.

“Is that your brother’s?”

He laughs. “Not exactly. It’s mine, but it’s his number. We all got them to support Finn.”

“We at least need to put some black liner under your eyes or something. This is weak, Dec. We’re going to have to up your Halloween game.”

"I promise to do better next year," he proclaims, his words throwing me off-balance. I'll likely see him next Halloween whether we're together or not. My stomach churns.

Don't do this to yourself, Alex. You'll get in your head again.

The thought of spending our baby's first Halloween with the three of us together brings about thoughts of my mom. "My mom loved Halloween." I smile.

"Tell me about her," he requests, his eyes soft, squeezing my heart.

Gulping down the sudden lump in my throat, I try to focus on the memory without getting emotional, but I want to share. "She always dressed up with Aidan and me on Halloween. But she loved to dress in these beautiful costumes, looking like a princess. Me, on the other hand, I wanted to be scary. One year Aidan dressed up as one of the killers from one of the Halloween horror movies and I dressed up as a creepy voodoo doll. She wanted to make us happy, so she tried to do something similar to me, but she ended up looking more sweet than scary." I laugh at the memory.

"She sounds wonderful."

Nodding, I agree. "She was," I affirm, my voice cracking.

The doorbell rings interrupting us and Declan rushes to pull it open. Echoes of tiny voices reciting the familiar phrase, "Trick-or-Treat," sounds around us. The onslaught of kids laughing and having a good time leaves me nearly breathless.

Taking a step back, I'm suddenly overwhelmed thinking about the past and the future. Making my way to the living room, I sit down on the couch. "Are you all right?" Declan asks, his eyebrows drawn down in concern.

Nodding, I claim, "I just need a minute."

He hesitates, but the doorbell rings again. Forcing a smile, he open the door, greeted to the same chorus of words. When the door closes again, with an apparent break in the kids, Declan returns to my side. Reaching towards me, he tenderly tucks a lock of hair behind my ear. "Talk to me, Alex." He looks deep into my eyes, his own pleading.

"I want to try," I admit, my voice cracking.

"Take your time."

Gulping down the lump in my throat, I whisper, "Okay." Remaining silent, he grabs my hand, entwining our fingers together. Lifting my hand to his mouth, he brushes his lips over my tattoo, sending a chill down my spine and calming me at the same time. His simple gesture gives me the strength to give him another piece of me. "Halloween is a day I've seen as so many different people, but it's one of the few days that has always been a good day for me."

Taking a deep breath, I continue, "Before my mom passed, it was a Halloween like everyone else's, and I enjoyed every minute of it. Things changed after she was gone. Trick-or-treating became the one day we were guaranteed to eat the treats we wanted. Plus, we would have sweets for a long time because I would stockpile most of mine and hide them. But it also became the day I could become anyone I wanted to be. For me it was better than Christmas." I force a smile, Declan's thumb rubbing soothing circles on my wrist.

"Better than Christmas?" he arches his eyebrows.

I shrug. "I want that for our baby. For them to be able to enjoy Halloween like the kids Trick-or-Treating at your door."

"They will."

"How do you know?"

"Because they have a mom and a dad who will do anything they can to make that happen."

My chest tightens, appreciating his declaration although it's not something he can guarantee. Cradling his face in my hands, I press my lips to his, pouring my emotions into this kiss. My tongue sweeps into his mouth, tangling with his.

The doorbell rings and we pull back, breathless. "Guess I have to answer that," he mumbles.

"Let's go." Grasping his hand, we walk to the door together, handing out the candy to a line of kids dressed in colorful costumes. Some I can figure out who they are, but others I have no clue. And somehow, I'm at peace with being on this side of the door standing alongside this beautiful man.

When we run out of candy, Declan turns out the light and locks the door, a mischievous glint in his eyes. "Now that you're here, you're never getting out."

I laugh. "If by never, you mean not until tomorrow morning, that works for me. We could definitely have some fun tonight."

He laughs, scooping me up into his arms, eliciting a squeal in surprise. "So, you'll stay the night?"

Looping my arms around his neck, I pull my face towards his, holding his gaze. "As long as you promise to take good care of me."

"Oh, that's a promise I'll make and one I intend to keep," he claims as he sits on the couch, holding me in his lap.

"Good, but that's the only one you'll keep?" A giggle escapes, but my laughter is quickly silenced as he seals his mouth over mine. Everything about him–his smile, his laughter, his taste, his touch–soothes my soul. I don't ever want this to end.

He pulls back, staring down at me with a look I can't quite decipher, making my stomach flip flop. "I'd like you to meet my parents if you're ready."

I gasp in surprise. That's not at all what I thought he was about to say. "Okay," I mutter, drawing out the word.

Resting his forehead against mine, his eyes search mine, attempting to read me. "You already met all my siblings, and my parents are eager to meet you. I promise you'll like them, but I don't want to push you. More than anything, I want you to be comfortable."

His concern for me warms my heart, but I think this is something I can do for him. I'm ready. "Thanks, but as long as you're with me, I'll be fine."

He gives me a slow easy smile, heating me to my core. "I'll be right by your side, but they are going to love you, probably better than they like me." He smirks.

"How many women have you brought home to your parents before?"

"If you count my homecoming date or my prom date, then that makes two." My mouth drops open, my lips forming a perfect O. How is that possible? "But that was more of my mom telling their moms to come over for pictures." I laugh.

"This will be a first for me." Placing my hands on his shoulders, I straddle him, my dress riding up.

He groans, his hands sliding up my thighs. "I always wondered if she wore panties under this dress."

"She's a cartoon."

"Sure, but you're one hundred percent real."

My laugh quickly turns into a moan as his thumbs skim my thong. "Dec," I whimper as he does it again. My body heats and my juices begin pooling, soaking the thin fabric.

Pushing the fabric aside, one finger and then two slip inside my pussy. "You're so wet for me." His fingers make quick work of me, thrusting and curling inside while his thumb circles my clit. My hips move, grinding into his hand, meeting him with every thrust. My heartbeat races and my breathing picks up its pace. I'm swiftly climbing towards a climax, much faster than expected.

Before I fall, he withdraws his fingers, eliciting a gasp of complaint. "Hey."

He chuckles, putting his fingers in his mouth and sucking them clean. "Damn, you taste good."

My eyes flare, my entire body feeling like a live wire. "Dec, please."

Holding my gaze, he declares, "I want you to ride me."

Fire shoots through me. I stand, instructing, "Then take off your pants."

He gives me his sexy crooked smile causing me to nearly trip as I slip off my panties, leaving my heels and tugging my dress up past my hips. He sits back down, and I grab his shoulders, holding tight as I straddle him once again.

Tilting my head, I kiss him hard, our tongues clashing, fighting for dominance. I pull back, his lips falling to my collarbone. Lining myself up, I slowly lower myself onto his cock. My head falls back the moment I'm fully seated, a groan falling from both our lips.

We begin to move, his hips rising to meet mine. Gliding his hands down my sides and back up my legs, he grabs my hips, holding me tight and helping me move up and down his hard shaft. "Alex, you are so fucking sexy and you feel so good. Damn, there's never been anything that feels like this."

Finding a perfect rhythm, I bounce up and down, my body electrified with every thrust of our connection. Uneven breathing, skin slapping, and our ragged grunts and moans are the only sounds besides our thundering hearts. "Yes," I groan, my body on fire.

"This view of you, fuck, Alex." The desperation and the awe in his voice urges me on.

I whimper as he hits the perfect spot inside me making my body quake. My insides ignite, my body swelling around him every time I drive my body onto his. Swiftly, he's driving me towards the edge. My fingers dig into his shoulders knowing I'm done for. "I'm gonna come," I gasp.

"Please. You feel amazing. It's too much. I need you to come." Obeying, I ride him harder, faster, chasing my orgasm. My walls clench around him, spasming and squeezing him tight as he fills me up hitting my g-spot and he falls over the edge along with me. His movements become erratic, and I hold on to him, trying to keep my eyes on him, watching as we come down from our high together. With a heavy sigh, my body slouches against his, my head resting on his shoulder and his on mine, both of us spent.

"I thought I was supposed to go easy on you."

"If your definition of easy is no sex, I'll find someone else."

"The hell you will."

My lips twitch, enjoying how much I rile him. "Okay. Maybe we should try a different room next time."

He laughs, kissing me hard. "You got it, Firecracker."

Lifting me, he stands, my legs wrapping around him. "Let's go get cleaned up and then you need to get some rest."

I hold on to him a little tighter as he climbs the stairs. For the first time in my life, this feels right, but I can't help the gnawing doubts at the back of my mind. I just refuse to let them take hold of me.

Maybe if I tell myself that enough, I'll believe it.

Chapter 30

Declan

Alex and I walk out of the doctor's office hand in hand, smiles on both our faces. We climb into my car and Alex holds up the black and white picture of a sonogram once again. "Can you believe this little thing is a baby?"

"Our baby," I emphasize, everything about the moment feeling surreal. "It's our little peanut."

"Peanut?"

I chuckle. "It fits, doesn't it? Whether it's a boy or girl?"

She laughs. "It does." Pausing, she shakes her head. "Do you have a preference? I mean if it's a boy or girl?"

"Honestly, no. I just want them to be healthy." My voice cracks, suddenly overwhelmed with emotion as thoughts of Ella fighting for her life flood my mind. As her older brother, it wasn't easy, but the possibility of going through something like that as a parent is fucking terrifying.

Refocusing, I start the car and pull out, trying to drag my head away from my fears, but they begin spinning out of control. With my left hand on the wheel, I rest my right on the console between us, my hand tight on the gear shift, reflecting the grip my head seems to have on my heart.

"Me too," Alex agrees, her voice soft. She places her hand over mine on the gear, intertwining our fingers together and giving it a gentle squeeze. Her delicate touch soothes my racing heartbeat. As I stare at the road in front of me, my breathing evens out, my thoughts drifting to the woman beside me.

November has been flying by. If time continues to speed by at this rate, our baby will be here before we have the time to get to a good place–a place she sees what I see; that the two of us are meant to be together.

Alex draws me closer every day, with an abundance of moments just like this. We connect, she's there for me and allows me to be there for her, yet she continues to hold me at arm's length. I'm not sure if it's intentional, but every time things turn more serious–unless it's about sex–she tenses. It's as if she's humoring me for a few moments before she flips the switch and becomes playful once again. That shift feels like her building her walls. Just when I think she's letting her barriers crumble, that's the same time her thick fences become higher, stronger, nearly impenetrable, but I'm determined to find a way through.

She's worth it.

We get back to my place, carrying a bag of Italian takeout. I grab the dishes and two waters, sitting down at the table, across from Alex. She scoops some chicken penne on her plate and dives in. A quiet moan escapes her lips bringing a smile to my face. I'm happy to see her eating and grateful she's not throwing up like before. It's good to see her feeling better most of the time. Her appetite has been insatiable in and out of the bedroom. My mouth waters, my thoughts turning dirty, but I can't help it when I'm around her. Then again, I can't even when I'm not. I just cannot get enough of her.

"Thanks for staying last night," I tell her, giving her a crooked smile.

"The orgasms you gave me show me how thankful you are. But you can show me your appreciation any time you want." She smirks, while my dick jumps at the thought. "Is Finn excited?"

Clearing my throat, I readjust in my seat, trying to remember what she just asked me. "Oh, yeah. Finn. He can't believe they're going to state and he's ecstatic both him and Jace signed on with James Baxter University. Their dream has always been to be able to go to the same college and play together, but it's not very common. They're damn lucky. It has been an incredible week. We're going to celebrate together on Thanksgiving since everyone has been so busy."

Alex drops her gaze, stuffing another bite of food in her mouth. "That should be fun for all of you."

My heart clenches thinking about the loss she's endured. I want her to be with me wherever I am, but will she be ready for a holiday with my family or will she think I'm pushing her? Taking a deep breath, I make the leap. "I would love to have you and Aidan join us. Do you two have any plans for Thanksgiving?"

Her gaze snaps to mine, her eyes wide. "You want Aidan and me to spend the holiday with you and your family?" she asks, her disbelief palpable.

"Well, yeah. Of course, I do."

"What about your parents? And the rest of your family?"

"They would all love to have you. Besides, my birthday is next week," I add, hoping to give her extra incentive.

She gasps in surprise. "Oh, my gosh, you're going to be thirty! That's so old." She smirks.

"This old shit again? I'm gonna make you pay for that," I say, struggling to keep a straight face.

"You better," she taunts, my dick jumping in anticipation. But I'm not going to let her redirect the conversation this time. Not yet.

"Please. I really want you there, Alex." Reaching across the table, I grasp her hand, giving it a squeeze, hoping it gives her the comfort she's looking for to decide and say yes.

Her Adam's apple bobs up and down gulping hard. "Dec..." her voice cracks and she pauses, clearing her throat, trying to conceal her emotion, but there's nowhere for her to hide. "I'll talk to Aidan, but I think we'd both like that. Thank you," she murmurs, her voice barely a whisper.

A grin covers my face. "Awesome." Lifting her hand, I pull it to me, brushing my lips over her knuckles. "Thanks."

Nodding in affirmation, she redirects the conversation, likely needing a reprieve. "Thanks for taking off work, so you could come with me to my doctor's appointment this morning."

"You don't have to thank me, Alex. I want to be there for everything for both you and the baby."

Shrugging, she adds, "Still."

"I'm glad you want me there, but you need to understand that as long as I have something to do with it, I will always do everything in my power to be there for both of you.

No matter our circumstances." It's true, I just hope one day she'll believe me. I'll have to keep repeating myself until she does.

Pinching her lips tightly together she nods and grabs her plate, striding for the sink. "Well, I appreciate it anyway."

"You know, Grant raves about what you've done to help them at G & A. Do you think him and your brother will survive without you?" I tease, trying to ease her anxiety.

Her breath whooshes out of her, and her body sags, relaxing with a soft smile tugging at her lips. "Maybe. I've finally gotten them organized, but who knows what I'll walk into tomorrow." I chuckle. "I've even had some free time while I'm working to play around with jingles again."

"Jingles?"

She shrugs, her cheeks tinging pink. "Yeah, I used to freelance with writing jingles for a couple different companies, but recently I thought I'd lost my creative gene. Apparently, it was writer's block. That, I can handle."

My eyes widen. "You never told me that. I'd love to hear something you've done or something you're creating."

Her cheeks turn a deeper shade of red. "You would?"

"Definitely. Would I know any of the ones you've done?"

"Maybe." She sucks her lower lip between her teeth and releases it slowly making me groan. "Sorry." She giggles, knowing exactly what she's doing to me. "Well, do you remember the peanut butter commercials they did with pro-football players and at the end of each one it would sing, are you ready for some peanut, peanut butter?" She sings the last few notes, the sweet sound of her voice squeezing my heart.

"Damn, I didn't know you could sing like that. Your voice is beautiful."

Her cheeks turn crimson. "Thanks."

"Yeah, I remember those ads. I'm truly impressed, Alex. Those peanut butter commercials are one of those that get stuck in your head and you can't get out, but you grow to love them."

She laughs. "Kinda like we already love this peanut."

My heart lurches. Holding her gaze across the table, I murmur, "Yeah, something like that."

Her lips twitch up. "Apparently I have a thing for peanuts."

"Hey, I was the one that came up with that," I claim, grinning.

"That's not how I remember it. I did write the song."

"And everyone knows the brand because of that song. Have you ever wanted to write anything besides jingles?" I ask, my curiosity piqued.

"I used to want to write songs when I was younger."

"Why not anymore? Do you not enjoy it?"

She shakes her head. "No, I do. It's just, I don't want to be the one to sing them. I like creating them, but finding a singer who wants to make one of your songs theirs is not that easy. Then, at one point, I guess I didn't think it would ever happen."

"Just knowing that jingle was yours and hearing you sing, I'm confident you're talented. And I believe you can do anything you want if you work hard and chase after it with everything you've got."

She huffs a laugh as if my words are ridiculous. "Thanks, Dec. I appreciate your support, but it's not a big deal," she claims, brushing off my comment. But that's something I'll definitely be coming back to. I want her to be happy. If writing songs is one of her dreams, she should be able to take the chance.

My lips tug up in a small smile.

Chapter 31

Alex

Thanksgiving

My nerves are going haywire, my insides battling an internal war and it has nothing to do with the peanut I'm carrying in my growing belly.

A knock sounds at my door, making me jump. Aidan's muffled voice sounds through the door. "Are you almost ready to go, Alex?"

"Yeah. Just give me another minute," I snap, showing my anxiety.

"Okay," he replies, his footsteps instantly retreating.

Heaving a sigh, I glance in the mirror one more time, smoothing out the sleeves of my white button down shirt hanging out, with a dark purple sleeveless sweater over the top. My black short-shorts balloon, making them appear almost like a skirt with a ruffled hem over slightly ripped fishnet stockings and my black combat boots finishing off my ensemble. Declan said it was casual, but I want to look nice and feel like myself at the same time.

Taking a deep breath, I run my hands through my long, violet hair cascading over my shoulders, noticing my roots starting to show. I frown. Maybe it's about time for another change.

Yanking the door open, I straighten my shoulders and walk towards the front door, calling over my shoulder to my brother. "Are you coming?"

Chuckling, he steps up behind me in dark jeans, a black button down shirt with the sleeves rolled up and his black boots, similar to mine bringing a smile to my face. "What are you smiling at?" he asks, feigning annoyance.

"Nothing at all. Just wanted to say thanks for coming with me," I tell him as we walk out to his jeep.

He gives me a small nod in acknowledgement. The moment he pulls away from the house, he asks, "You sure you're ready for this?"

I glare at him out of the corner of my eye. "It's not like it matters anymore."

He glances at me before returning his gaze to the road. "It always matters. If you don't want to go, we'll find somewhere to eat, just me and you."

"Thanks, Aid, but I do want to go. I'm just nervous," I admit, grimacing. "I've never done something like this before."

"It's no different than any other Thanksgiving as long as we're together," he insists making me laugh.

"Sure, it is, except there are other people there I've never met and I actually want them to like me. Plus, there's all these expectations."

"Just be yourself, Alex. That's all anyone wants or expects."

Exhaling slowly, I feel my shoulders start to relax with his encouragement. "I hate to give you a bigger head than what you already have, but I don't know what I'd do without you, Aid," I tell him sincerely.

"You don't have to ever worry about that. I'm not going anywhere. You will always have me."

"That's not something you can promise," I remind him, both of us frowning at my words causing my stomach to churn.

"Yes, I can. I'll be here for you, even when I'm not."

Knowing what he means, his words squeeze my heart, making my chest tight. Gulping down the sudden lump in my throat, I declare, "The same goes for you, Aidan."

He nods and continues driving to Declan's parents' house with both of us riding the last few minutes in silence. The moment before the door swings open, he whispers in my ear, "You've got this."

Declan stands in the doorway grinning at us; at me. My breath catches, his intense look disarming me. He's dressed in tan pants and a blue button down, making his eyes appear to be even brighter blue. The shirt is open at his neck and the sleeves rolled to just below his elbows. "You look beautiful," he tells me, and leans in, giving me a chaste kiss. My cheeks heat as he shakes hands with my brother.

"Thank you for having us," Aidan says, handing him a bottle of wine and a bottle of bourbon. "The bourbon is for you."

"For me?" Declan questions, arching his eyebrows.

"Alex said it was your birthday," Aidan explains.

"Yeah, it was yesterday. But you didn't have to do that. The two of you coming here was more than enough for me. But thanks," Declan says.

"So that's how you got her to come today," Aidan teases.

My eyes narrow on my brother. "You don't have to stay."

Aidan ignores me and steps inside, waiting for Declan to lead. Declan's hand falls to the small of my back shooting tingles up my spine.

As we greet his family, I take in our surroundings, fall decorations adorning every room. Garlands of orange, yellow and red leaves drape around the windows, gourds and pumpkins are placed strategically, adding tastefully to the décor and tiny turkeys sit at every place setting at a large dining table, the cream dishes complimenting the auburn tablecloth.

The cacophony of chatter, laughter, and dishes clanging as Ella and Charlotte help their mom with the final touches of dinner reminds me of how Thanksgiving used to be before my mom was gone and makes me question if we should really be here. Aidan says something I don't hear before he walks across the room towards Grant standing with Finn and Mr. Howard in front of the television watching football.

"Alex," Declan says as if he's been calling my name. Lifting my gaze, I stare at him. His eyes soften and he steps closer, tucking a loose strand of my hair behind my ear. "I'm really glad you're here."

A smile tugs at my lips and my heart stutters. His simple words easing the knots from my gut. "Me too." Tilting his head down, he gives me another chaste kiss.

"Declan, let the poor girl breathe," Mrs. Howard prods.

"Yeah, Dec," Finn says, chuckling. He steps past us, swiping a meatball off a platter, his mom swatting him away.

"Hey, I thought we couldn't have any of those yet," Mr. Howard complains walking towards his wife.

"That's because Finn's her favorite," Charlotte jokes.

"You know I don't have favorites," Mrs. Howard claims.

"We know, Mom," Finn states, smirking, and winks at his mother.

"My favorite tonight will be the ones who help me finish with this dinner so we can all eat," she claims, giving Finn a pointed look.

Everyone laughs and pitches in, my own shoulders relaxing further every minute. "What can I do to help?" I ask.

"If you want to grab the rolls and the butter plates and set them on the table, that would be great," Mrs. Howard replies.

Everyone scurries around the kitchen, snacking on appetizers, stopping when a cheer erupts on the football game to watch the replay of whatever we missed. It's not long before we're all helping to bring the food to the table, the savory scents assaulting my nostrils, thankfully with no sudden bursts of nausea. The golden turkey steams at the head of the table with sides of sweet potatoes, mashed potatoes, green beans, stuffing, cranberries, rolls and more. "This looks delicious."

"Thank you, Alex," Mrs. Howard replies, smiling broadly.

"My mom's cooking is always fantastic," Declan claims, earning a grin from his mom.

"Suck-up," Finn mumbles under his breath. Declan's laughter is his only response, his eyes focused on me.

Tears well in my eyes, suddenly overwhelmed with emotion. Aidan scoots his chair closer to mine, his hand running adoringly over the top of my head. Glancing at him, I give him a shaky smile. He always knows how to read me. My hormones are leaving me unsettled; at least that's what I'm blaming it on.

Declan sits down on my other side and reaches for my hand, giving it a squeeze.

Mr. Howard stands at the head of the table, carving the turkey as he speaks. "We have a lot to celebrate tonight." He pauses, lifting his gaze and looking around the table. "Our family, both old and new, our health..."

"A football championship," Finn adds.

"And Declan's birthday," Ella chimes in.

Declan glances at me. "You and our baby, an unexpected, but welcome gift."

"Yes," Mr. Howard agrees with a smile. "I'm thankful to have every single one of you, here, at this table today. Happy Thanksgiving."

A blast of warmth rushes through me, feeling as if I'm embraced by not only Declan, but everyone here.

Maybe I can fit in with Declan.

Chapter 32

Alex

Christmas

Time starts to go quickly, and we fall into an easy routine, our messages back and forth making me smile like I'm a teenager in love for the first time. I may not be a teenager, but the love thing is feeling more real every day. I thought he was sexy as hell the first day we met; his broad shoulders, ridged abs and narrow waist, the way his blue eyes pierce my soul with fire and heat, or the way he looks at me from underneath his long eyelashes as he runs his hand through his hair like I amuse him, or he's captivated with what I'm saying–like he really cares about me and my interests.

My body desires him, my heart craves his, but my head warns me to be wary. He's showing me everything I've been missing, but I'm terrified it's an illusion and will be ripped away the second I decide to let go of my hesitations.

When we first met, I never realized how much more there is to him. He's not only sexy and an absolute god in bed, but he's smart as hell, and he knows how to bring a smile to my face whether he's making me laugh or doing something to make me feel good to my body and my brain. I've never had any man besides Aidan who really listens to me, but he does, remembering the little things and encouraging or supporting me with everything big and small. Even Aidan likes him and that's saying a lot.

Surprising myself, I don't want this thing between us to end. I want him to stay in my life and not just for our little peanut but for me too. That thought feels dangerous as if I'm hanging off the edge of a cliff, just not the kind I want to be on. But what if it's a good thing? What if it's exactly what I need?

Thanksgiving with Declan's family went well, but this is Christmas. It feels like the ultimate family holiday. Would I feel like an outsider? He invited both me and Aidan, likely knowing that was the best way for me to say yes, but it still isn't easy.

Declan pulls the chicken pot pie out of the oven and sets it on the counter, the smell of the chicken, vegetables and spices draws my attention. "How does it look?" he asks.

Closing my eyes, I inhale deeply. "Mmm, it smells delicious."

His head falls to the crook of my neck, his teeth nibbling and I moan for a different reason. "That's the wrong sense. You have to keep your eyes open. Maybe I'll have to teach you a lesson later."

"Okay," I agree, making him chuckle, the vibration making my skin tingle.

Lifting his head, he gives me a chaste kiss. "Come on. Let's eat."

Opening my eyes, I meet his gaze, pressing my lips to his for one more kiss. Planting my hands on his shoulders, I jump down, his hands instantly going to my hips and steadying me. He serves us each a piece and we walk to the table with a glass in one hand and plate in the other, sitting down across from one another. "My mouth is watering, ready to dig into the crust. That's the best part."

He chuckles. "It's all good, but I've never made one before. Thank you for teaching me."

"You're welcome."

Grabbing a fork, he digs in. His mouth closes over the fork, his eyes sparking with pleasure as he swallows. "Oh, wow. This is delicious, Alex."

"It was one of my mom's recipes. I remember having it when we were kids. As soon as I had my own kitchen where I could make anything I wanted, it was one of the first things I tried. It took me a little while to get it right, but it's one of my comfort foods." I shrug like it's no big deal when we both know it is.

"Thank you for sharing this with me."

"The last time my mom made this for us was the day before Christmas Eve the year before she died. We made Christmas cookies and then had this for dinner before a family Christmas movie night," I share, my chest tight, but it feels good to share stories about my mom.

Unfortunately, those same memories bring bad ones to the forefront of my mind as well and my face quickly falls. "The next year, Aidan and I ate in his room with a box of dry cereal and tap water." I don't add that it was for three days in a row, but it was. My dad was too lost in the bottle trying to forget it was his first Christmas without his wife and forgot that he had two kids who lost their mom. "We didn't celebrate Christmas that year at all."

Declan drops his fork and rounds the table. Picking me up he sits down and sets me on his lap, gathering me in his arms. "I'm so sorry you went through that, Alex. No one should ever have to suffer like that. I'm not naïve, I'm aware people suffer like that every day, but that doesn't mean it should happen, and it shatters me that one of them was you."

A sad smile curves my lips. Cuddling closer, I rest my head on his shoulder, enjoying the feeling of being safe and loved in his arms.

Love. Is that what this is?

I don't know how long I sit in his warm embrace, but eventually, he kisses the top of my head and leans back to look at me. "I think it's time we start some of our own traditions if you're up for it?"

"Like what?"

"Well, since it's Christmas Eve-Eve, let's make it a true week celebration."

"But we only have three days."

"This year, we can add more next year."

"Okay," I say, dragging out the word, not sure where he's going with this.

"Why not open a present right now and then another on Christmas Eve and everything that's left on Christmas? And tonight, afterwards we can have some hot chocolate and find a holiday movie to watch together."

A smile lights up my face. "You have something for me?"

He chuckles, pecking my lips. "I have more than one something, but let's just go with one thing tonight."

"But I left my present for you at my brother's house."

His hand slips beneath the hem of my shirt, skating across my belly to my side and giving it a gentle squeeze. Pressing his forehead to mine, he licks his lips and rasps, "That's okay. I have exactly what I want to unwrap from you right here."

"Dec," I whimper, feeling his hard length stiffen against my ass. Closing my eyes, I press my lips to his, and wiggle just a little.

Instantly, he's standing and setting me back on the chair making me giggle. He grins and gives me a chaste kiss before taking a step back. "Wait here."

I arch my eyebrows and watch as he strides towards the stairs and jogs up them. But he's back moments later with a small gift bag and hands it to me with a hesitant smile. "Open it," he urges, bouncing on his feet.

"Okay." I pull out the tissue and find a small square box and rip the paper off. Holding my breath, I flip open the top and peek inside. Two cuff bracelets sit on black velvet bed; one silver, one gold.

"Read it," he urges, kneeling in front of me and resting his hands on my knees. Pulling them out, I glance at the gold one, a small set of wings engraved on the top. Underneath it reads, "One day, I may no longer walk beside you, but I will love you forever and watch over you with pride, smiling as I live on in you and my future grandchildren."

My hand flies to my mouth as I gasp and tears stream down my face. "Aidan has this tattooed in his angel wings he got for our mom. These are her words."

Declan nods. "Yeah. Your brother told me a while ago when I asked about the tattoo. So, I asked him if it would be okay if I had something made for you with the words. I hope it's okay." I nod, looking at him through blurry eyes, while he attempts to wipe away my tears. "I wanted you to be able to keep your mom close to you while you were going through the rest of the pregnancy and even after the baby is born. You're not alone, Alex. I hope it's okay I did that," he repeats, his nerves showing.

"Oh, Dec, thank you so much." Lifting my gaze to him, I sniffle, giving him a teary smile. "I love it. Thank you." I sniffle again and he walks across the room and returns with a box of Kleenex, making me laugh.

Stuffing his hands in his pockets, his cheeks heat as he mumbles, "You're welcome. I had a feeling I should give it to you when we were alone."

"So, that's what gave you this idea…"

He shrugs. "Maybe. Do you want to read the other one?"

Nodding, I wipe my eyes one more time and reach for the silver cuff. A tiny set of footprints is engraved on the front making my chest tight. "You're smart, strong, and brave. You listen to me, laugh with me, and love me unconditionally. I'm the luckiest soul to be able to call you, Mom."

This man.

Standing, I close the distance between us. Curling my fingers around his neck, I pull him to me and push up on my tiptoes, pressing my lips to his. My lips tingle, feeling the emotions between us as if it's a physical being. Tilting my head, I deepen the kiss, our lips moving in a slow dance. My tongue juts out, twisting with his, the savory taste of the pot pie and him consuming my senses.

Breathless, I fall back on my heels, smiling up at him. "I really do love these. They couldn't be more perfect. Thank you, Declan."

My chest tightens and I take a step back, staring at the man in front of me, almost wondering how we got here, although we already know. A dark thought crosses my mind, causing my stomach to churn. "Um, you know Dec, all this talk about my mom and my past, makes me think about our future."

"I get that."

"No, I mean, about the baby. What if something happened to one of us or even both of us? I don't ever want this baby to suffer."

He shakes his head, his palm cradling my face. "It never would, even if the worst happened. This baby has so much family, who I know would do anything for them. They have Aidan, Ella and Grant, Char, Finn and my parents just to start."

"You're right. Sloane and Kelly would be there too; I know it."

"And probably Laine."

I smile. "Most likely."

"Sounds like this baby is going to be spoiled to me."

Laughing, I wrap my arms around his middle and hug him tight. He kisses the top of my head and whispers so quietly, I almost don't hear. "I love you, Alex."

My heart skips a beat and restarts at a rapid pace. I question if what I heard was right, but I know it was. *I love you too, Declan,* but I'm not as brave as he thinks; I can't yet say it to him out loud. That would make it real. Instead, I stand unmoving in his warm embrace knowing there's nowhere else I'd rather be.

Chapter 33

Declan

It's been a busy week with the majority of my team off and an elite client that wants his campaign ready for the new year. So, with me staying late at the office, Alex has been at her brother's and I've been fucking miserable. I can't wait to have my eyes on her, to kiss her, to touch her, to hold her close and just be with her. She brings a smile to my face and has a way of making the bullshit disappear.

Tonight needs to be special. I want to show Alex how much she means to me. The way she accepted her presents last week gave me the impression she might be ready for more. But at the same time, she still has skittish moments and the last thing I'd want to do is push her too fast and run her off.

Tugging at my collar, I grimace, constricted. At the last minute, I strip off my tie. Rolling it up, I place it in the cup holder, and unbutton my top two buttons. I run my hands down my navy blue suit and white button down shirt, now open at my neck, feeling like I can breathe again. Reaching for the flowers I bought her, I climb out of my car and stride up to the front door with a confidence I don't yet feel.

"Coming," Alex calls, over the muffled tapping of her approaching footsteps against the wood floors. She pulls the door open with a hesitant smile causing my breath to catch in my throat. "Hi." She's beautiful, dressed in a shimmery golden gown, clinging to her curves. A nearly imperceptible bump at her belly, along with the deep V between her breasts and high slit showing off her thigh make my mouth water.

"Wow. You're absolutely stunning, Alex."

Her cheeks turn pink, my gaze falling to her plump lips as she smiles, the look taking my breath away. "Thank you. Happy New Year."

Not able to help myself, I step towards her and tip my head down, brushing my lips over hers. "Happy New Year." Leaning back, my knuckles caress her velvety cheek. That's when I notice something is different. My eyebrows draw down in confusion and I move a little further back to get a good look at her. "What..." I begin, trailing off when I realize I have no clue what I'm asking.

Alex arches her eyebrows in challenge, her lips twitching in amusement. "Something wrong, Dec?"

"No, not at all, you're perfect. It's just..." Taking my time, my gaze roams slowly over her from head to toe and back up again. My eyes widen and I gasp in surprise when it finally hits me. "Your hair."

"What do you think? New Year, new Alex." She shrugs. "Or maybe it's old Alex. This is pretty close to my natural color." Shuffling her feet, she appears to hold her breath, waiting for my reaction.

"Well, you were gorgeous in violet and it's no surprise you're gorgeous in red. It's a lot like your brother's."

"Gee, thanks. What every girl wants, to be compared to her brother," she grumbles sarcastically, but she's not able to hide her small smile.

"I'm serious. You're beautiful. I am curious though, what made you dye it?"

She arches her eyebrows and reaches for the flowers, making me wonder if she's going to answer me. "Thanks." Spinning on her heel, she brings them inside, her exposed bare back facing me sending chills down my spine.

"Whoa." What did I ask her?

My dick twitches, begging for attention and I have to readjust. That gown is dangerous for so many reasons. I feel like a lucky bastard that I'm the one that gets to bring her home tonight...at least I hope I do.

A moment later, she returns with the flowers immersed in a tall, crystal vase. Pausing, she grabs a small purse, assessing me as she pulls the door shut behind her and tugs, making sure it's locked. Glancing at me, she smirks, her fingers hooking underneath my chin. "Close your mouth."

Nonapologetic, I give her a rakish grin. "Then I need to find another way to show you what I think of you in that dress."

"For a minute I didn't think it would fit."

"Oh, it definitely fits, and you look absolutely breathtaking in it. But, I admit, I can't wait until you let me take it off you."

"If," she emphasizes.

"Oh, believe me, I know."

"Anyway, I asked the doctor if I could dye my hair and he said it was fine after the first trimester," she begins, reminding me what I asked in the first place. "Lately, I've either been too busy, or I don't feel well. I don't want to have to worry about getting my roots done with everything going on. This will be easier to maintain for a little while."

"I didn't realize you had to worry about that," I say, reaching out and pulling the passenger door open for her. She laughs in response as she climbs in. Carefully, I shut the door and jog around the front of the car.

The moment I slip behind the wheel, I glance at the woman beside me, holding my rolled-up tie in her palm with her eyebrows arched in question. "What kind of plans do you have for us tonight?"

I chuckle softly, my cheeks heating. It's not that I've never thought about it, but that's not the reason for the length of fabric between us. "Nothing nefarious."

She frowns. "You sure about that? You're not thinking of all the dirty things we could do with this tie?" She wraps one end around her wrist.

Tugging at my collar, a growl escapes before I can stop it. My body ignites, my eyes flare, and my dick hardens making me grateful I'm in suit pants, but still wishing it were already the end of the night and there was nothing between us. "You know I am now." She knows exactly what she's doing to me.

Her head falls back against the seat as she laughs, the sound melodic to my ears. "Where are we going for dinner?"

"My place."

Her eyebrows draw down in confusion. "But I thought we got all dressed up to go out somewhere."

"With you this frisky, I'll never make it through the night in public." She laughs, sitting a little taller in her seat, but I'm not really joking. She does something to me that I don't quite understand, and I lose all my common sense, so I give her the honest answer. "We're going to Theodore's."

Her eyes widen. "I've heard that place is fantastic. The food is supposed to be absolutely incredible."

"So that's okay with you?"

"That sounds wonderful, Dec." Smiling, she sits back as I drive us to the elegant seaside restaurant.

A few minutes later we step inside Theodore's, with a glossy mahogany bar in the center of the room, cream walls, and a darker stained, wide-plank wood floor. The candlelit round tables adorned with a black tablecloth skirts the floor to ceiling windows overlooking the ocean. It's hard to see at this time of night, but a few strategic lights on the outside of the building helps maintain a small glimpse of the view, at the same time giving you the feeling there's no one else around for miles.

Placing my hand on the small of Alex's back, we follow the host to a table along the windows. Alex pauses as we pass by a woman softly playing the strings on her violin, adding to the romantic ambiance. She glances back at me and arches her eyebrows, sitting down in the chair the waiter pulled out for her.

The moment we're alone, Alex lifts her eyes to mine. "We didn't have to do something like this. It seems so extravagant."

Reaching across the table, I grab her hand with both of mine and give it a gentle squeeze, holding her gaze. "I know we didn't, but I want you to know how special you are to me, Alex." Pausing, I lick my lips, three little words at the tip of my tongue. "You're worth it." Those weren't exactly the words I was thinking, but these were the better choice with her–for now.

"No one has ever–" her voice cracks and she pauses. She smiles, her eyes shining, welling with tears, my thumb running over the tattoo on her wrist in comfort. Gently, she tugs her hand away, dabbing at the corners of her eyes. Clearing her throat, she appears to shake away her emotions. She grabs her menu and begins perusing it. "It all looks so delicious. What are you thinking?" she asks, taking a breath.

"You're right, everything sounds so good. Maybe I'll go with the Chilean Seabass. What about you?"

"The Mahi-Mahi." The rest of dinner we fall into easy conversation, talking about music we listen to and what she likes to create. Her laughter has a way of lighting me up every single time I find a way to pull it out of her.

"Come home with me," I request.

She laughs and gives me a look that makes me want to leap over the table. "Why don't we see if we can get through dinner first, and then I'll let you know."

"Damn, woman. You are so much trouble."

"You're the one that wants to skip dinner and jump right into dessert."

I laugh, my entire body alight with a tingling sensation, an energy that's filled with anticipation and happiness of what this is between us, and I don't want to miss a single second of it.

Chapter 34

Alex

Curled up in a blanket on Aidan's couch with my acoustic guitar sitting next to me for the first time in a while, I smile to myself. A notebook, a blank stack of sheet music, two pencils and an eraser sit on the coffee table. It all makes me feel like I'm in my element once again. While playing around with writing a new song, I feel the music all the way to my soul. It's as if waking up and seeing the world anew after being under a dark spell for years. I don't remember the last time I really felt this way, or if I ever really did. Back then the music I wrote was much darker because I used it to deal with what happened with my mom. It was my solace, my peace, and this is anything but dark.

"Opposites in every way, except when it comes to our hearts. We're magnets of love. La-dee-la-love," I softly murmur a tune, working on a song for the first time in a very long time. A love song, no less, but I feel inspired. Maybe they're right and I can do this again.

It's hard to remember being this happy, but I am–happy. Why don't I deserve to have that? I do. So, apparently, I'm driven to write some songs about it. This is definitely a first. I'm excited to see what I come up with, but I need to run to the bathroom and get myself a glass of water first.

Laughing at myself, I jump up giddy.

Realizing my mistake too late, I trip over the blanket, my limbs getting tangled as they struggle to break free of the cocoon I'm encased in, desperately trying to break my fall. But it's no use. Attempting to twist my front away from the impact, my body slams against the wood floor, my right shoulder and my head getting the brunt of it as the wind gets knocked out of me.

"Ugh," I groan in pain, gasping for air. The moment I catch my breath, I feel like I'm going to throw up and attempt to get myself onto my hands and knees. Instantly I'm dizzy. That's when I feel it, blood dripping down my cheek and in between my legs. My face turns ashen, and I crawl towards the coffee table only two feet away and grab my cell phone.

Taking a deep breath, I tap Declan's number and wait. I frown when it goes to voicemail, forcing myself to leave a message. "Hey, Dec. I need your help. I fell and I think I need to go to the hospital. Please, call and come get me."

Disconnecting, I try Aidan's number and leave the same message before trying Sloane and just asking her to call me, not telling her why so she doesn't worry if she gets it when I can't respond. With great effort, I try Declan and Aidan once again. "Hi Declan. It's me again. I don't know how to get in touch with you besides your cell, but I really hope you get your messages. My head is really starting to hurt and I need your help."

My front door bursts open, and Aidan rushes into the room, looking about as pale as me, followed by Ryder. "What the fuck? We need to get you to the hospital," Aidan bellows.

"Do I look that bad?" I try to smile, but it only makes my stomach roil.

Aidan glares at me, demanding, "Why didn't you call an ambulance?"

"I didn't think it was an emergency."

"Damnit, Alex."

Aidan sweeps me up into his arms and I wince as my right shoulder bounces against his chest. "Ow! Take it easy," I mumble, my words slurring slightly, but the swift movement is too much.

Ryder steps in front of him, looking down at me. "What hurts besides your head?"

"My right side."

Aidan flinches, realizing the unnecessary pain he put me in. "Sorry–"

Ryder interrupts, taking control. "Carefully hand Alex to me. She'll be better on her left side and grab her wallet and insurance card."

My body is gently jostled, my head falling against Ryder's hard chest.

He carries me out the front door. Carefully, Ryder lays me down across the back seat and buckles me in, pressing his lips to my forehead. "You're going to be okay, Lex. We've got you."

The care and tenderness he gives me, along with the name only he called me gives me an unexpected sense of calm. He jogs around to the other side, just as I hear Aidan through the open passenger door. "Found it." Almost immediately followed by, "What the fuck are you doing here?"

Trying to push up, I drag my gaze towards him and squint, wondering if my eyes are deceiving me.

"Dad, we need to get Alex to the hospital. We don't have time to have this conversation with you."

"Dad," I mutter, in pure shock.

"Alex, my baby girl, are you alright?" he asks, trying to peek his head inside.

Blinking hard, I give a slight shake of my head, wondering if hitting my head conjured my father. "What are you doing here?"

"I'm here to see you both, to apologize."

"Dad, we need to leave now. Meet us at the hospital if you want to talk to her," Aidan interrupts.

"I want to talk to both of you."

"Whatever," Aidan grumbles and yanks the door out of our dad's hands, closing it. My eyes start to drift closed wanting to shut all of it out as I sink bank into the seat. I don't want to deal with him. I'm not sure I can.

"Stay awake, Alex!" Aidan demands, climbing over the seat to get to me as Ryder pulls away from the curb.

I wince. "You're so loud."

"Just stay awake until the doctors see you. Please," he begs, placing my head carefully in his lap. His hand tenderly runs over the back of my head, trying to stay clear of all the blood, the action soothing me.

Attempting to do what I'm told. I try Declan one more time, but leave another voicemail, my words coming out garbled. "Declan, I need you. There's so much happening. Please, I'm scared."

The moment I disconnect, my phone rings. I answer without checking the caller ID–looking at the screen hurts too much. "Declan?"

"No, it's Sloane. What happened? Are you okay?"

"Aid and Ryder got me. They're helping me," I state trying to focus on each word as it leaves my mouth.

"Ryder? I'm on my way to your house."

"It's okay, we just left. I'll call you later and tell you all about it."

"Okay. If you're sure," she says, sounding hesitant. "But I'm here if you need me, Alex."

"I know, Sloane. Bye."

"Goodbye."

Disconnecting, I drop my phone in my lap. "Aidan, I hurt so much."

"I know, baby girl. I've got you. I promise. And I'm not going anywhere," Aidan answers, his concern evident in the sound of his voice.

"Okay. Who's driving?" I ask, confused.

"Fuck," I hear someone mumble under their breath, but I'm not sure who.

"Ryder," Aidan replies.

"How?"

"He was at the shop getting his bike tuned and luckily saw your name on my phone when it was ringing," Aidan informs me.

A smile tugs at my lips. "Thank you, Ryder."

"I've still got you," Ryder reiterates, giving me a small reminder he never left of his own accord, at the same time letting me know he's here for me in this moment.

"I need you to stay awake though, Alexa. We're almost there."

Ryder parks in front of the hospital and runs around to my door, gently cradling me in his arms as Aidan scrambles out and runs ahead. We step through the sliding glass doors of the Emergency Room, Aidan's booming voice heard above all else making me wince. "We need help! Please. My sister fell. She's bleeding and she's pregnant."

Struggling to stay awake, I feel myself going in and out of consciousness, catching snippets of what people are saying and what's going on around me. But the moment I'm given consent to close my eyes and sleep, I do as I'm instructed.

I'm not sure how long it's been when I open my eyes again, but I see Aidan standing over me with tears in his eyes. "Don't ever do that to me again."

"Okay."

Forcing a hesitant smile, he proclaims, "There she is. It's good to see your eyes open. How are you feeling?"

"Like shit," I grumble, my voice raspy. "What happened?" My heartbeat begins racing and my eyes widen in fear. "The baby?"

"The baby will be okay. You both will."

"Thank God."

"But you got a few stitches on your head and you have a concussion. Besides, you're going to be a little bruised."

"A little? My entire body hurts." I groan, pouting. Slowly, my gaze searches the sterile room.

"Where's Ryder?"

Aidan frowns. "He went to grab some food, but he'll be back. He seems to know you pretty well," he states, fishing for information.

"I did live with the man," I retort, frowning. "Was dad really at the house?" I ask, my stomach churning with anxiety as a slew of questions run through my mind.

Aidan heaves a sigh and nods reluctantly. "Yeah, that was him; he was really there," he states as if he's still trying to believe it himself. "He's here too. I made him sit in the waiting room at the end of the hall. He said he didn't want to leave until he knew you were all right. But I didn't want him to be the first thing you see when you wake up."

"Thanks," I say, not sure how to process any of it.

He pinches his lips tightly together and looks out the window. "What do you want me to say to him?"

Gulping down the lump in my throat, I try not to think too hard. "I guess you can tell him I'll be okay." My brain catches up with reality and I gasp, suddenly startled as to what he might know. "Does he know I'm pregnant?"

He shrugs. "I'm not sure, but I didn't tell him. He might have an idea though, since this is a maternity floor."

"Great." I frown, overwhelmed with no way out. "Okay, just tell him I'm going to be okay. He doesn't deserve to know more than that."

Aidan gives a firm nod and turns from the window. "Okay."

"Aidan?" He halts, glancing at me. I gulp hard and force out the single word, needing to know. "Declan?"

Aidan winces and clenches his jaw, shaking his head. "I'm sorry, Alex, but I haven't heard anything from him–yet. But I did text him the room number for when he gets his messages."

Pinching my lips tightly together, I nod in acceptance. "Okay." My stomach churns and my body prickles with a heartbreaking pain. I close my eyes as a couple tears slip out of the corners without my consent. Of course, he's not here.

I knew what I had with him was too good to be true. But it's fine. I'm so much stronger than that. I'm not about to let a man change that about me.

Like everything else, I can raise this baby alone. Besides, I have Aidan when I really need someone and maybe even Ryder. I can't believe he's here. Sloane has always been more than a good friend, but I don't want to be a burden to her, especially now that she has Kelly. But they don't disappoint me.

There was a reason I was hesitant to trust Declan and let him in and he just gave it to me on a silver platter. Maybe this fall was good for something and showed me his true colors before I was in too deep. Who am I kidding? I'm barely keeping my head above water, already drowning. He broke through my barriers and with my walls a crumbled heap, my heart hurts even more than the rest of me.

Now what am I supposed to do?

"It's going to be okay, Alex," Aidan whispers the words he knows I need to hear. Gulping down the lump in my throat, I nod, too choked up to speak, but still grateful. I close my eyes as he walks out to go talk to our dad.

This is all too much.

Chapter 35

Declan

After spending all day with clients without a minute to myself, I'm completely exhausted. I just want to call Alex and see if she wants to spend the evening with a pizza and a movie on the couch. I'm grateful as fuck it's Friday. Now, where did I set my phone? It beeps with a text, and another. I follow the sound in search of it. Several messages sit waiting, one from Charlotte right at the top.

I can't, Dec. Please. I'll explain when you get here.

Instantly, I sit up straight, my body taut, rigid.

I'm on my way, but are you okay?

Charlotte

Yes, but please hurry.

Seeing Alex will have to wait a little longer. I'm already out the door and jumping in my car before her message comes through. My heart pounds against my ribcage, afraid something more is wrong. Why can't she take a rideshare? Why does she want me to come get her? Is there something she isn't telling me? I will find out what's going on.

My foot falls heavy on the gas as I drive the normal hour and a half drive to Kane's apartment in close to an hour. The moment I pull up outside, I'm out of the car, but Char is already striding quickly for me. "Are you okay? What happened?"

"Dec, can we just go?"

Taking a moment, I look her over from head to toe, finding her eyes red and puffy, but seemingly okay besides. It's hard to tell in the dark. "Fine, get in the car, but you're not getting out until you talk."

"Okay," she agrees in exasperation, but does as I request and buckles her seatbelt.

Taking my time, I start the car, giving her time to talk, but she doesn't even look at me, let alone open her mouth. "Have you been outside this whole time?"

She scoffs. "No."

"Char, what happened?"

Heaving a sigh, she shakes her head, another tear running down her face. Her shoulders sag in defeat as she finally glances at me out of the corner of her eyes. "We got in a fight."

They've fought before, so what the fuck does that mean? "Did he hurt you?"

She grimaces. "Not physically."

"What were you fighting about?"

"I'm pretty sure he's cheating on me with someone in the cast," she whispers so quietly I almost don't hear. My jaw clenches. "I confronted him about it, and he denied it, gaslighting me like I'm delusional. The more I challenged him, the more he got in my face, screaming at me." Pausing, she gulps, looking at her lap. "I've never been scared of him before, but tonight–tonight I was terrified."

My heart clenches making it difficult to breathe. I'm livid. How fucking dare he. "You need to stay away from him."

"How? Until my contract is up, I can't get out of it. If I quit, I just look like an undependable, spurned ex-girlfriend and no one will ever hire me again. I might as well give up my dreams now."

"Give me the contract. I'll have a friend of mine take a look at it and see if there's anything we can do. In the meantime, I need you to look for another job far away from that asshole. Hell, I'll find you a job."

She shakes her head. "I'm not going to work doing something I have no clue about. I want to at least try to stay in the business I want a career in somehow, but I won't just quit, Dec. I can't."

I grind my teeth, taking a deep breath to get my anger under control. Char is not the one I blame. I always knew that asshole was bad news. "Fine," I grunt.

"So, you want to tell me why I was the one who had to come get you? Why not mom and dad or a ride share?"

"Because I'm a mess and I didn't want anyone to see me." She huffs in frustration. "I'm starving, can we get something to eat?"

Grateful for the subject change, I nod. "Yeah, we can do that. I'll get off at the next exit."

A few minutes later, we stop at a diner just off the road. We walk inside, the atmosphere reminding me of a fifties soda shop with red booths, stainless tables, and a jukebox on the other side near the bathrooms. The moment we sit, we order burgers and fries, and I relax back into the booth, looking across the table at Char.

My heart stops. "What the fuck?" I mumble under my breath.

Charlotte pales instantly, shifting in her seat and looking anywhere but at me. "Wh–what?" she stammers.

"You said he didn't hurt you," I speak slowly, enunciating every word, attempting to keep my anger at bay.

"He didn't," she denies, shaking her head.

"Then what the fuck happened?" I point to her jawline, from just behind her ear to mid-jaw.

Grimacing, she claims, "That was an accident."

"The fuck it was. You need to report him, Char."

She shakes her head vehemently. "No, I can't, Dec. It was an accident. I swear. He spun around and his hands were flying like they always do when he's mad. He had no idea I was right behind him."

My heart is fucking shattering. "You can't let that asshole get away with this."

"It wasn't his fault."

I huff, feeling completely helpless. "Char, please. Move home, move in with me, or with Ella. I honestly don't care where, but you need to quit your job and come home where we can all be there for you."

"No, Dec. Ella is busy planning her wedding, you have a baby on the way and I'm not moving back in with mom and dad. It doesn't matter either way, I can't go home. You may not understand it, but there's nothing there for me except all y'all. I have no future in Genesis Beach. Don't you get that?"

I wince. She has no idea how much I understand that. "Fine but staying near him is the worst thing you can do."

"So, help me figure out a way to get out of my contract."

"You know I will. Just please stay away from Kane."

She looks down at her hands, shredding a napkin in front of her. "I promise you, Dec, it was an accident, and he's never hurt me intentionally."

I scoff, knowing I can only take her at her word, but struggling to believe there's even a sliver of the truth in her claim. Slipping my phone out of my pocket, I notice a string of missed texts and calls. Before I go through them, I send a quick text to a lawyer friend of mine.

> Hey Kenney! I need some urgent legal advice on a contract for Charlotte. Can you help us out?

His reply comes instantly.

Kenney

> Anything for you. Send the details and contract my way and I'll get back to you ASAP.

> Thank you! I owe you.

Kenney

> Yes, you do.

"Kenney will look at your contract. He said send him the contract and the details right away."

Her body sags in relief just as her food is placed in front of her. Char smiles at the waitress. "Thank you."

"Thanks." I force a smile.

Char takes a bite of the burger. "Mm, this is so good, Dec." She gestures to my phone still sitting in front of me. "Your phone is lighting up like a Christmas tree."

My eyebrows draw down and I grab my phone, glancing at the screen. Messages and missed calls from both Alex, and Aidan. My stomach drops as I scroll, one word standing out.

Hospital.

"Fuck. We gotta go."

"What's wrong?"

Jumping up, I drop one hundred dollars on the table. "Bring your plate, there's more than enough money to cover it." My heart pounds as I rush for the door, hoping Charlotte's following me, but I can't stop to look. I'm behind the wheel, holding my breath as I wait for her to shut the door so I can back out.

"What's wrong?" she repeats, her own voice frantic.

"I don't know. Alex is in the hospital."

"What?"

"I'm fucking trembling. Check my texts from her and Aidan and listen to my messages so I can focus on getting us there without crashing."

"Should you be driving?"

"It doesn't fucking matter when you can't." She flinches. "Sorry, Char. We just need to get there. I'm sorry."

She nods in acknowledgement. "What's your password?"

"927575." Charlotte remains quiet, going through my phone. It's not long before I'm frantic and about to lose my shit. "What's wrong?"

"No matter what, it's going to be okay, Dec. We're almost there," she says in response, only causing my stomach to churn like a hurricane. My heart thrashes against my ribcage, the sound of my blood flowing through my veins and my beating heart makes everything else fade in the background.

"Is she in a room?"

"Yes, she's in maternity. Room 414."

"Are you going to tell me what's wrong?" I repeat as I pull into the hospital parking lot.

"I don't know. Neither of them say but I think it's the baby."

Without another word, I park in the first vacant spot and sprint into the hospital towards the elevators.

"Sir, can I help you."

"Alex—Alexa Schoeller, room 414."

"Let me just grab you a visitor's pass. Driver's license please?"

With hands shaking, I reach for my wallet and yank it out, handing it to her and bouncing on my toes while I wait. She hands it back with a Visitor's badge and I snatch it out of her hands. "Thanks."

My body vibrates impatiently as I take the elevator to the fourth floor. Having spent so much time in the hospital with Ella, I'm extremely familiar with the layout, although she was in pediatric oncology on two, the setup is the same. But this situation is different.

Ironically, I finally understand what Grant was going through. When it comes to Ella, I would do anything for her and I love her more than anything, but she's my sister. With Alex, it's different. My fear of something happening to her and the baby consume me and has me bursting into flames like a blazing inferno with no way out. I would do anything to protect them.

My feet stutter the moment I reach her room finding Aidan sitting on the edge of her bed, watching over her, and Ryder leaning against the wall with his arms crossed over his chest. What the fuck is he doing here? I can't worry about that now. My eyes rim with tears, my focus solely on Alex.

"Alex," my voice cracks and three sets of eyes swing to me.

"You came," she whispers.

"Are you all right? What happened?"

"I...what are you doing here?"

"I'm here for you, for..." Pausing, I gulp down the lump in my throat, trying to get my emotions under control. "I'm sorry I wasn't here sooner. I haven't been able to look at my phone and then I had to pick up Char."

A man steps cautiously into the room, holding flowers.

Ignoring him, she shakes her head. "It doesn't matter just go."

I take a step closer to her, my chest tightening. "Please, tell me you're okay, that you both are."

"Go, Declan. Please, just leave. I can't do this with you right now. I'm sorry, but I just can't."

Aidan stands and walks up to me, placing his hand firmly on my shoulder. "Ryder, stay with Alex," he requests before taking a step towards me. "I think you need to go, Declan." I'm struggling to breathe, feeling like I'm being crushed by a steamroller. Stumbling backwards, Aidan urges me out the door.

"Alex, please," I beg as Ryder approaches her.

"You need to leave. You're only upsetting her and that's the last thing she needs right now," Aidan insists, blocking the doorway.

His words feel like a punch to the gut. The last thing I want is to cause her pain or stress. Reluctantly, I nod and turn to go.

Charlotte steps off the elevator and rushes to me, her eyes wide with fear. All I can do is shake my head and lean on my sister, this time allowing her to be my support.

Chapter 36

Alex

"Can you make sure he leaves?" I ask my brother.

"Of course." The minute Aidan practically pushes Declan out of the hospital room, I almost feel like I can breathe. It's too much to deal with all at once. Declan, Ryder, my dad, falling like a klutz. I'm so mad at myself, but mostly, I don't want Dec to be here for whatever is about to happen with my dad. At least Ryder knows my history–he was there for part of it.

Narrowing my eyes at my father, standing just inside the doorway shuffling his feet back and forth, I glower. I'm angry, hurt and completely lost. He's dressed in khakis neatly pressed and a red polo shirt, strangling a bouquet of sunflowers between his palms. He definitely looks more put together than the last time I saw him; the last few years I remember him. It's almost as if he's the dad I truly remember before we lost everything, except older with more wrinkles and gray hair.

"Hi, Alexa."

A frown mars my expression. "What are you doing here, Dad?" I ask, spitting out the word like it's poison.

Cautiously, he takes a step closer, looking at me with clear eyes. "I, ah, came here to see you and Aidan."

"Well, you've seen us. Now, you can go."

He takes another step. "Alexa, that's not what I mean."

"My name is Alex," I snap.

He pinches his lips tightly together and gives me a stiff nod. "Sorry. Alex."

"What do you want?" I question, my chest tight.

"Aidan said you'll be okay. And the baby?" I give him a look and he holds his hand out, looking around. "You are in the maternity ward."

I nod, and heave a sigh, defeated. "The baby is fine."

"Congratulations," he says, glancing between me and Ryder, his eyes full of curiosity, but I remain silent. He's welcome to come to his own conclusions. "How far along are you?"

"That's none of your business!"

Flinching he glances at his feet, mumbling, "I deserve that." Clearing his throat, he lifts his gaze and takes another step closer. I glare at him causing him to stop. "I'm here to apologize to both of you."

"Don't you think it's a little late for that?"

"It's never too late, until it is."

Although, I understand what he's saying, I refuse to respond. That doesn't mean it doesn't hit me square in the chest. I bite the inside of my cheek to keep the tears at bay.

"Alex, are you okay?" Ryder asks, closing the distance between us.

"I'm fine," I grit to my teeth, breathing a silent sigh of relief as Aidan strides back into the room, his gaze narrowing on our dad.

"What the fuck are you still doing here?" Aidan questions, demanding an answer.

"I needed to see for myself that she's all right."

"Great. She's fine. You can go now."

"Look, Aidan, I know I messed up."

"Yeah, you did. Over and over, and over again," he emphasizes.

"I'm trying to apologize."

"What are you apologizing for, Dad?" he asks, sarcasm thick on his tongue. "Are you saying sorry for not being there for us when we were just kids and lost our mom? Or, maybe for forgetting to feed us, buy us clothes that fit or just make sure we were clean and safe? Or, maybe not making sure we went to school? Or are you apologizing for being so drunk all the time that you forgot about us completely unless we were in trouble for something? You probably didn't even realize when the state came and took us away from you and separated Alex and me. I had no way of protecting her when we were apart. Do you know that it took me another year of fighting after I turned eighteen to even get my own sister back where she belongs?"

Dad flinches, but nods as tears stream down his face with blatant regret. "I'm ashamed of what happened and who I became without your mom, but I want to do what I can to make it right."

"That's impossible. You can't make it right," Aidan rasps, his visible pain mirroring my own.

"I have to try."

"Stop." Tears blanket my cheeks, while my breathing picks up its pace and my heartbeat hammers harder and faster against my ribcage with every word. The heartrate monitor I'm currently attached to gives away my anxiety, setting off an alarm of distress. "Please, just stop fighting," I beg, not able to take anymore.

Instantly, all three men rush to my side. "Alex, are you okay?"

"Yes, just please, no more fighting. I can't do this anymore. No more arguing."

Aidan and our dad nod in agreement, appearing justly chastised as a nurse rushes into the room going straight for me and flipping off the alarm.

"What's going on in here?" she asks, a hint of accusation in her voice.

"Nothing. I'm okay," I insist, hoping it's true.

"Y'all need to leave. Whatever is going on, this isn't good for Alex or the baby," she insists keeping her attention on me.

"No," I argue, my brother's face wracked with guilt. "Ryder didn't do anything and I want Aidan to stay with me."

Reaching for my hand, Aidan steps closer. "I'm sorry," he whispers, but I shake my head, understanding all the emotions going through him.

"I'm glad you're okay, Alexa, I mean, Alex," my dad states. "You two may not believe it, but I love you both and I only want what's best for you."

Aidan scoffs and I squeeze his hand, remaining silent.

"Y'all should know, I found help and I've been through rehab. I know I should've done it sooner, but I promise, I'm not that man anymore." His Adam's apple bobs up and down as he gulps hard. "I'm leaving, but I'll leave the flowers for you, Alex. I left my cell phone on the card hoping either of you would be willing to have a conversation, but I know better than to expect anything after what I put you both through." Turning, he trudges out of the room a tear spilling onto his cheek.

Without a word, Aidan looks into my eyes, questioning if I'm all right, his own watery with his pain. My heartrate settles and the nurse looks at me advising, "Okay, it looks like you're going back to normal. I don't want you even thinking about anything that might cause you stress."

"Got it," I affirm.

The moment the nurse exits, Aidan wraps his arms around me and holds on tight. "I'm sorry, Alex."

"Don't apologize to me, Aidan. Are you all right?"

Leaning back, he looks down at me, surprised, and huffs a laugh. "You're asking me if I'm okay?"

"Of course, I am."

Offering me a small smile, he nods. "Yeah, I will be. What about you?"

"Yeah. I've got you."

He chuckles. "You scared the shit out of me twice in one day now. Please, don't do it again."

I roll my eyes. "I'll try not to." He chuckles softly, opens his mouth and then snaps it shut. "What, Aid?"

"Why did you kick Declan out?"

"It was just too much. Him, Dad, Ryder, and this." I frown, gesturing to myself sitting in the hospital bed.

"I don't want to cause you any stress. I should go," Ryder says.

"Wait a minute, Ryder." I reach out my free hand and he steps towards me. Aidan moves back, making room for him. With tears in my eyes, I rasp, "Thank you."

He nods, giving me a sad smile. "I've still got you, Lex."

"Come here," I urge lifting my arms.

The corners of his lips tug upwards as he bends down, giving me a hug, and kissing me on the top of my head. "Aidan has my number. Call if you need me, okay?"

"Sure," I agree easily making him chuckle.

Releasing me, he stands. "Don't know why I say it when I know you won't take me up on it, but I will be checking on you."

I huff a laugh. "I've missed you."

"Me too, Lex."

We wait until Ryder exits, Aidan lowering himself onto the edge of my bed. "You know I have a couple questions about that." He points towards the door.

"Leave it alone, Aid. It's nothing."

With a slight shake of his head, he moves on. "Okay. At least tell me if you're going to call Dec and tell him you're okay?" I purse my lips. "He was really freaked out, Alex. And he did show up. I know what you're thinking, but this is not going to be your excuse to push him away."

"Aren't you a know-it-all." I glower at him.

He chuckles, shrugging as if the answer is obvious. Then his smile drops, his face turning serious. "Just do me a favor and don't do something you will regret."

"I'll try. Thanks."

He nods. "Since I know you're going to be okay and they want to keep you overnight for observation, do you want me to go and let you get some sleep?"

"I think that's a good idea."

"You'll be okay?" I nod. "All right. I'll be here early to get you out of here unless you tell me otherwise."

"Got it. Goodnight."

I wave as he walks out, swiping my phone off the side table and pulling up Declan's name. My fingers hover over the screen, but I set my phone down without sending a message. Something inside me is telling me I'm being irrational, but I can't do it.

I'm just not ready.

Instead, I reach for the card on the sunflowers, and open it. Taking a deep breath, I exhale slowly and read.

Dear Alexa,

I'm probably the last person you want to hear from, but I needed to know you're okay. I want to apologize in person, but I'm aware this isn't about what I want. I'm sorry for all that I put you and your brother through. I know it's not nearly enough, but I am sorry. The love I had for your mom was all consuming and when she died, I was devastated and couldn't even take care of myself. It's not an excuse, just the truth. I wish we could go back and I could fix what I did to you and Aidan, but I can't. All we can do is try to figure out how to move forward. If you find it in your heart to give me a chance to talk to you in person, I would be eternally grateful.

Love, Dad

P.S. My cell is below.

Chapter 37

Alex

Ryder looks at me from the other end of the couch, a small smile on his face. "I'm glad you're okay but hanging out with you while you're down is not the way I wanted to catch up with you."

I giggle, wincing instantly from the pain. "Don't make me laugh."

"Sorry, but it wasn't a joke."

Heaving a sigh, I concede. "I know."

"I can't believe you've been so close all this time and I had no fucking idea."

"And I can't believe you're friends with my brother."

Chuckling, he shrugs and we sit for a moment in comfortable silence before he inevitably brings up our past. "You know, I go over that week in my mind over and over again, wishing I could've done something or said something different, so Jeffrey would've been the one removed."

"Don't blame yourself."

Shaking his head, he asks, "How can I not? I told you I'd be there for you."

"And you were, Ryder. I don't blame you."

"It wasn't enough. Even after you were gone, I kept trying."

I shrug, knowing there was nothing else he could've done. "We were kids. They believed what they wanted to believe."

"Yeah." He runs his hand through his hair and drops it to his lap. "It crushed me that they wouldn't tell me what happened to you. I'm just glad you're okay." Me too, but I can't think about that today, there's too many other things consuming my mind. Taking a deep breath, he changes the subject, "So, about Declan..."

A quiet laugh falls from my lips, grateful to move on from the past and amused at his topic choice. It's like he's reading my mind. "Very subtle Ryder."

He smirks, unapologetic. "You like him?"

I press my lips together in thought, debating what I want to say, but this is Ryder–I know I can tell him the truth. "Yeah, but it's complicated."

"It probably doesn't help that he showed up at the hospital so late," he states, watching me close for my reaction.

"You still know me so well."

"Look, I honestly don't have a bad word to say about the guy from what I know about him. It's up to you if he's right for you."

"I know and I promise the baby isn't swaying me. It's just the catalyst that brought us back together."

"Knowing you, I have no doubt. But if he's not the one for you, I'd be here in a heartbeat for you and the baby."

Arching my eyebrow in challenge, I say, "That's a big offer, Ryder. It's been a long time since we've seen each other."

Shaking his head he refutes, "For me, it would be the easiest decision I ever made."

My heart squeezes and I look away from his intense gaze, blinking back the tears welling in my eyes. "Thank you," I barely squeak out.

"Before Aidan kicks me out, I'm gonna get out of here and let you get some rest."

"Probably a good idea."

He stands up and steps close to me. Holding my gaze, his hand covers mine. "Whatever you do, now that I know where you are, I'm here for you and I'm not going anywhere," he insists. Closing the distance between us, he hovers over my lips for a moment before tipping his head up and kissing me on my forehead. "Get some rest, Lex."

"Thank you, Ryder."

He nods, calling to Aidan, "I'm headed out. Let me know if you need anything."

"Thanks," Aidan states, walking back into the room. He shakes Ryder's hand and gives him a firm pat on the back, escorting him out the door.

Walking back to me sitting in the living room, he asks, "You okay?"

"I'm good."

"I have a few more things for you," he offers.

Aidan places a notebook, pencil and a buzzer from a board game that's annoyingly loud down on the coffee table next to the bottle of water, snacks, and remote for the TV, he left there earlier, along with my guitar leaning it against the nearby chair.

"Now that Ryder is gone, you can buzz me if you're cell isn't fast enough."

"Seriously?" I mutter, giving him a look. After being discharged, we came right here, so he could help me get comfortable, but he seems to be going over the top in my opinion. "I can handle myself, Aidan."

"Just like you handled yourself when you fell?"

"Fuck you."

He arches his eyebrows in challenge. "Anyway, I'm going to check on you every couple of hours."

"You don't need to do that anymore. It's been long enough and that makes it so hard to get any sleep."

He gives me a look making me giggle, but I flinch, the simple action painful. "Are you okay? Do you need anything else?"

Heaving a sigh, I grumble, "I'm fine, Aidan. Go get something done instead of standing here hovering over me and annoying the shit out of me."

Spinning on his heel, he stalks away, muttering under his breath.

My cell phone rings, and I glance at the screen, Declan lighting it up. That's the fifth time he called today. I know I need to talk to him, but I'm not sure what to say and I don't know if I'm ready to hear what he has to say. His explanation when he finally showed up last night felt like what it was–an excuse.

Granted, I didn't really listen to all of it, but how am I supposed to compete with his family for his attention? That's not what I want. But I'm not the kind of woman to stand in the background and wait. I don't have that kind of patience. He should want to be there for me, protect me, the same way he does for his brother and sisters. I'm no one's after thought.

Then again, am I doing exactly what Aidan claims I'm doing? Am I using this as an excuse to push him away? Admittedly, seeing my dad and then reading the card from him got to me. I don't want to end up like him, and not be able to take care of myself because I loved too much and lost. The thought of my baby suffering the way we did is heart wrenching. I'll do anything to protect this peanut.

My phone pings, alerting me to a text coming through. I already know it's from Declan before I even look.

Declan

> I'm sorry. Please tell me that the two of you will be okay.

Guilt washes over me, but my fingers are frozen, tightly gripping the phone. I should tell him we're okay.

Declan

> I know it's no excuse, but my boss kept me away from my phone all day. I'll quit before I let that happen again. In fact, my phone will be glued to my side from now on with an alarm anytime it's you.

Declan

> But that doesn't account for Char. You know my family is important to me, but that doesn't mean they're more important than you. I will do better, just give me a chance. Please.

Declan

> Wanna pick the alarm that goes off when you call? You can make it really embarrassing if you want.

A giggle slips from my lips without my consent. Damn him. How can he make me laugh when I'm pissed at him? I picture calling him as he stands in line at the grocery store, with "It's Raining Men" playing or "I Touch Myself". My imagery only causes me to laugh harder making me cringe. "Ow!"

Aidan rushes in the room. "Are you okay?"

"Yeah, laughing hurts."

He arches his eyebrows. "What's so funny?"

Shaking my head, I mumble, "Nothing."

"Okay." Sighing, he turns and walks away just as my phone beeps with another text.

Declan

> I'm kicking my own ass if it makes you feel any better.

Biting my bottom lip, I hesitate, my fingers hovering over the phone before I tap out a quick reply and press send, not giving myself time to second guess.

> *A little.*

Declan

> Seeing your message just made my day. Does that mean you're going to be okay? I sure as fuck hope so. I'll keep working on doing anything I can to make you feel even a little bit better. I'm sorry, Alex.

Declan

> What about the baby? I need you both to be okay.

His words squeeze my heart, but I'm not ready to jump right back in with him. I need time. Not being able to get in touch with him didn't only hurt, but it was terrifying. I can't have another unreliable person in my life, no matter how much I want to forgive and forget, I'm just not ready. Unfortunately, I know I need to ask myself if this is the real reason.

I set my phone down and close my eyes, instantly realizing I still haven't told him we're both okay. I'm exhausted. The nurses kept me up half the night checking my vitals. Declan isn't going anywhere right now, and hopefully he won't be pissed at me because I can't keep my eyes open. I need some sleep.

A soft hand on my arm, nudges me awake. "Alex, time to wake up," my brother's voice rings in my ears.

Groaning, I roll over and slowly blink my eyes open, squinting into the light. "But I just closed my eyes."

He chuckles softly. "Maybe it seems like it but, you've been asleep for almost four hours."

"Impossible."

"I just wanted to tell you that Declan is here."

My eyes widen, and I attempt to sit up, suddenly more than awake. Instantly, I'm dizzy and cautiously lower myself back to the couch cushions. Rubbing my eyes, I look at my brother and clarify, "He's here right now?"

"Yes, but I left him standing on the front porch. He's here to talk to you. Should I send him in?"

I start to shake my head, but it hurts too much. "No. I don't want to see him. Tell him to leave."

"You sure about that?"

"Please, Aidan. I'm not ready. I wasn't his priority before, so why am I now when I need rest?"

"Are you sure that's all it is?" he asks, arching his eyebrows in challenge. I don't respond and he pushes. "Don't you wanna know what he has to say? You've gotta know there's more to it than that, Alex."

"And you know I don't care, Aidan," I snap, heaving a sigh at my tone. "I'm sorry. I didn't mean to bite your head off." He pinches his lips tightly together and nods in understanding. "I know I'm being irrational, but he ghosted me when I needed him. It shouldn't take him nearly an entire day to check my messages."

"I'm not arguing with you there, but you and I both know that's not what's going on here."

"Whatever. Tell him to go. I'm not ready to let go of that yet."

"Okay, I'll let him know."

"Thank you, Aidan."

"You're welcome. Go back to sleep, Alexa," he whispers, likely so the speaker won't pick up his voice. I feel him hovering over me before he presses a gentle kiss to the top of my head. "I love you, sis. I'm just thankful you're okay."

A soft smile tugs at the corners of my lips. "Love you, too, Aid and me too." I sigh, closing my eyes once again.

Chapter 38

Declan

Not able to stay still, I shuffle my feet back and forth, impatiently waiting for Aidan to return after shutting the door in my face. My chest hasn't stopped aching; I feel like shit. Yes, I fucked up, but she has to give me another chance. Right? Her text–two simple words–gave me hope and I'm clinging to it like I'm hanging off the edge of a skyscraper without a safety net.

In reality, I kinda am.

The door swings open with Aidan blocking my path making my heart plummet. "She doesn't want to see you." His words rip my heart from the pit of my gut and kick it around like a soccer ball. Shit.

"Please, Aidan. Can you at least tell me if her and the baby are going to be okay?"

Something flashes in his eyes, but he doesn't give anything away before speaking. "Yeah, they're both going to be all right."

My breath rushes out of me as I exhale in relief, my entire body sagging as if just freed from chains holding me prisoner. "Thank you." He nods in affirmation, his eyes still narrowed. "But I still have to fix this. I need to talk to her, Aidan. How am I supposed to make this right if I can't even explain myself?"

He scoffs. Stepping outside, he forces me to take a step back as he softly closes the door behind him. Glaring at me, he crosses his arms over his chest, a challenge in his gaze. "And you think explaining yourself will work?"

"Yeah, I'm hoping. Why wouldn't it? I have a very good reason why I missed her call. You should understand. It was about Charlotte, my sister."

"Don't compare our situations. Of course, I understand wanting to protect my sister, but no matter what happened with your sister yesterday, the situation is not the same," he insists, emphasizing each word.

"You're right, but Alex has a good heart. I know she would've wanted me to be there for Char."

"Whatever it was, you're right, she absolutely would have."

My eyebrows draw down in confusion, every part of me desperate. "Then, why won't she talk to me?"

Arching his eyebrows, he takes a step closer, but I stand strong, unmoving. "Why couldn't you even answer a simple text?"

My stomach twists. "You're right and I'm sorry."

Exhaling harshly, he drops his hands to his sides in exasperation. "Don't you get it, Declan? Alex doesn't want you to turn your back on your family. You're right; that's the last thing she would want. But she does want to know that you will be there for her when she needs you."

"I am."

He scoffs, his disbelief apparent. "Like yesterday when she had an emergency and it took you almost the entire day to show up? No, you're not."

"I..." I open my mouth to argue and quickly snap it shut, guilt overwhelming me.

Shaking his head, he declares, "You're there for Ella. You're there for Finn. You're there for Charlotte. I'll give you that–you're a damn good brother. *If* they're good, then you're there for Alex. She's an afterthought." I shake my head, but he pushes through. "If she's not, you would've answered her messages or picked up the phone to make sure she was okay. Sometimes you can't be there for everyone, and we all get that. I wouldn't ever want anyone to go without help, but you have a big family and a great support system. All of you have each other's back. I know Grant is part of that too; he would do anything for all of you. Yeah, if any one of them need you, she'd expect you to be there. But this time Alex *really* needed you and you weren't fucking there."

Remorse overwhelms me, carving out my insides with a rusty knife and leaving it to rot. He's right. "I'm sorry."

"She has me, and I'm not going anywhere if I can help it. But what sucks? This time, I wasn't enough, and we don't have any other family we can depend on. *We* only have each other."

His words hit me like a bullet train causing me to gasp for air. We have a big family, although we almost lost Ella more than once, she's still here. That grief was hard enough. Being the oldest, I've always been the one to watch out for my siblings, but we all can depend on each other for anything, and we do. On top of that, we still have our parents. My chest tightens. "I would do anything for her."

"That's not enough. Through her eyes, I'm the only man in her life who puts her first. And maybe Ryder, I haven't figured that one out yet," he adds as if he's talking to himself, making my stomach turn. Shaking his head, he continues, "After everything we've been through, she doesn't ask for much. But she has to know she means something to you, and she isn't just a fucking convenience or an obligation."

Visibly, I flinch as if he just punched me. "She's so much more than that."

"Yeah, she is, and I probably shouldn't tell you this, but the man that was there today when you were there was our father." My mouth drops open in shock. "We haven't seen him in I don't even know how many years. He treated us like an obligation after we lost our mom and even then, he couldn't handle it, handle us. She deserves more than that."

"She deserves everything."

He nods, clenching his jaw as if debating with himself before he opens his mouth. "Her not wanting to talk to you isn't just about her or even the baby."

My eyebrows draw down, puzzled, but I quickly put the pieces together. "Do you mean when your mom died?"

He huffs a humorless laugh and shakes his head as if ridding himself of a bad memory. "Didn't she tell you?"

My stomach churns, knowing there's so much more to the story than what she was willing to share, but I was afraid to push her too far. "She told me your mom died when you were kids."

Aidan heaves a sigh, his hands falling low on his hips, and his head dropping. "Shit." Taking a deep breath, he exhales slowly. Squaring his shoulders as if preparing for battle, he lifts his gaze, meeting mine. His voice comes out much quieter than before when he finally speaks. "Did Alex tell you how she died?"

"No," I mumble, dread building in my gut.

"Our mom was murdered, and Alex was there to witness the entire thing. She's lucky nothing happened to her."

"Wh... what?" I stammer, my eyes going wide. My heart drops to the pit of my stomach like a cement block descending to the bottom of the ocean and my face goes pale. "No. Fuck. No."

"She bled out on Alex while the police took down the guy who did it. The EMTs rushed in after it was secure, but it was too late—our mom was already gone. Alex was only ten years old." He cringes his eyes welling with tears but fighting to keep them at bay.

"I'm so sorry."

Ignoring me, he continues, "Our dad, the man you saw at the hospital, he stopped being our dad after that. He became an alcoholic and not a functioning one." He huffs a humorless laugh and grimaces. "We were both better off staying out of his way. Two years later social services took us away from him. I'm not about to go into what happened in those two years for that to happen. That's on her if she wants to share that with you. But we were both in the system for two years before I turned eighteen. As soon as I did, I started doing everything I could to fight to get her back, but it took me another year before I made it happen. Alex was fifteen before they finally gave me custody and she went through hell during that time. She is the strongest and bravest woman I know."

"Shit," I mutter, overwhelmed. My entire body aches for her, for both of them, but devastatingly for her. It's as if I'm continuously being poked everywhere with a knife while my heart is squeezed in the palm of someone's hand. No one should have to go through any of that, especially a child. I wonder if the stories she told me about not celebrating Christmas or eating a box of cereal with her brother have more to do with neglect.

Fuck.

"I've been the only man who has always made her a priority. She deserves a man who will do at least the same and so does your baby. All it would have taken was for you to answer her text or answer the phone, but she wasn't important enough." I flinch, his words another punch in the face. "How can she trust that you'll be there if you're already showing her it's conditional?"

My eyes close, and my chest clenches making it difficult to breathe as overpowering regret washes over me. "Fuck. It's not. I'm an asshole."

"I know that's not true, but when it comes to Alex, you need to be a fuck-load better." Pausing, he takes a step closer to me, getting in my face, emphasizing, "This isn't even close to good enough. Not for Alex."

"Thanks, Aidan. I promise you I will be."

"Yeah, you will. And don't let her push you away. She's worth it. I know you won't regret a minute of it."

"As long as she wants me, I'm there. And even then, I can be annoyingly persuasive. At least that's what I'm told."

He chuckles. "Good because it looks like you may have some competition."

His words hit like another blow knowing exactly who he's referring to. Reluctantly, I force myself to walk away and attempt to figure out what to do next because I'm not giving up on her–on us.

Chapter 39

Alex

"Thanks y'all for letting me barge in," I say to my best friend, Sloane and her boyfriend, Kelly. I wanted to go somewhere that I could hide; somewhere it wouldn't be that easy for Declan to find me again. At least not until I'm ready.

Sloane huffs a laugh. "You're talking like you broke in. I'm happy you're here. It's about damn time! We haven't been able to spend any real time together." She frowns. "Besides, Kelly is going to visit his grandma today anyway and it will give them some time together without me intruding for once."

"She loves seeing you every single time," he proclaims, emphasizing each word, his focus on Sloane. Leaning over the back of the couch, he brushes his lips over hers and pulls back with a small smile on his face. "But Alex, Sloane has been talking about you nonstop since you came back to town, complaining about not being able to see you. I think it's fantastic that you came over and you're always welcome."

I glance up at Kelly and force a grin. He stands about six feet tall with broad shoulders, dark, wavy, brown hair, a killer smile and a constant five-o-clock shadow. Kelly works as an architect and Sloane does landscape design. Although, they didn't meet at work, they have fun doing projects together when they can. He's perfect for Sloane and spoils the hell outta her. I'm happy she has him.

She deserves it. "Thanks, Kelly."

"No problem. I'll see you two later. And congratulations again, Alex," he says before slipping out the door.

My face falls and I groan, resting my head on Sloane's shoulder. "I don't know what to do about Declan."

"What do you mean?"

"One minute he seems perfect, and I know there is no such thing as a perfect man, but I thought he was perfect for me. Then, the next minute he's not answering any of my calls or texts."

"Did you ask him why?"

I frown. "Something with his sister, but it's not that I'm mad he helped her and not me. He should absolutely be there for his family. My problem is I really needed him and he basically ghosted me."

"Why did you need him? What happened? What's wrong?" She sits up, and pushes away from me, looking me over, assessing me.

"I'm fine, but I had a scare." I bite my lip, hoping she won't be pissed I didn't tell her what was going on sooner.

"What do you mean you had a scare?" Frowning, I tilt my head towards her, so she notices my stitches and fading bruises on the right side of my face.

She gasps, her eyes widening to the size of saucers. "Holy crap! What the hell happened?"

My nose scrunches up, not wanting to talk about it, but I need to with someone besides my brother. Taking a deep breath to gather my courage, I exhale slowly, revealing, "Um, I haven't been feeling well lately like a lot of pregnant women and then yesterday, I was feeling better, so I was sitting up and writing a song–"

"You were writing music again? That's great!"

"Yeah, but I was excited too, which was part of the problem. When I jumped up off the couch a little too fast, I got tangled in the blanket I was wrapped in and fell pretty hard. Besides getting a mild concussion and bruising half my body, I was spotting."

Her lips pinch tightly together, her hand immediately covering her mouth as she processes the information. "Okay. What did the doctor say? Are you all right?"

Grabbing her hand clenched at her side, I quickly reassure her, "I'm okay and so is the baby."

"Thank God," she mumbles under her breath. She breathes a sigh of relief, her hand by her mouth dropping back into her lap.

"I knew I needed to go to the hospital to get checked out, but there was no way I could drive. I couldn't get ahold of Declan or Aidan at first. Well, apparently Ryder was at the shop and noticed me repeatedly calling Aidan and they flew to the house."

"Why didn't you call an ambulance?"

I shrug. "I don't know. When it comes to stuff like this, I have trouble trusting that help will come, so I call someone I believe would come get me in a heartbeat. They got there in time, so it's fine."

"Wait, that's why you called me, isn't it?"

Nodding, I apologize. "I'm sorry."

"You should've told me in your message, Alex. I didn't think it was an emergency when you called."

"I know. I'm sorry. But I didn't want you to worry if you got my message too late. Then, I was too tired and out of it to call you after."

"Okay, fine. I understand, but next time, call me, or even Kelly. We would both do anything for you."

"Thanks, and I promise, I do know that Sloane."

"Now, who the hell is Ryder? I've heard the name before, but I can't place him."

"He's the high school history teacher and the assistant football coach."

Her eyebrows furrow in confusion. "That's not at all what I thought you were going to say. How do you know him?"

I shrug. "We were in the same home for a while when we were kids."

Her eyes widen in surprise, knowing that time was tough for me. "You were friends?"

My cheeks heat, knowing we were a little more than friends at the time, but I nod. "Yeah, maybe more."

"Oh." She wiggles her eyebrows making me laugh and lightening the mood. "Is he hot?"

"Does it matter? My life is complicated enough."

"So," she begins dragging out the word, "speaking of complications, what kind of messages did you leave Declan?"

Flinching, I admit, "Ones that would definitely make you worry on both his voicemail and his text messages." I shake my head in frustration. "But that's my point, Sloane. The entire day was gone by the time Declan showed up at the hospital. The crisis was already over. They wanted to keep me overnight for observation, but it was no longer an emergency. Dec wanted to stay, but I said I didn't want to see him. How could I forgive him so easily and let him stay if he wasn't going to be there when I really needed him?"

Frowning, she pulls me back into her arms. "I'm sorry, Alex."

A few tears slip out of the corner of my eye and down my cheek. Sniffling, I wipe them away. "Sloane, I was so fucking scared."

"I believe it. I would've been too."

"You know, maybe I'm being irrational, but I don't know how to be any different. I get his family needs him sometimes, but so do I. I'm pregnant. What if it was more serious and something happened? Why didn't he have the courtesy to answer a fucking text from me? Even if he couldn't get there, he should've tried to get in touch with me."

"Your feelings are completely valid, especially knowing everything you went through growing up. But try to remember that those things happen to everyone. I'm sure he won't let it happen again."

I snort, blushing, both of us laughing. "You can say that again. I kinda lost it. I'm not sure if it was my pregnancy hormones, my fear, my lack of sleep or my past that drove it, but I kicked him out of my hospital room without telling him anything."

She scrunches up her nose. "What do you mean without telling him anything? It couldn't have been that bad."

I scoff. "You know me better than that. He was begging me to tell him if me, and the baby we're going to be okay, and I ignored him while screaming at him to leave. Aidan practically pushed him out the door for me when my dad came back in the room."

"Wait, what?!"

I wrinkle my nose. "Yeah, my dad showed up at the house just as Aidan was taking me to the hospital, so he followed us there and waited to see me."

"Oh, wow. How did that go? What did he even say?"

Shrugging, I confess, "Okay, but his words gave me more of a reason to hold back with Declan."

"What the hell are you talking about girl?"

"Loving and then losing my mom is why he became an alcoholic. He couldn't deal with life. He seems better, but..."

She winces. "He's not who you should be taking advice from. I didn't think I would meet Kelly and fall in love with him, but I did. Even if something happened," she flinches and continues, "I wouldn't trade our time together for anything in the world. Do you think your dad would even do things differently if he had the chance? I don't think he would."

"I don't know," I mumble under my breath.

"Well, whatever you decide, Declan will forgive you for going overboard. He's crazy about you."

"Will he?" She nods and I heave a sigh. "Okay, I hope he does, but should he? He didn't deserve that from me. No one should treat him like I did. Pregnancy hormones or not."

"Alex, he'll understand."

"But he shouldn't have to. He's been through so much. I think about his sister being sick for so long and then I get hurt and ghost him. I'm such a bitch."

"Apologize. You're allowed to make mistakes, just like he did and you're going to forgive him just like he will forgive you."

My heart clenches. "I sure hope so."

"Don't push him away because of your doubts and insecurities. That's not fair to either one of you."

Frowning, I look away. She knows me so well. "That's not what I'm doing."

She arches her eyebrow in challenge. "Have you told him about your mom? Or your dad?"

I flinch. "Yes, but not really. It's so hard to talk about. Now, with my dad showing up and my nightmares back, I'm a mess when I simply think about it," I confess, tears streaming down my face once again while I swipe them away in frustration. "I hate being this emotional."

Sloane squeezes me tight while I cry on her shoulder. "It's going to be okay. But I really think you need to talk to him about everything and give him a chance. It will help him better understand."

Heaving a sigh, I concede, "You're right."

"I usually am," she teases, attempting to lighten the mood.

The corners of my lips tug upwards as I lean back. "I don't know about that, but it was bound to happen sooner or later." She laughs. "Maybe it's all the orgasms you're getting from Kelly."

Her head falls back as she laughs harder and shrugs. "Maybe. It's a great reason to ask for more."

"Why do you need a reason?"

"True."

"All this talk about orgasms makes me want to go see Declan and figure this out." She arches her eyebrows in challenge bringing a smile to my face. "But maybe we can have some ice cream and I can hear what's going on with you first?"

"Sounds good to me."

Chapter 40

Declan

Scowling at the inside of the refrigerator, I slam the door as if it's not my fault it's nearly empty. I run my hand through my hair in frustration. My house is a mess, I'm tired, hungry, and irritable as fuck. Realistically, I know my bad attitude is because I haven't seen Alex since she kicked me out of the hospital almost a week ago, but I can't pull myself out of this hole. I'm desperate to see her at the same time wondering if she's spending the time with Ryder instead.

True, Alex and I haven't been living together but we were spending more nights together than not, so even one night where she's not speaking to me has made it hard to sleep. I'm not sure how to get her talking to me again, but I know we can figure it out when we get over that hump. My dick jumps like a teenage boy at the internal innuendo, causing me to groan in frustration. Fuck me.

Maybe I'll order a pizza. I swipe my phone off the table, my eyes sliding over Alex's name with zero updates. Attempting to ignore her silence, I begin scrolling for somewhere easy to grab food. Just as I tap order, there's a knock at my door. Not expecting anyone, I frown. Trudging towards the door, I yank it open, determined to tell whoever is standing on my doorstep to fuck off.

"Alex," I gasp. My eyes widen, swiftly scanning her from head to toe and drinking in every detail from her simple white sneakers to her olive-green pants and a striped tan and ivory cropped sweater, with a small baby bump peeking out. My entire body sags in relief at the site, pale yellow and blue bruising on the right side of her face the only remnants of her accident. "You're okay. You both are."

She flinches as if I just stole her favorite stuffed animal, tucking a fallen lock of her red hair that had fallen from the high ponytail behind her left ear. Damn, she's beautiful. "I'm sorry, Dec. I didn't mean to keep that from you," she blurts out.

"It's okay, Alex. I thought you would tell me if something had happened to either of you, and Aidan gave me something, so I didn't completely lose my mind, but I'm just happy to see for myself that you're both all right. "Does it still hurt?" I ask, my hand beginning to reach out for her, but I pull it back before I get too close, dropping it awkwardly at my side.

"Not really, but my shoulder is a little stiff sometimes," she claims.

My eyebrows draw down in concern. "I didn't realize it was your shoulder too."

"My face wasn't the only thing that hit the ground," she grumbles causing me to wince. She swiftly amends, "I'm fine though."

Knowing I can only care for her as much as she'll allow it, I nod. "I...ah...I wasn't expecting you, but I'm really glad you're here."

She nods stiffly, giving me a faux smile. "Me too, but I think we need to talk."

Although, it's exactly what I'd been hoping, the words alone cause me to flinch. Gulping down the sudden lump in my throat, I attempt to ignore my hammering heartbeat and take a step back. "Of course. Please come in." She slips past me, her sweet floral scent washing over me and giving me a sense of peace, I didn't realize I needed. "You smell so good."

Her steps falter as she looks around the room, seeing all the way into the dirty kitchen. "Whoa. What happened in here? I didn't realize you were so..."

Recognizing the mess she's seeing, I feel my cheeks heat and rush towards the couch, swiftly clearing it of the dirty clothes I abandoned, before grabbing the dirty dishes off the coffee table. "I'm so sorry, the house is normally not this bad."

She sighs, nodding. "Don't worry about it. I didn't give you any warning before showing up on your doorstep."

"You can do that anytime. Please, sit."

She does as I ask, sitting at one end of the couch, while I rush into the kitchen with the dishes and come right back. Cautiously, I sit down next to her, making sure to give her some space. Staring at her, I sit quietly, my body tingling with nerves.

"About last week," she begins.

But I interrupt, "Alex, I'm so sorry. I–"

"You've already told me, well, mostly. And I believe you meant it when you said you didn't want it to happen again."

"It scared the shit out of me."

"Me too. But I need to explain my reaction. The problem is I don't really know how to even begin."

Inching closer, I tell her, "Take your time." Clenching my jaw, I briefly hesitate, but then confess. "The day I came to see you Aidan told me to leave. He also shared a little bit about what he thought and why."

Her head snaps to mine, her eyes wide. "What did he say?"

"Well, he told me how your mom died. He said you were with her when it happened and witnessed everything."

She flinches, her gaze falling to her lap. "Yeah," she says, forcing out the word. "We went to the pharmacy to get medicine for my dad because he was sick. While we were waiting, a guy came in with a gun. He was robbing the pharmacy for oxycodone. When he heard the police sirens, he lost it and shot the pharmacist then my mom. There was so much blood. She died in my lap," she murmurs, her voice dull, lifeless. I sit frozen in utter shock, listening to her confession. "My life was never the same after that."

Taking a deep breath, she exhales slowly, pulling her knees up to her chest. "That day, Declan," her voices cracks and she tries again. "That day I lost everything. My mom, my dad, and even my brother as I knew him. He became more of a father to me after that. One by one, everything in my life kept disappearing. I lost my friends, my home and that feeling of being safe and loved." Her tears spill over onto her cheeks. "Damn it! I haven't cried this much in years and it's really starting to piss me off!"

Her declaration drags me out of my stupor. Closing the distance between us, I reach out for her, and this time I don't shy away. I fucked up, but I'm not letting her deal with this alone. When she doesn't pull away, I wrap my arms around her, tucking her small body protectively into my chest. "You're allowed to cry as much as you need to. Take your time, Alex. I'm here for you."

"That, right there. That's the reason I was so pissed at you." I want to ask what she means, but something is telling me to just let her talk and hold on tight. "You kept telling me you would be there for me if I needed anything, but when I did, you didn't answer your phone. I know you had valid reasons, but you said one thing and did another. I've had too many people who don't show up for me, and I don't need another one."

"I'm sorry." I wince and hold on tighter. "I promise I'll do better."

"My brother was there. Ryder was there, but you weren't there." I grind my jaw at the sound of his name, but now's not the time to ask. "How can I trust that your promise will be enough?"

"I'll just have to prove it to you."

She laughs. "How do you plan on doing that?

"I don't know. Time and determination," I mutter honestly. Slowly, I run my hand up and down her back, trying to answer that exact question when suddenly it hits me like a tidal wave. "I know what I want," I blurt out.

"What do you mean? For what?" Alex asks, her eyebrows drawn down in confusion.

"Our bet. I know what I want."

"Okay," she mumbles, dragging out the word. She holds her breath as she waits for me to tell her, as if she's afraid to hear what I'm going to ask for.

"Move in with me."

"What?"

"I want you to move in with me."

"Have you lost your mind? We weren't even talking five minutes ago and now you want us to move in together? That's absurd!"

"No, it's smart." I shake my head. "What happened the other day scared the hell out of me. I want to have you close to make sure you're okay."

"That sounds a little controlling."

"I promise, you still have full control."

"Are you sure you're not doing this because of Ryder?"

"Why would you say that?" I ask, already knowing the answer.

"Because he helped me that day and was at the hospital and you heard him ask me out at Grant's. You're not jealous?"

"Of course I am, but I promise this has nothing to do with that."

"Ryder and I are friends."

"I'm happy to hear that." I grin, breathing a sigh of relief, taking her at her word. "But I'm asking because I want to know your safe and happy. I'm not missing another call or text from you either. I already attached an alert on my phone for your name, even when my phone is silenced."

"You don't have to do that."

"Yes, I do because I would never forgive myself if anything happened to you or our baby."

"It still could, you know."

Wincing, I nod in agreement. "Yeah, I know, but if there's something I can do, I'm going to make sure that happens. And either way, I will be there for you. I'm sorry, Alex."

"You already said that Dec."

"I know, but I'm really fucking sorry."

"Fine. Okay." She looks away, sucking her bottom lip between her teeth and slowly releasing it before turning back and meeting my gaze, defiant. "That doesn't mean I should move in with you."

"You're right, it doesn't, but it does make sense. I'll be there for you and the baby when you need me."

"You can't promise that."

Flinching, I take a deep breath, gathering my thoughts. "True, but I want to be and if we're living together, it's likely. Plus, I have the space. Your brother's place is only two bedrooms. And what if he or she is up all night crying?"

"I didn't even think about what I would do once the baby was born," she admits, her eyebrows drawn down. She sucks her lower lip between her teeth once again, concern etched on her brow, the opposite of what I want.

"That's okay. We can figure that out together. Think about it. We can turn the spare bedroom across the hall into a nursery. Most importantly, I want to be close to you, to hear you when you laugh so hard you snort, to hold your hair back when you're not feeling well and to make you dinner, even if you don't want to eat it. I want to hold you if you're having a nightmare, lift you up when you need encouragement or support and catch you when you fall because we all do and with this little boy or girl, we're bound to end up falling into the mud and struggling to get up–at least I am–but we'll have each other to lean on."

"I don't know, Dec. Are you going to be this much of a slob if I live here with you? I'm not cleaning up after you all the time."

"No, I usually keep things neat and clean. I just had a rough week."

"Because of me? You can't stop living because things aren't going well."

"You're right, but on top of things with us, work has been a nightmare the last few weeks. Yeah, I was upset about things with us, I'm not going to lie about that, but I came home late and completely exhausted all week too."

She frowns, processing my response. I get why that would bother her after hearing about her dad, but I'm not him. Pressing my lips tightly together, I grind my jaw, hoping she'll agree to my proposal. "Keep in mind, If it doesn't work for you, your brother is right around the corner." My words are meant to comfort her, but they do the opposite for me, my concern growing that she'll bail and that's the last thing I want. It has to work. I've never wanted anything so much in my life.

"I don't know why I'm doing this, but okay, a bet is a bet."

My heart skips a beat. "Okay, you'll move in with me?"

She nods, my stomach doing somersaults. "Yes, I'll move in with you."

"Yes!" I cheer, pressing my lips to hers in a celebratory kiss, her giggle quickly turning into a sweet moan, two of my favorite sounds.

Chapter 41

Alex

Declan sets down one of my bags in the living room as I look up from the couch. "I still can't believe I'm moving in with you but at least I'm not the one doing all the hard work since you two ogres think being pregnant means I can't do anything."

"What are you talking about?" he asks, huffing a laugh, arching his eyebrows in question. "You can do anything you want to do, like you always do."

"True. But me not having to carry any boxes or move in all my stuff is not necessarily a bad thing. Apparently, it's more of a you and Aidan problem. I'm used to doing everything on my own; well, mostly, but if you two need the workout and the ego boost, go for it."

He chuckles and strides over to me, pressing his lips against mine. "You know I don't mind doing it for you. I want to make this as easy as possible, so you don't change your mind." I laugh and he continues, "But mostly, I want you to take care of yourself whether you think you need to or not." Reaching up, I pull him closer, kissing him again. Tilting his head, he deepens the kiss, a soft moan escaping my lips. Weaving my fingers into his hair, I hold him tight, tangling my tongue with his. It may have only been a week, and partially my fault, but I fucking missed this.

A loud bang reverberates off the walls, startling us apart when Aidan walks inside, his dropped box sitting at his feet. "Damn, Alex. Don't do that shit in front of me."

"You weren't here yet," I claim as Declan chuckles, straightening.

"The door was wide open for anyone to walk in."

"Sorry, but not sorry." I smirk. "Besides, I had to do a lot more than kiss the man to end up pregnant."

"Alex, what the fuck? I like to pretend it's immaculate conception, so let me live firmly in my fantasy world." He heaves a sigh and shakes his head, muttering under his breath, "You're going to be the death of me."

I giggle, enjoying pushing my brother's buttons. Looking at Declan, I ask, "Would you mind giving me a minute with Aidan?"

"Of course." He gives me a chaste kiss and grabs the box Aidan just dropped on the floor. "I'll bring this upstairs to the bedroom and make sure there's space cleared out for you wherever you might need it."

"Thank you."

"Separate rooms," Aidan jokes, calling after him. Declan laughs in response, disappearing upstairs.

Aidan strides towards me and sits on the opposite end of the couch, facing me. "What's up?"

Running my teeth over my lips in thought, I decide to start easy. "Are you okay with this?"

"Are you?" he echoes.

"Yeah, I am. I'm nervous, but I'm excited too."

"Then, yeah, I'm okay with it. But why do I think there's something more you want to say to me right now?"

Scrunching my nose up in displeasure, I concede, "Because there is."

"Don't hold back now, Alex. What is it?"

Closing my eyes, I take a deep breath and exhale slowly for courage before opening my eyes and focusing back on Aidan. "So, I opened the card from dad when I was in the hospital." He clenches his jaw, but remains silent, waiting. "He didn't put pressure on me or anything, but he apologized and said he would love to have a conversation with both of us if we were willing to do that."

He nods, his body taut, watching me, assessing me just like I'm doing to him. "What do you want to do?"

"Honestly, that's why it took me a week to say anything to you, I was thinking about it and I don't want to influence you one way or another."

"Right now, my answer will only pivot with yours."

How did I know that's what he was going to say? "Okay, so, first, I want you to know I've worked through a lot of my issues with dad with my therapist. I'm not ready to forgive him, and I don't know if I will ever be, but I do think I need to hear what he has to say. I have a lot of questions I feel like I need answered."

His body sags as if in defeat before he nods, making my heart clench. "Then, that's what we'll do."

I shake my head. "That's not what I mean. I'm grateful you're my brother and you're always there for me, but I want you to do what's best for you with dad. It's okay if you don't want to go with me to see him or talk to him, Aid. But I need to," I emphasize knowing I should tell him why. "There's something dad said in the card that keeps running through my mind and I need him to explain."

"What did he say?" he asks, his eyebrows drawing down.

"Basically, he said he loved mom so much that when she was suddenly gone, he couldn't even take care of himself."

"That's an understatement," he mutters with disgust.

"He claims it wasn't an excuse, but I'm afraid that I'm like that too."

Aidan's eyes widen in realization and he swiftly gathers me into his arms. "You are not him, Alex," he insists vehemently. "If you love someone, whether it's Declan or someone else, and something happened, you would never neglect or abandon your own child."

"I believe that, but..."

"It's the truth! Of course, it would be hard, but I would be there to yank you out of despair. You can always count on me no matter what you're going through."

"Sure, but...we weren't enough for dad, how do I know I'll be enough for whomever I'm with."

"Fuck, Alex." Releasing me, he grips my shoulders and looks into my eyes, insisting, "You are always more than enough. Whatever asshole can't see that is not the man who will be lucky enough to be by your side. Got me?"

Forcing a smile, I nod, gulping down the lump in my throat. "Got you." He pulls me back into his arms, squeezing me tight before letting go. "Thank you, Aidan, but I still think I need to see him."

"Then, I want to go with you. Just tell me when and I will be there."

"Okay."

We both get back to work, getting me settled. While I start unpacking the boxes as they come inside with Declan and Aidan doing the heavy lifting, we quickly move in the rest of my things. It's not like I have a lot of stuff and besides, I'm still wondering if this is only temporary. I don't want to get my hopes up.

"Thank you for helping with everything, Aidan."

"You're welcome, Alexa."

My breath hitches and we both freeze as if waiting for a speaker to sound, but it remains silent. "Yes!" I laugh.

Aidan chuckles. "You need a new smart speaker. I know what I'm buying Declan for his birthday."

"No, you're not." I smack him lightly in the stomach, then wrap my arms around him. "I love you, Aid."

"I love you too, Sis." He kisses me on the top of the head and releases me. "I'll see you later and you know you are always welcome to come back, for an hour, a day, a week, a year or forever. Just give me a heads up when you're on your way so you don't get an eyeful." He smirks.

Rolling my eyes dramatically, I shove him outside. "Goodbye, Aidan." I wave, shutting the door behind him, giggling.

Declan steps up behind me and wraps his arms around me. Leaning back against him, a smile lights up my face. I feel truly safe and happy, everything about today feeling surreal. I'm just trying not to second guess myself.

"It's fun to listen to you two. Y'all sound like me and my siblings. You may give each other a hard time, but you know it's out of love.

"Yeah. He's a good brother."

His lips fall to the crook of my neck, his heated breath tickling my skin causing goosebumps to erupt and eliciting a soft sigh. "I can't believe I get to come home to you every single night," he says reverently, his voice low. He kisses a trail along my collarbone, his tongue joining in, licking, followed by another kiss.

"But you had to win a bet to get me here and a bet is not permanent," I claim, my own words turning my stomach.

"I sure hope it's forever," he mumbles so quietly, I'm almost unable to decipher his words, but I swear being pregnant I can hear better than I ever could before. His claim causes my body to ignite and my brain to go haywire.

Spinning around, I loop my arms around his neck, push up on my tiptoes and kiss him hard hoping to satisfy my body and silence my brain. I'm not ready to think about forever. I need to go one step at a time and focus on today.

Right now, Declan is exactly what I want. "Time to start christening the rest of the rooms in your house."

He growls, sweeping me up in his arms as his lips crash into mine, my heart instantly racing as I melt into him.

Chapter 42

Declan

A smile tugs at my lips as I pull myself from sleep. Lying on my back, I hold her loosely in my left arm, her head resting on my chest. Inhaling deeply, I savor her sweet floral scent dipped in sex. Her warm body presses up against my side, her arm resting on my belly and her leg draped over mine. I'd love to be able to wake up like this with her every day. I'm still having trouble believing she agreed to move in with me, but I'm happy as hell I won that bet to help coax her. And after two weeks, I'm happier every day. I believe she's my forever, but now I have to convince her without scaring her away.

A soft moan escapes her lips and I feel her start to stir. Her fingers begin lightly tracing the ridges of my bare chest. I hum, relishing the feeling her touch elicits from me. "Good morning, Alex."

"Good morning," she whispers, the sweet sound of her raspy morning voice going straight to my heart. "You're still here."

Chuckling, I affirm, "I am."

"I thought you had to work this morning."

My fingers tangle into her hair, running through it. "I'm going to call in. It's Friday anyway and I don't want to be late for your appointment." I know it's an excuse, but I don't really have it in me to give a fuck anymore. It's not like they give a damn about me, or any of the team for that matter.

She smirks, arching her eyebrow. "You would've had plenty of time."

"Trying to get rid of me?"

She pushes up off my chest and looks at me, my oversized t-shirt I put on her, last night, gaping at her neck, giving me a peek of her cleavage. Damn, I love her in my clothes. "No, not at all, but you obviously hate your job. You should quit and find something you love. Why do you still work there again?"

Sighing, I confess, "You're probably right."

"You know I'm right."

I give her a half smile. "Before it was for my family, but now I think I'm still there because of insurance and I want to make sure you and our baby our taken care of."

She scowls at me, and I bite the inside of my cheek to hold back my laugh, already knowing exactly what she's going to say. "I can take care of myself."

"Yes, you absolutely can and that's one of the reasons why I–, why I like you so much," I stammer, redirecting my thoughts. "But that doesn't mean I don't want to do more than my part for both of you."

"Caveman," she grumbles, rolling her eyes dramatically.

Chuckling, I tease her, "Cowboy, ogre, caveman, you've got all the names."

"At least it's not asshole, but none of those men are allowed in my bed."

"Are you sure about that?" I smirk.

"Not today anyway," she retorts and we both start laughing.

"So, it's a big day at the doctor," I say attempting to change the subject.

She looks at me, narrowing her eyes. "This conversation isn't over. But..." She grins. "We have the twenty-week sonogram today and if the baby cooperates, we can find out the gender of the baby."

"Is that what you want?"

She tilts her head to the side and sucks her lips between her teeth in thought. "I don't know honestly. What about you?"

"I don't think I want to know, but I'll go with whatever you want."

"Might be a last-minute decision."

"It's okay either way."

She smiles in response. "So...," she murmurs, dragging out the word, "since you're not going into the office..."

Her hand trails down my chest, and over my thigh, cupping me, she awakens my morning wood turning my cock impossibly harder. Holding my breath, I wait, anticipating her next move, but this time, she moves too slow for my taste. Grabbing her wrist with my free hand, I roll out from under her, and reach for her other hand, pinning them above her head.

"That tie would do me some good right now."

Her face turns red and her lips part, her tongue jutting out as if ready for a taste. My dick twitches, and my hips roll into her heat, feeling her through my pajama pants. Her belly pushing against mine, making me all too aware of the growing baby inside her. "Too many clothes, Dec," she whimpers, pleading.

Pushing off her, I release her hands. Kicking off my pajama pants, I keep my eyes glued to her as she sits up, pulling my t-shirt over her head and tossing it to the floor, completely naked underneath. She looks down, her hands going to her belly, suddenly appearing self-conscious. This is new and it isn't her. I don't like it. "Don't cover yourself from me. You're absolutely gorgeous, Alex."

She scrunches up her nose in displeasure. "I feel fat."

"You're anything but. I love that you have this bump. You're carrying our baby and that makes you even more sexy." She hesitates, prompting me to push. "You weren't at all shy last night when you did a strip tease for me, or when you rode my cock."

She blushes again. "Dec..."

Getting back on the bed, I move over her, looking into her eyes. "Alex, you're beautiful," I pause, kissing her lips, "confident," moving down, I kiss the spot on her neck that makes her shiver, "independent," I press my lips between her breasts, "strong," sliding further down, my tongue flicks out, licking her sweet and salty skin by her belly button, followed by a kiss, "and everything about you makes me want you." I maneuver myself between her legs, my tongue licking between her folds. Planting one arm on each side of her, I push up and lift my gaze, holding hers, while hovering over her. "Your body changing to carry our child will only make me want you more, so please do not cover yourself. I want to see every inch of you and worship you like the sexy goddess you are."

Her chest starts heaving, taking big breaths, her pert nipples pointing in my direction, begging for my touch. My mouth closes around one, gently sucking, my tongue swirls around her nipple and then flicks it back and forth, her back arching, pushing her breasts towards me. Humming, I release it with a pop, eliciting a desperate whimper from her lips. Taking her other breast in my mouth, I give it the same treatment.

One hand goes to her breast, my thumb grazing her nipple, while the other slides to her belly, caressing her smooth skin. Sliding my hands down towards her sex with my lips following, I press tender kisses along the trail. Settling myself between her legs, I close my eyes, inhaling deeply. "Mm," I murmur, enthralled with her scent, drawing me in. I kiss the inside of each thigh and brush my lips against her core.

Opening my eyes, I meet her lustful gaze and give her a wicked grin a moment before diving in, covering her with my mouth. My teeth graze her clit and my tongue juts out, pushing into her pussy as I watch her head fall back, a loud moan falling from her lips. "Ah..." Laying my tongue flat against her, I press firm and lick slow to her clit. Her body reacts, arching towards me. I do it again, starting inside her, pulling out and spreading my tongue wide to push against her hard and drag it to her clit. Her hands weave into my hair, grabbing on for leverage as she tries to get closer. "Declan," she gasps. Her insides heat, swelling around my tongue as I lick her again, maintaining my torturously slow pace.

"Please," she begs as I do it again, relishing her desperate plea of my name on her lips.

Pulling back, I hum in appreciation, my mouth vibrating against her skin. "Come for me, Alex." My tongue, lips and teeth continue their measured assault on her pussy. Pressing, licking, nibbling, sucking. My own heartbeat races, my cock begging to be part of the action with every response she has to me.

Pulling my hair, her body bows off the bed as she screams my name. "Declan, yes! Yes! Dec!" She convulses against me, her insides spasming against my tongue. Moaning, I lick, lapping up her juices and suck her dry. Her body slows and I soften my touch, releasing her with a low growl as she falls limp underneath me. "What did..." she pauses, attempting to catch her breath. "What did you do to me?"

Chuckling, I claim, "I'm not done worshipping you yet." I climb up her body, propping up on my elbows, hovering over her, afraid my weight will put too much pressure on her belly. Aligning my rigid cock with her opening, I pause, pressing my lips to hers. Tilting my head, I deepen our kiss, my tongue slipping into her mouth, giving her a taste of herself. Our tongues tangle together, pushing, licking, twisting in a deliberate, playful dance. Slowing, I break our kiss, both of us gasping for breath. "Are you ready for me?"

"Yes."

Holding my breath, I ease in, not wanting this to be over before it begins. She lifts her leg, attempting to wrap it around me, but I grab her ankle and bend her knee, pinning her foot to the bed. "I need you here this time."

"Okay, just move."

Focusing on her, I do as she asked, pausing when I'm all the way inside her. Taking a deep breath, I exhale slowly, trying to get myself under control before I move again. Pulling back, I thrust inside, circling my hips before backing out and doing it again. "You feel so damn good," I tell her as I look into her eyes, forcing myself to maintain my relaxed pace while my body is revolting, begging me to speed up.

Reaching up, I push her hair out of her eyes, needing to see her, brushing my lips over hers. Wrapped in her beauty, I breathe her in, share in our heat, feel her rubbing against me and completely lose myself in her. Our bodies, our breaths and our rapid heartbeats are all soon in perfect sync.

I feel the warmth of her insides, closing in on me. Cradling her face in my hands, I hold her gaze, both of us picking up our pace with every part of the two of us following suit. Gasping for breath, I feel her body give in, squeezing me, giving me permission to let go along with her. My movements become erratic as I thrust inside her. Staring into her blazing eyes reflecting my own, skin slapping against skin, the sweet sound of her gasps mingling with my grunts, I lose control, my vision blurring as we both fall over the edge into oblivion.

"Dec," she rasps, her walls milking me for every drop.

Dropping my forehead to hers, we try to catch our breaths, our breathing ragged. Without thinking, I mumble almost imperceptibly, "I love you." Reality slams into me almost instantly and I press my lips to hers and roll away, my stomach churning. "Let me go get something to clean you up. I'll be right back."

I stride towards the bathroom, grabbing a pair of boxer briefs out of my dresser on the way and hoping like hell she either didn't hear me, or doesn't run. I'm not sure she was ready for my confession, but it's too late now.

Chapter 43

Alex

Humming a tune, I pick at my guitar, attempting to find the sound I'm imagining in my head, but my concentration is haywire. Between moving in with Declan, him telling me he loves me, me pretending it never happened, this baby on the way, my dad showing up, Ryder being here, and all the nightmares about my mom, it's hard to focus. Throw in work, and I'm screwed. Heaving a sigh, I set the guitar to the side and grab my laptop, searching for ideas for a nursery. There are so many themes, I almost don't know where to begin.

Declan strides out of the kitchen with two glasses of water and hands one to me. Sitting down next to me, he asks, "What are you looking at?"

"Different Ideas for the nursery. You said you wanted to use the room across the hall from yours, right?"

"You mean our room?" He arches his eyebrows in challenge, but I remain silent. Shrugging, he says, "I just thought that would be the easiest, but we can use one of the other two bedrooms at the end of the hallway if you would prefer."

"Maybe we should soundproof our room. We'll have a baby monitor to hear the baby, but I don't want them to hear us."

He chuckles. "I can look into getting it done, but there is somewhat of a barrier between the rooms. Better across the hall than on the other side of the wall. Do you see anything you like?"

"I don't know. There are a lot of black and white themes, fairy tales, sports, princess, animals, nursery rhymes, colors, the ocean. Ugh. Do you think we should've found out what we we're having so we could plan this better?"

"No, that doesn't matter. Let's just find something you like."

"Maybe zoo animals."

"Do you want to go to a store tomorrow and look at some setups or do you want to do it all online?"

"Um, I ah, I can't tomorrow," I stammer, closing my laptop and setting it on the coffee table.

"No big deal. We can go look on Sunday if you want. Do you have plans tomorrow?" he asks, brushing my hair behind my ear.

"Sort of. I, um, I have plans with Aidan," I say, wanting to tell him more, but my stomach twists into knots with anxiety. It's not that I'm nervous to tell him about my plans, but the idea of confessing everything about my past makes my heartrate skyrocket. But, at this point in our relationship, I feel like he has a right to know. I can do this.

"What do you and your brother have planned?"

Clasping my fingers tightly together, I begin twiddling my thumbs. Declan reaches for my hand and gives it a squeeze, grabbing my attention. I lift my gaze, and he insists, "I'm here for you, whatever it is."

Nodding, I take a deep breath and flip my palm up, grasping him for support. "We're going to take a ride to my mom's grave." The words hurt, turning my stomach, but at least I'm able to get them out without losing it. "We try to go together sometimes, and I like to stop and talk to her when something big is going on; good or bad."

"I think that's great you two go together."

"We don't go together every time, but this time we want to. Then, we're going to meet our dad for lunch," I blurt out, his eyes widening in surprise. "I didn't tell you this, but my dad brought me flowers when I was in the hospital."

"I saw him, but I don't remember much, I was very focused on you."

Nodding, I huff a laugh. "Yeah, that was him. Well, he left me a card with the flowers. He said he's been getting help and he's doing better. He asked if we would talk to him. I wasn't sure, but I think I need to hear what he has to say."

"That's okay, you know."

"I do, but I'm not ready to forgive him. Unfortunately, I think I need to talk to him for some answers whether I like them or not."

"Do you want me to go with you?"

A small, appreciative smile curls my lips. "Thank you, but no. I think this is something I need to do alone or just with Aidan."

"Okay. I'll be there if you change your mind though. My phone will be glued to my hand until you're home."

"Don't do that, I like what your hands do to me," I say, attempting to lighten the mood. He chuckles at my lame joke.

Taking a deep breath, he hesitates before asking, "No pressure, and you don't have to answer me, but I'm going to ask anyway...What happened to you and your brother after she died?"

Briefly, I pinch my lips tightly together and take a calming breath. "Okay, Dec, I'm going to talk and tell you what happened, but this isn't easy for me. I need you to not say a single word until I'm done. Can you do that?"

"I'll do anything you need me to do."

Nodding, I gulp down the lump in my throat and let go of his hand. I readjust, laying down on my side and curl my legs up towards my belly, a hand protectively covering it. Putting my head in his lap, I face the black screen of the television, my nightmares already playing in my mind. His hand automatically falls to my head, his fingers running through my hair, the action soothing.

"At first, I completely shut down..."

Gulping hard, my dreams play in my mind as I speak.

Blood drips from my hands as I beg my mom to wake up, but I'm the one who wakes up, screaming at the top of my lungs. "Ahh!"

Aidan jumps up from the floor, wrapping me in his arms. "It's okay, Alex. You're okay."

"M...M...Mom," I stammer, crying into my brother's white t-shirt.

"I know. It's okay. I'm here. We have each other. We're going to be okay, he insists as I cling to him, his own silent tears falling on top of my head."

A loud crash from the living room startles us both making us jump. Aidan stands, cautiously approaching my bedroom door. Looking back at me, he holds out his hand, commanding, "Stay here."

"I'm not staying here alone."

He scoffs but puts his finger to his lips as we quietly sneak out of my bedroom, tiptoeing towards the living room. Aidan suddenly jumps back, making me stumble. Lifting his bare foot, he pulls out a piece of broken glass and shows it to me, both our eyes veering towards the floor. A picture of our family, happy, lay discarded amongst the shards.

Carefully inching around the broken glass, we make our way to the living room, finding our dad in Mr. Miller's face, his best friend. "She's gone. The love of my life is gone, and I'm supposed to figure out how to take care of these kids alone when I can't even take care of myself? How, Dave? And now Alexa is having nightmares after witnessing it and Aidan is getting into trouble at school. I can't do this. I don't know how to fucking do this without her." He picks up a vase and smashes it against the wall before Dave can stop him.

Aidan and I gasp, bringing their attention to us. Dad's angry glare has Aidan shoving me behind him and both of us scrambling backwards towards my room and locking the door behind him.

"Our dad would drink until he passed out and then it would start all over again. Nobody really blamed him, they all just felt sorry for him, sorry for all of us." I scrunch up my nose in displeasure. Declan's lips brush the top of my head, his fingers, continuing to play with my hair.

"We had a lot of family and friends that checked on us right after it happened, making sure we had food, clean clothes, or just to get us out of the house for a little while so my dad could have time to deal with it, but he never did. Eventually, all our family and friends stopped coming around because it was too depressing to be around us; nobody knew how to handle it, so they didn't. After a while, it got pretty bad..." I say, falling back into a memory.

"I think the coast is clear," I tell Aidan with my ear pressed to my bedroom door.

"I'll go check," he offers. "Wait in your closet."

Not wanting to argue, I don't bother telling him I'm going too. Opening my door, he walks down the hall, glaring at me as I follow. Defiant, I only shrug in response. He shakes his head but keeps moving. Both of us breathe a sigh of relief when we find our dad on the couch, passed out with a nearly empty bottle of scotch on the coffee table and a tipped glass on the floor near his hand. But at least he's not awake and screaming.

Picking up the glass, Aidan sets it on the coffee table, cluttered with food, wrappers, spills, and old pictures, some already ruined. Both of us look around, taking in the mess surrounding us. It's obvious the house hasn't been cleaned since the last time Aidan and I scoured it.

"Let's get something to eat and then maybe we should clean up a little bit," Aidan suggests.

"Okay," I nod in agreement and head towards the kitchen.

Aidan and I search the refrigerator and cabinets, finding nothing but liquor, beer and, sour milk and a stale box of crackers. "Change of plans. Let's go find some food and we can clean up later."

"What if he wakes up?" I ask, anxious.

Aidan frowns, stepping over to me and giving me a hug. "I won't let anything happen to you, Alex." My stomach growls making me frown. "And that's why we're going to get food first."

"Fine," I grumble.

"After a while, Aidan would just come home with food, knowing there wouldn't be much in the house. I'm not sure if Aidan got food from some of his friends, bought it somewhere or stole it and I honestly didn't care; he at least took care of me."

"Fuck," Declan quietly mumbles under his breath, but I ignore it and keep going.

"We both missed a ton of school. Eventually we were told we had to go back to school, but showing up was hit or miss. The days our dad woke up without a hangover, we'd make it, but I honestly think he was probably still drunk and it was too early for a hangover. They sent a police officer with a truancy officer from school when we missed too many days and I think that's what started the Child Protective Services investigation, although it still took them a long time to do anything and I'm glad it did.

"Aidan and I didn't want to lose each other, so we started walking nearly two miles to school every day, cleaned the house and tried to be presentable when they showed up. But there were a few surprise visits from our assigned case manager that didn't go so well and that's when they removed Aidan and me and put us in a foster home." Sniffling, I wipe away my tears I didn't realize had fallen, remembering the day they took us away.

Aidan and I sit side by side in a cold room, with his arm protectively around me, staring at a woman with dark hair and streaks of gray pulled up in a bun on top of her head and glasses perched on the end of her nose as she looks through our records, alongside something else on her screen.

"Please, I don't want to leave my brother. I need to be with him. Please," I beg, tears streaming down my face.

"I promise, we're looking for a home that will take both of you, but it really depends on what's available."

"You have to find one. You can't separate me from my sister. I have to protect her. Please," Aidan begs.

"We will try."

"We'll stay here, or anywhere until you find somewhere, but we have to be together," Aidan insists.

They give us both a look of pity and that's the moment I knew we wouldn't be that lucky.

"The first home was only temporary while they looked for somewhere for us. I don't remember much about it, but I was only there a week before they moved me. They never found someone who would take us both. There were four of us at the second place–all girls and I was the youngest. We all shared one room with two sets of bunkbeds. The oldest, Tandy, she decided she was in charge of me and when I wouldn't listen, she hit me." I flinch at the memory and sink deeper.

I limp out of the living room towards our bedroom, my face streaked with tears, trying to hold my head high after Ms. Stapleton spanked me in front of everyone in hopes it would deter us from lying. But I didn't lie and I had the bruise on my cheek from Tandy to prove it.

Cheryl follows me inside and I turn towards her accusingly. "Why did you lie and say I hit my face falling out of the top bunk?"

She flinches. "I'm sorry, but Tandy made us corroborate her story. I can't be on her bad side."

Wiping my tears, I stand taller, making a decision to learn to fight. I'm not going to let anyone control me. "One day, you'll wish you weren't on mine."

"Tandy kept pushing me and trying to control me. I stayed silent and did what I had to while I learned to fight. The day I was removed and put in a new home was the day I finally fought back, but I was there for almost a year, enduring her torture.

"The next foster home I stayed in for more than a year and a half. They had two boys there too and at first they let me stay in my corner and do my own thing. The older one, Jeffrey, was two years older than me and the younger one, Ryder, was my age and as I got more comfortable, we became friends, the first friend I had since my mom died. I started high school and kept to myself, but

Ryder and I got really close. He was my best friend, and my first boyfriend. We shared a lot of firsts...”

Declan freezes at the mention of Ryder's name, but quickly forces himself to relax, running his fingers through my hair.

After seeing Ryder so recently, my mind can't help but fall back into the one time I remember feeling safe and not so sad, until it all got ripped away in a heartbeat once again.

Ryder tips his head down and presses his lips to mine, once again, making me giggle. "You're supposed to be doing homework."

"But I'd rather be kissing you." He grins and kisses me again, my hands looping around his neck as we tilt our heads, his tongue plunging into my mouth.

I moan, kissing him back, his hand slipping underneath my shirt and squeezing my breast. He lays me back on the couch and pulls back, looking down at me. "Is this, okay?"

"Yes," I murmur, pulling him closer. My hands glide up and down is back as I kiss him, feeling him press into me. Breaking our kiss, I say, "Ryder, I think I want to try more."

He arches his eyebrows in surprise. "You sure?"

"Yeah. I'm sure."

He kisses me again, but slips off me, laying beside me, staring at me. Tentatively, his hand rubs over me through my leggings making me whimper. Pulling back, he looks down at me, his eyes flaring. His hand falls to my waistband, and I nod. He slips his hand into my pants, my body tenses, nervous but he kisses me, helping me relax before his fingers reach their destination.

"Holy shit!" Jeffrey's voice startles us both.

Ryder rips himself away from me and I quickly cover myself, although I still had all my clothes on. "Get the fuck out!" Ryder commands.

"I didn't know you were such a little slut, or I would've taken a ride."

Ryder tries to leap over the couch, but I reach out and grab him. "Don't," I beg, knowing it won't be anything good for either of us if he hits Jeffrey.

Seething, he does as I say, instead grabbing a pillow and whipping it at Jeffrey. "Get the fuck out," he repeats.

Jeffrey laughs and walks out.

"The next day at school, people started making crude gestures and comments, calling me a slut. Ryder and I both got into a lot of fights, but mostly me. They did a lot of pretending when he was around and I didn't want to get him in trouble so I didn't always tell him what happened."

Declan's lips brush my head, but I'm not sure if it's for his comfort or mine.

"One night, our foster parents had gone out to dinner and Ryder was in the living room watching TV, but I went to bed early because I wasn't feeling well." My mind dives right back into the nightmare of that day.

Clumsy hands roam over my body, waking me. Moaning, I try to shove them away when I'm suddenly weighed down. A body pins me to my bed, the scent of alcohol flooding my senses. "That's it, baby," Jeffrey slurs, slamming reality into focus. Fear consumes me as his hands grope me. "Come on little slut, I'll make you feel good."

I open my mouth to scream and he kisses me, slobbering on me like a dog. I squirm shoving against his chest trying to pull away. "Get off me!" Finally, I break my leg free and jerk it up between his legs, kneeing him in the balls.

He screams, "Fuck! You bitch!"

Ryder runs into the room, takes one look at me crying with my arms wrapped protectively around my legs and swings at Jeffrey, hitting him over and over again. Jeffrey fights back, but his reflexes are slow and takes more hits than Ryder.

Our guardians storm into the room, breaking them up and glaring at me. "What the hell is going on?"

Ryder gestures to Jeffrey. "This asshole was trying to take advantage of Lex."

"I didn't do shit," Jeffrey spits.

"Ryder stood up for me and tried to take the heat, but I got blamed for all of it since I had a history of violence." They probably just didn't want to deal with having a girl around if it brought problems like that. I scoff at the ridiculousness of it all, but after that, I always wanted to make sure I remained in control of my relationships. It wasn't Ryder's fault but seeing him brought back those memories.

"The last place I was at wasn't too bad, but I wasn't there for long. I only wanted to get back to Aidan. When he finally got the courts to release me to his care, it was the happiest day of my life."

Turning around, I crawl into Declan's lap finding his face streaked with tears for me making my heart both clench and soar. Wrapping my arms around him, I hold on tight as his snake around my waist, pulling me close. "Will you just hold me and never let go?"

"I will hold you forever if you let me," he claims, his voice cracking with emotion as he presses his face into my neck.

My mouth opens to tell him how much he means to me, how much this means, but the words escape. I close my eyes feeling safe and loved in his embrace, a place that has always seemed more like a fairytale than reality to me.

Chapter 44

Alex

Aidan's arm drapes protectively around me as we walk through the tombstones towards our mother's grave. Every time I come, being here helps me feel closer to her and gives me a sense of peace by talking to her aloud, as if she were standing in front of me. We find her black marble stone, etched with white writing and a beautiful, small, oval smiling picture of her in the corner. I remember the day Aidan and I picked that image out. It's the way we remember her.

Beloved Wife and Mother

Diana Schoeller

Always in our thoughts and forever in our hearts.

We love you!

"Hi, Mom," I say.

"Hi, Mom," Aidan echoes.

"Aidan and I wanted to come see you. We have a lot to tell you."

He huffs a laugh. "Alex has a lot to tell you. I'm here for her and to tell you I love you and I'm doing my best to make you proud."

"She's proud of you, Aidan."

"Today, we're here for you." He nods, urging me to speak.

"Fine." Sighing, I do as he says and swiftly blurt everything out in one fell swoop. "So, I met someone and you're going to be a grandma." The reminder that she won't ever meet her grandchild causes my heart to stagger.

"Smooth, Alex."

Ignoring him, I continue, "I know you'll watch over him or her, but I wish you could be with me when they're born to help me figure out what to do. We couldn't have asked for a better mom and I want to do the same with my baby. I miss you, Mom," I say, my voice catching and tears welling in my eyes. Aidan pulls me a little closer, giving me a squeeze in encouragement.

"As for the man I met, his name is Declan. I think he's a really good guy. Even Aidan likes him."

Aidan chuckles beside me, "It's true."

"I'm not really sure how it happened. Well, I understand how I got pregnant, but I mean the feelings part of it. That's all new to me. It's funny–I had years of therapy, and it barely made a dent in my armor, but after just a few short months with this man, I feel like myself again and the feeling can be incredibly overwhelming." Taking a deep breath, I confess what I've been too afraid to admit to myself, "I'm in love with him, Mom, but I'm afraid I love him too much."

"Wait. What do you mean, you love him too much?" Aidan questions.

Shrugging, I explain in simple terms. "He's already broken through all the barriers I've built. What would I do if something happened to him? I don't want to break like dad did and fail my child."

"Fuck, Alex. Is that what you think?" I shrug in response, my answer obvious. "Alex, I wouldn't let that happen. Hell, neither would Sloane or Declan's entire family. You will never be alone and if the unthinkable would happen, and you fall, you have an army that will be there to catch you."

"How do you know?"

"Nothing is one hundred percent," he concedes, wincing. "But answer this, do you think Declan is worth taking the chance?"

His question runs through my mind although I already know the answer. He's more than worth it. It doesn't mean it's easy to take the leap. Squinting, I look up at my brother, my heart pounding out of control. "Aid…"

He chuckles softly. "You don't have to tell me anything. Your eyes say it all."

We stay and talk to our mom together for a little while longer, leaving a bouquet of yellow roses, next to a fresh bouquet of sunflowers, both Aidan and me believing they're from our dad.

The ride to the diner remains silent with me deep in thought. When we walk inside, I look around at the white tables and blue cushioned benches lining the wall, with similar tables scattered around the room and colorful, retro art hanging on the wall. I stride towards an empty booth in the back corner facing the entrance, scooting all the way in. Aidan sits down next to me, and we both start fidgeting as we wait for our dad.

"Can I get y'all something to drink?"

Lifting my gaze to the waitress standing near our table with a polite smile, I request. "Can we just have three waters to start?" She nods and slips away, quickly returning with the water.

A few minutes later, our dad steps through the door dressed in tan pants and a blue polo, neatly pressed, similar to the other day. Carrying three small gift bags in blue, pink and yellow, he approaches and sits down across from us with a big smile on his face. "Aidan, Alexa–"

"It's Alex," Aidan interrupts.

"I'm sorry, I mean, Alex." His eyes shift from Aidan to me and back again. "You're both so beautiful. I see your mom in both of you. Alex, you look just like her."

"Thanks."

"I'm so glad you're both here."

"I wouldn't be here if it weren't for Alex," Aidan proclaims, clenching his jaw.

"Well, whatever the reason, I'm still thankful you're here." We all sit silent, our dad's gaze continuing to bounce between the two of us and then he shakes his head as if clearing the fog, setting the gift bags on the table. "I brought a little something for both of you and something for the baby."

"Thank you," I say, Aidan adding nothing but a grunt.

"Look, I know this isn't easy. I always wondered if I'd ever look across the table at either of you again. My life is filled with regret, but my biggest one is and always will be not being the father either of you deserved when we lost your mom." Aidan scoffs but says nothing. Glancing at Aidan, he adds, "If you don't want to see me after today, I'd understand."

Aidan only emphasizes, "I'm here for Alex."

Dad winces and nods his head sadly. "So, I want to let you know, I've been through rehab seven times."

"What makes you think this time it's gonna stick?" Aidan asks accusingly.

"Because this is the only time I've been sober for over a year. I'm nineteen months sober and I can't go back if I want to survive."

"What do you mean if you want to survive?" I ask.

He pinches his lips tightly together before revealing, "I have cirrhosis and although they caught it early, it's not something that's reversable. Alcohol would only speed up the disease."

"So, you came to tell us your dying? Do you want us to feel sorry for you?" Aidan questions nearly spitting out the words.

He shakes his head. "No, I want to give you answers, or peace. As for me, I never said I was dying. It's inevitable if I don't get a transplant, but I've been on a donor list for a new liver since I hit one year of sobriety."

"How likely is it that they'll find a liver?" I ask, my heart picking up its pace.

He shrugs. "I'm not sure. I try not to pay attention to how many people are in front of me and someone at immediate risk would be moved to the top of the list. All I can do is stay healthy, try to take care of myself and wait. But I don't want you to worry, I did this to myself."

My heart sinks. I'm not even sure if I want to know him but hearing that I have a timeline to decide makes it all the more real. With a small shake of my head, I attempt to remind myself why I'm here and focus on that. "I wanted to ask you about mom."

A sad smile curls his lips. "She was an incredible woman, but you already know that, so what do you want to know?"

"Anything I was too young to know," I admit, giving me my answer to his unasked question, at least a part of it. I want to know everything he's able to share about our mom before he can't.

He chuckles. "That's going to take some time."

"I'm okay with that." Aidan shifts in his seat next to me, his body taut, and his eyebrows drawn down in concern. Trying to brush it aside for now, I say, "But today maybe we can start simple." He nods, urging me to continue. "In the card you gave me with the flowers, you said the love you had for mom was all consuming and that's why you couldn't take care of yourself."

"That's not exactly what I meant and it's not an excuse," he reiterates. "It's hard to explain."

"I get that, but what do you mean?"

"Your mom was perfect in my eyes. She was all that was good in this world. Before I met your mom, I partied a little too hard and found myself in too much trouble. Nothing serious, but she saw the good in me beyond having a good time. After that, I turned myself around because I could only see her, and I knew I didn't have a chance in hell if I didn't make an effort.

"Everything else around me was static when she was there. She made the sun shine, the rain fall, and everything not just better, but electric. Then you two came along and we had our perfect little family.

"Without her I was nothing. You two would eventually have your own lives and she would never be a part of our worlds again. Then, I'd be alone. I was hopeless. My beliefs changed. I didn't think I would ever be enough for anyone, especially the two of you. It took me too long to pull myself out of that depression–way too long. The grief was eating at me from the inside out and drinking temporarily numbed my pain, but it only made it worse.

"I fell back into old habits, but in my grief, I wasn't the good time guy anymore. Instead, I was the man who was desperate, would do anything to erase the pain, and I was angry as hell at the world and took it out on anyone around me. It was selfish."

He sighs, running a hand down his face in exhaustion. "And when it came to you two, I fucked up every little thing. I never said or did anything right if I was able to do anything at all. You were better off without me."

"That's not true! You have no idea what either of us went through," I snap, shaking my head.

He flinches. "You're right and I was too blind or drunk to notice." Pausing, he gulps hard, his Adam's apple bobbing up and down. "It should've been me, and I've had to live with failing both of you and your mom every single day."

"Now he's a fucking martyr," Aidan grumbles under his breath. "Did you know my friends gave me food to bring home for me and Alex? What I didn't get from them I stole, so we could survive. We were the ones cleaning up your puke along with everything else in the house and checking to see if you were still alive, but at least we had each other. You could have made sure it stayed that way."

"That's what I should've done."

"Yeah, you should've. But we got to deal with CPS instead. When they came and took us, it didn't seem to matter to you, but you sure as fuck should know it fucking mattered to us. We needed each other but no one cared. We had to fight for ourselves alone until I finally got Alex back three years later. Three years, *Dad*!" He seethes, sarcasm thick on his tongue as the words leave his lips. "You know what can happen in that time?" Aidan grinds his jaw so hard I think his teeth might crack, glaring at our dad. "Fuck you!"

Dad flinches but nods as if he were expecting Aidan's outburst. "It will never be enough, but I'm sorry."

Aidan huffs a humorless laugh and stands, looking at me. "I'm sorry, Alex, but I need some space from him. I'll be in the Jeep. Please let me know if you need me, otherwise, come out when you're done. Take all the time you need."

"I'll be fine, Aidan. Go."

Giving me a firm nod, he spins on his heel and stalks out.

"Alex, I'm sorry. I'm not trying to make excuses; I'm just trying to answer your question. Yeah, I'm ashamed of what I did after your mom died. I regret falling into the bottle and most of all, I hate that you and Aidan took the brunt of all of it. I'm taking full responsibility for my actions and if there was something I could do to change it or make it better, I would do it in a heartbeat."

Sighing, I nod. "Thanks," I mumble, not sure what else to say, my mind reeling with what he's already said. "So do you think it's possible to love too much?" I ask the question I really need the answer to, so I can move forward one way or another.

He pinches his lips tightly together in thought, considering my question. "For me, it wasn't about loving too much but not loving enough." My eyebrows draw down in confusion. "Yeah, I loved your mom more than anything, but I didn't love myself enough. Without even realizing it, I put the weight of my life on your mom. That wasn't fair to her or to either of you. I still love your mom and I'm grateful for every day she loved me, but no one should carry someone else's burden of self-love, you have to find that on your own. If you love yourself, and grief hits you, you have a chance that it won't consume you until there's nothing left to love."

For a moment, I remain silent, thinking. Looking across the table, I take in this man, his eyes sad, but hopeful. I'm not the same. For so long I've pushed everyone out and put all my energy into surviving, then into loving myself and who I want to be.

Maybe it's time for me to have more.

"I'm not making any promises, but I think I'd like to hear more about mom sometime."

He smiles. "I would love that and if you're willing, I'd love to know more about you and your brother."

I nod. "I'm going to go check on Aidan. I'm sorry I'm not staying to eat."

Shaking his head, he claims, "It's okay. You don't ever need to apologize to me. It probably doesn't mean much, but I do love you."

Gulping down the lump in my throat, I slide out of the booth and stand. "Bye, Dad." Holding my breath, I stride out the door recognizing I'm stronger than even I realized and I want more with Declan, if that's what he wants too.

I spot the Jeep and see Aidan repeatedly slamming his fist on the steering wheel, squeezing my heart. It looks like it's my turn to be there for Aidan just like he's always been a rock for me.

Grabbing my phone, I send a quick text to Declan.

I'm staying at my brother's tonight.

Chapter 45

Alex

I set down the aspirin and a glass of water on the nightstand next to Aidan's bed. "It's here when you need it," I whisper but he only grunts in response. I'm worried about him. Our dad showing up really messed with his head. Ironically, it did the opposite for me, as if telling me exactly what I will never be.

Knocking pulls me out of my thoughts and I turn, striding towards the front door. Pulling it open, I smile, both surprised and happy to see the man scowling down at me. "Declan, hi. Come in." I step back and shut the door behind him. "What are you doing here?"

"What am I doing here? I was worried, so I came to see you. You never came home last night."

Arching my eyebrows, I remind him, "I texted you to say I was staying at my brother's house."

"Yeah, but that was it and this is the first time since you moved in with me. And after everything you shared the other night, I was afraid you were overwhelmed."

"I've honestly never felt better. The thing I feel more than anything is relief that you know it all."

"I'm happy to hear that, I really am, Alex. But before when you disappeared on me, it was because you were running. Stop running away from this, from me."

My eyes widen and I shake my head. "You're right, Dec, but this time I'm not running away from anything or anyone."

He takes a step towards me, arching his eyebrows in challenge. "Are you sure about that? Not even to anyone? Like Ryder?"

Fighting not to roll my eyes I glare at him. "Are you fucking kidding me? Are you jealous of Ryder because we have a history?"

He clenches his jaw, taking a slow breath before he responds. "I already told you I'm jealous, but I'm trying really hard not to be. Finding out you had history with him was hard to take."

"I thought you trusted me," I state, accusingly.

He shakes his head vehemently. "I do trust you. I trust you more than any-thing, but that doesn't mean it's easy to hear or process."

"Then maybe I shouldn't have told you."

"That's not what I meant."

Crossing my arms over my chest in defiance, I question, "Then what exactly do you mean?"

Hesitating for barely a moment before admitting, "He has a big piece of you that I never will."

I scoff and shake my head. "That may be true, Declan, but you have a lot more than he does," I insist, my hand falling to my stomach.

He flinches. "You're right. I'm sorry."

"Besides, the fact is there are a helluva lot of women I could say the same thing about when it comes to you. You don't see me standing here starting a fight."

His shoulders sag in defeat. "I know it's not fair to ask you to help me feel better for my own insecurities, and I'm sorry for that. But this relationship thing is new for me. I've never wanted anything more in my life. Trust is not the issue. I just don't always know how to handle it."

"That's obvious," I grumble under my breath.

He grimaces. "But I will always be honest with you, and I know you will do the same." I nod in affirmation. "I can also tell you I never had feelings for another woman–no one but you and I can't imagine ever loving anyone else."

His words send tingles down my spine. Sighing, I concede, giving him something more to help ease his concern. "Yeah, but Ryder and I will only ever just be friends. For better or worse, when I look at him, I remember the good things about our friendship, but also the tough things about my life at the time I'd rather not ever think about again. He's a good man, but he's not the man for me." He gulps, nodding in acknowledgment. "But when I see you, Dec, I see happiness and hope."

"Yeah? What about sexy?"

Narrowing my eyes in warning, I tell him, "Don't push me, Declan."

"Look, I'm sorry. I was just asking you a question. I don't want to lose you," he admits, his voice cracking. He pauses and clears his throat. "Since it's not Ryder, please, just tell me what's going on and let me be there for you. Why are you running again?"

I shake my head, both amused and frustrated. Ugh, this man. "I'm not running, Dec. See?" I point towards the floor. "Two feet planted right in front of you," I state sassily.

"Then, prove me wrong, firecracker."

"This isn't a game, Dec."

"You're right, it's not. It's your life. It's my life. And it's that baby's life–our baby. No matter how far you run, that will never change."

Heaving a sigh, I insist, "And I don't want it to."

"Then, prove me wrong," he repeats, stepping into my space. "Don't move back in with your brother. Stay with me. I like finding your stuff all over the house, I like hearing you humming when you're doing things around the house or sitting and playing your guitar. I like coming home and talking with you about everything big and small, having dinner with you, and just relaxing on the couch together. I like having you in my bed and waking up with you in my arms every morning." I hesitate and he licks his lips, pushing further. "I'm in love with you, Alex. I'm so head over fucking heels in love with you. And I'm asking you to stay, please. Come home with me. It's not home without you anymore."

My heart soars, making it difficult to breathe, and my entire body tingles with pure happiness, but I also need to stop his line of thinking. "Declan! If you would stop being such a caveman and just shut up and listen to me, then you would know I'm not going anywhere."

"You're not?" he asks, his eyes still full of concern.

"No. I stayed here last night because after talking to my dad yesterday, I was worried about my brother. He drank way too much, so I'm still here, making sure he's okay this morning."

"Oh." His face heats, turning beet red. "I'm sorry." He runs his hand through his hair and drops it to his side. "I know it's no excuse, but I was really worried about you and all I get is a text saying you're staying at your brother's house." He gives me a crooked smile, gripping my waist.

"That look is not going to do it this time. You need to have more faith in me if this is going to work between us."

"I am sorry, Alex." Frowning, he shakes his head at himself. "Now I feel like a jackass."

"That's because it fits. I'll add it to my list of names for you, right next to ogre and needless hero."

He chuckles. "I deserve that."

"At least that and more. That's me going easy on you for storming in here like a barbarian."

"And another one. I'd be happy to show you my barbarian side." He wiggles his eyebrows making me laugh, not able to hold it in any longer.

"I'll tell you when that side can come out of the cage. But no more alpha male assuming the worst or trying to tell me what to do in anything except the bedroom and we'll be good." I smirk.

He grins, his eyes sparkling once again. "I'll work on that."

"You damn well better," I tease. "But I think I have one or two ideas on how you can make it up to me."

"Oh, yeah? What's that?"

Arching my eyebrow in challenge, I prompt, "Well, there are still some rooms in the house we haven't christened yet."

"I'm all in." Leaning in he brushes his lips over mine, making my lips tingle.

Pulling back, I say, "Oh, and Declan?"

"Yeah?"

"I love you too," I say almost flippantly, testing the words on my tongue, but they feel exactly right.

A soft gasp leaves his lips, his eyes going wide. Grabbing my hips in a firm grip, he asks, "What did you just say?"

My hand falls to his chest, and I look into his eyes, saying the three words I know are true with complete confidence and conviction. "I love you, Declan."

"Damn. I love the sound of that coming from your lips. I love you, too, Alex."

Keeping one hand on my hip, he slides the other up my side, and into my hair as his lips descend on mine. Our mouths move together in a slow dance, finding a perfect rhythm. My tongue juts out, slipping into his mouth and turning our kiss deeper. Tangling our tongues together, we lick, suck, and nibble eliciting a moan from me. I'm quickly lost in his kiss, my body heating and vibrating with need.

Lifting my leg, I loop it around his back feeling his hard length rubbing against my belly. "I want you, Dec."

"Damn, I want you too. I need to get you home so I can devour every part of you," he claims with a low growl, nipping at my lower lip.

Tilting my head, I request, "Yes, please."

"Seriously?" Aidan asks as he steps out of his room, his exasperation apparent. "Can't you do that at your house?" He groans and I drop my foot to the ground, smiling as I turn to face him.

"How are you feeling?"

"Like shit. Came out for some food."

"Need some help?"

"Nah, I'm good." He turns and walks towards the kitchen.

"What happened?" Declan asks as soon as Aidan is out of earshot.

"I'll explain later. Although, I will say that I think talking to my dad was a really good thing for me and you, but it was different for Aidan. It will take him more time to deal with it and I want to be there for him."

He nods in understanding. "And you will be. I'm sorry again. Please let me know if there's anything I can do to help."

"Thanks. I will." Pointing towards the kitchen, I say, "Give me a minute. I want to check on him."

"Okay," he murmurs and presses a kiss to the top of my head before I slip away.

Quietly, I step into the kitchen. My brother's hands are pressed to the counter, his shoulder slumped and his head down. "Aidan?"

Startled, he spins around, facing me. "When did you get so quiet?"

"All those times I used to sneak out," I smirk, answering honestly.

He sighs. "Thanks for taking care of me last night, Alex. I'm sorry you had to deal with my shit."

"You've done it more times than I can count for me." Pinching his lips together, he nods in acknowledgement. Taking a step towards him, I ask, "Are you all right?"

Huffing a humorless laugh, he shakes his head. "Eventually. I just need to figure out my shit."

"With Dad," I finish.

He clenches his jaw but doesn't respond. Tipping his head towards the living room, he asks, "Everything good with you two?"

A smile tugs at my lips. "Better than okay."

He gives me a half smile. "Good. You shouldn't leave him out there alone too long," he jokes. "I'll be fine."

Nodding, I close the distance between us and wrap my arms around my brother's waist, resting my head over his heart. His protective embrace soon envelopes me. I only hope I can do for him what he always does for me.

"I love you, Aidan and you can talk to me too, you know."

"I know, Alexa and I love you too."

"That's so nice of you to say," the speaker sounds.

He chuckles and I shove him away. "I'm not even mad right now."

"Go back to your boyfriend. I'll be fine."

Knowing that's as much as I'm getting today, I walk back out to the living room and sit down next to Declan. "How was your day and night?" I ask, needing a subject change.

"I spent the day with my family doing stuff for the wedding."

"Is Ella getting nervous?"

"No, she's just excited. It's good to see her so happy. We should have a good time. I'm happy you're coming with me." He gives me a chaste kiss. "But my night sucked without you. Charlotte called this morning, though, to share some good news."

"She did? What?"

"My friend Kenney was able to get her out of her contract without causing any problems for her. She said one of the swings will be able to take over for her until they hire a replacement. So, she'll finally be able to get away from that asshole."

"That's great news. Does he know about this plan yet?"

"Yeah, and he has no choice but to accept it. She already started auditioning for some other jobs. I've been reaching out to some friends too."

"You know people in theater?" I ask, my eyes going wide.

"Not exactly, but I reached out to a few of my clients I'm on a friendly basis with that work in TV and film in Chicago and New York."

"How did I not know this?"

He shrugs, smirking. "I've made a lot of connections at this firm over the years and a lot of them request to work with me."

"If that's the case, and you hate being there so much, why don't you start your own marketing company? You obviously already have a big network."

"Yeah, I've actually thought about it, but there was a non-compete clause in my contract when I started with the company. If I quit, I'm not allowed to take on work with my clients from the firm for an entire year. I'm not sure I could do it without being able to depend on some of my current clients."

"Are you sure there's not a way to get creative with that?"

"Maybe, but I won't take a chance and put any of us at risk. I would have to consider all the details before I do something like that."

"I think you should seriously look into it. You're miserable where you are, and I want you to be happy."

"You want me to be happy?" He gives me a mischievous grin. "All right. I promise I'll look into it and see what I can come up with. In the meantime, I'm thinking about everything I'm going to do to you when I get you home."

"After barging in here, it better be damn, good, cowboy."

He laughs. "I promise it will be." Tipping his head down, he gives me a chaste kiss and suggests, "Let's go say goodbye to your brother so I can take you home and you can find out just how good I can be."

"I'm in."

Epilogue

Declan

One year later...

Blindly reaching out, I feel around for Alex, but come up empty. Squinting into the darkness, I look around the room and frown. Where did she go? The sound of her soft voice echoes through the baby monitor making me chuckle. Smiling, I lay staring at the ceiling and listening to the sweet and sexy notes Alex sings. I think this is the new song she's working on for that relatively new band in the northeast. She sold one other song to them already and they were interested in more from her.

They said her songs feel like them.

"And then came you,

Challenging me at every turn,

Making every part of me burn.

And then came you,

Taking me by surprise and

Standing right by my side,

Then, came you."

"What do you think, Diana?" Alex asks our ten-month-old baby girl, named after her grandmother, Alex's mom. "Maybe we should ask daddy."

"Dada, dada," Diana murmurs.

Gasping, I shoot out of bed, and stumble across the hall, not bothering to grab a shirt, my eyes glued to my little angel. "Did she just say, Dada?"

Alex giggles in excitement. "She did. Her first word. Is that Dada?"

Diana waves her arms frantically and bounces in her mother's arms, looking at me and squealing in delight. "Dada, Dada."

My chest tightens as I cross the room in two long strides. Wrapping my arms around both my girls, I press my lips to the smooth velvety skin of my daughter's forehead, inhaling her powdery scent. "That's me." I grin, my heart full, feeling like it's about to burst out of my chest. I almost wonder how I survived without them, but that's not something I want to dwell on.

"How's my baby girl?" I ask, keeping my voice soft and low. "Aren't you supposed to be sleeping?"

"Dada, Dada," she continues her chant.

"She doesn't look like she's going back to sleep anytime soon," I say, frowning.

Holding my hands out, she tries to launch herself at me and does a nosedive. Chuckling, I catch her, pulling her into my arms. One hand embraces her bottom and my other hand palms the back of her head, holding her close to my heart, gently swaying back and forth. It's my go to for when we want her to go to sleep.

Alex sighs, resting her head on my other side, with her face close to our girl. "Yeah, but we're going to try anyway."

Peering down at them, I smile. Diana's hair gets thicker every day and looks just like her mom's when Alex's hair isn't dyed, while her blue eyes are nearly a mirror image of my own. Diana appears to be a beautiful mix of both of us, letting me know I'll likely be fighting off the boys as she gets older, but at least I'll have some help with her uncles–Finn, Aidan, Grant and even Ryder. "I like the song you were singing," I tell Alex.

"Yeah? I'm not sure I have it quite right yet."

"I really like it, but I'm sure you'll figure out what you want too."

"Thanks, Dec."

"You're welcome, Miss Schoeller," I say, hoping I'll soon get her to accept my proposal and take my name. She smiles. Leaning in, I press my lips to Alex's, humming in appreciation.

Wet, tiny hands clap us both on the cheeks. "Dada, Dada."

Alex laughs. "I'm Mama. That's Dada."

"Dada wants Mama to come to bed," I say, playful.

"I will as soon as we get her down."

"Keep singing. She loves the sound of your voice, just like me."

"Charmer."

"My names keep getting better," I tease, giving her a crooked grin. "But it's true, I could listen to you all day. Unless you want me to keep her, and you can go back to bed and get some rest? I don't mind."

"No, you have the meeting with the music media agency tomorrow morning," she reminds me.

I never thought I'd be on this side of marketing, but I love it. When I started letting people know I was starting my own marketing company, Hero's Pulse Communications, I had several clients I had to turn down, telling them I'd be happy to take them on in a year, but if they had any referrals that would help get me started. Plus, reaching out to help find Char some auditions or even a temporary job sent some new clients my way. Now, my company is on the rise for all aspects of marketing and media management in television, film, and even music. It's how I was able to help Alex sell her songs. It's surreal, but we both couldn't be more thankful.

"I forgot that was tomorrow. This weekend went too fast."

"It always does." She tips her head up and I meet her halfway, kissing her plump lips. "Plus, Char leaves in a few days and I know you'll want to spend some time with her before she goes."

"You're right. I can't believe she's doing a reality show."

"You should get some sleep. You have a busy week coming up," she tells me, gently taking Diana from my arms.

"Thank you, but I was thinking of other things we could do together if I could get you back in our bed," I tell her and kiss her again.

She giggles. "You're insatiable."

"That's one of the many reasons why we are absolutely perfect for each other," I say, nibbling on her neck.

She hums softly, pushing up on her tiptoes, attempting to lean into my lips. "It definitely makes things fun."

"Have I told you today how much I love you?" I ask, kissing a spot in the crook of her neck making her shiver.

"Not yet today. It is only three in the morning, though. You have plenty of time left in the day to tell me repeatedly."

"Well, I do. I love you, Alex."

"I love you, too, Dec."

Diana's eyes fall closed and I tenderly kiss the top of her head. "Goodnight baby girl. I love you." I move back, looking at Alex, whispering, "She's asleep."

She kisses her forehead and says, "Goodnight my beautiful girl. I love you so much." Carefully she sets her down in the crib and raises the side, both of us tiptoeing out of the room and into ours.

Alex lays her head on my bare chest, right over my heart and drapes her leg over mine. Reaching down, my hand runs over the curve of her ass and underneath the hem of her tank top. "Dec," she moans as I skate my fingers over her silky skin up to her breast, my thumb brushing her nipple.

"What?" I ask, feigning innocence, feeling her heart beating as fast as mine underneath me. Rolling her over, I pull her shirt off and toss it to the floor.

"What happened to sleep?" she asks, already breathless.

"I'd rather have you any way you'll let me every single time," I insist, my hips rolling towards her on instinct.

She moans in pleasure, her hands roaming the hard ridges and valleys of my chest, my shoulders and my arms. "Mm-kay."

Covering her mouth with mine, our tongues collide, instantly fighting for dominance. One hand grips the back of her neck as we kiss, tasting, exploring, our mouths hot and hungry. Every little move, taste, touch steers me towards the edge and my dick hasn't even gotten involved yet.

Gasping for breath, I rasp, "Alex, you drive me wild."

Sliding down, I brush my lips over her jaw and down her neck, relishing every moan, every quiver, every time she whispers my name. Cupping her breast with my palm, my mouth covers her nipple, my tongue swirling as I gently suck it into my mouth before giving the other one the same attention.

I continue kissing a trail down her body, my fingers snagging the waist of her violet pajama pants and sliding them down her legs.

Gripping my shoulders, she insists, "Your pants have got to go."

Rising, I kick them off in a heartbeat, my lips returning to her body. "Your wish is my command."

Brushing the inside of her thigh with my mouth, she whimpers, goosebumps erupting over her delicate skin. My tongue barely sneaks out for a taste when she grasps my hair and tugs, stopping me. "Wait."

Lifting my gaze, I ask, "Are you all right?"

She nods. "Yeah, but if my wish is what you're after, my wish is to have your cock buried deep inside me right now."

My eyes flare, my dick jumps and my heart catapults for her as I climb up her body. "Fuck, those words on your tongue just made me as hard as granite. You're so damn sexy, Alex." My fingers dip inside her pussy, finding her wet and ready.

"I need you now, Dec," she reiterates.

Settling between her legs, I line myself up at her opening. "I'm coming." Plunging deep inside her with a grunt, her walls sheathe my cock inside her wet heat igniting each part of me. I swear, every inch of her body and the way she moves was made just for me. Taking a deep breath, I pull out and drive inside her once again.

"More, Dec. I need you to fuck me hard."

"I won't last."

"Neither will I."

"Okay." Pulling out, I snag her legs behind each knee and bend it towards her belly, angling over her once again. "Ready?"

"Please," she begs. In one hard and swift motion, I thrust inside her, both of us groaning in pleasure as I hit her g-spot in the back of her pussy. I pause for a moment and then pick up the pace, plunging inside her hard and fast.

"Yes, Dec, yes, oh, my god, yes," she pants arching towards me, attempting to meet me halfway.

"Fuck, Alex, come for me, I'm gonna come." She muffles her scream in the pillow beside her as her walls swell, squeezing me, pushing me over the edge, the tingling sensations detonating deep in my core and spreading like wildfire. My vision blurs, and my movements become erratic as I pound into her, white, hot, fire burning through me while I shoot my seed inside her and she milks me for every drop.

I loosen my hold on her legs, and they instantly fall to the bed making me chuckle as I collapse next to her to catch my breath. Pushing myself off the bed, I tell her, "I'll be right back." She hums in response bringing a smile to my face.

Quickly cleaning myself up, I wet a warm washcloth and squeeze it out bringing it over to Alex. "Let me?" I request. She nods, unmoving, making me chuckle. Tenderly, I wipe between her legs, tossing the washcloth in the laundry basket by the closet. Tugging my pajama pants on, I crawl back into bed, pulling her into my warm embrace, her back to my front.

"I love you, Declan," she whispers, her eyes sealed shut.

Softly, I kiss her lips. "Those are the most beautiful words coming from you. I love you too, Alex. Marry me," I say, the same words I've said nearly every day since I knew she loved me too, but her answer has always been the same–no.

She smiles, peeking at me with one eye open. "Maybe."

My heart skips a beat and I gulp a quick intake of air. Fuck, yes! It's time to work on my proposal. I kiss the spot behind her ear she loves so much. "I'll take that. Damn, I love you."

"Goodnight, Declan. We're up in two hours."

I chuckle, holding her tight. "Goodnight, Firecracker."

The End

Acknowledgements

I'm thrilled to finally be able to share this story with all of you. It's funny how the characters take over no matter what I originally intended. I know this took a while, but it needed to be just right. I'm happy with the results and I hope you are too.

Thank you to my family for your constant support in doing what I'm passionate about. I know I can get in my head, lost in a story sometimes but you are all the most important things in my life.

Thank you, Dina for your expertise in editing. Keep asking me the tough questions and giving me your POV to see all sides! I'm grateful for you and what you do.

Thank you to Ren for agreeing to do the cover for this book. I knew you would be perfect for this one and I love how it turned out. Hopefully you do too. It was fun to finally be able to work together on this, especially since it had been so long since we worked on the last film project. I really hope we can work together again very soon!

And Dennis, thank you for jumping in and taking on this photo shoot for the book cover and marketing for the book. I love what you did for the cover and all the additional shots. I appreciate all your hard work and talent.

Thank you to my Street Team, my Beta Team and my ARC Team, I'm so grateful for all you do in helping me get my books out there. It gives me not only the chance, but also the motivation to keep writing. I adore each and every one of you. Thank you to All my Readers. I'm more than grateful that I'm able to share my stories with you!

Connect with the Author

Author Website

www.nikkialamersauthor.com

All Author Links

https://linktr.ee/nikkialamersauthor

About the Author

Multi-Award Winning Author, Nikki A Lamers grew up in Wisconsin and lived in Florida for a few years before ending up on Long Island in New York where she now lives with her husband and their two children. Writing, reading, coffee, chocolate, and wine all she needs alongside her friends and family. Since meeting her husband, they enjoy spending time in Maine and exploring different places, meeting new people and always looking for her next story. For her other job she freelances as a script writer, advisor and supervisor on and off set for TV, film and commercials. Now, Nikki is having fun working on her next (several) book(s)!